I0573954

I0573954

MARIANO MORILLO B.Ph.D.

THE PARADISE TYRANTS

To denounce is to liberate

ISBN:

Hardcover: 978-1-77419-062-3

The Paradise Tyrants

To order additional copies of this book, contact:

Maple Leaf Publishing Inc.
3rd Floor 4915 54 Street Red Deer, Alberta T4N 2G7, Canada
1-(403)-356-0255

DEDICATORY

To the God of my Being

To My Children

To my Readers

To those who thirst for Justice

To those who cry out in the desert

To Those Who Seek Justice as the Firmest Pillar of a Society

To the Occupy Wall Street Movement and its Ramifications.

Contents

CHAPTER 1

— The world was turning in an indefinite direction, man forgot his origins and the fight of one and another for survival had led the leaders of nations to chaos and despair.

And using the last resort of pressure and control, nuclear weapons and violence, had increased in all four directions.

Man had lost control of his own monster, and before pride and arrogance, a huge portion of the earth was lost in the abyss.

Nature also did its part, and great breezes blew, eradicating the forests, and heavy rains fell, muddying the land

An uncontrolled famine, scourged in different directions, and many confused in their ignorance snatched their lives, and amid so much confusion a nation rose, whose system gave room to mesocracy, theocracy, aristocracy and all terminologies, conjugated in that ending.

The fame of that nation expanded throughout the world, and the residue of inhabitants of other nations who had managed to escape from the effect of the cause and the inclemency of the weather, left to populate those new lands with promises and hopes.

Chaos justified his action, the man was still confused, violence was growing every day, and justice had gone astray.

From the depths of the world and from some corner of El mar, the waves dragged a new species of men who, by their charisma and their services, distinguished themselves from all others, with a magical leadership, which just by talking made itself heard by all.

They were like a government of governments, they organized chaos and applied honey and gall, resorting to democracy and violence, making it clear that when something was not achieved with music, they would resort to the gun, for them peace was like a chimera, because their great benefits came from war, and their system had evolved in violence, and they had imposed their throne on the world, defining their actions in the different cardinal points.

For a period of more than sixty years, the world tolerated their leadership, not without those who rejected them, but the time came when those who were asleep awoke, and questioned the style of government of those men from beyond El mar, resulting in the erosion of the laureate leadership, being recorded in the active consciousness of an exasperated public opinion.

By the very ostentatious condition of bonanza that those who emigrated to the land occupied by that nation in the continent reached, and by the strength of their currencies compared with those of other neighboring nations, the fame and admiration of that kingdom and its citizens, expanded to the ends of the earth.

Everywhere in the world there was an injection of restlessness, and a growing curiosity about that nation, which induced many to want to emigrate, and few to arrive.

From there, the news emerged that the kingdom was an empire that was trying to get its hands on every corner of the world where they knew there might be some source of wealth.

Those who traveled to the kingdom in search of better opportunities, and returned loaded with goodness, influenced the minds of those who stayed, giving rise to those who despaired and aspiring to the dream of that magical land, became masses of immigrants who after the adventure of a hope of "abundance" sometimes gave in to disappointment and disillusionment.

Others were ready to face the pain of misunderstanding, and trying to beat their frustrations, they were under the illusion that if they had left their nations, houses and family, it was after the honor of inhabiting the land of the sun, of the green light of splendor, which they would end up naming "the Paradise".

And so it was that the velvety name of its origin was cemented into the structure and condition of a nation.

The kingdom expanded its power, evil was generated in the name of good, the kingdom became an empire, riches of other nations were transported to the headquarters of that Paradise, its neighbors became dependent and the kingdom financed their causes.

There, free supply and demand were promoted, there was an apparent air of freedom

Where citizens thought they had everything, even if they had nothing, and where beauty was sold in scented soaps, and cosmetology.

And the constitution, which everyone called the visibility of justice, was a glorious text of jurisprudence, where the scholars of the time based their defenses, and the judges based their sentences.

Then, because of their eagerness to expand and control their political and economic power, their rulers began to be seen as tyrants, because when they wanted to hunt down an adversary, they spared no effort to achieve their goal, and many times they used to eradicate an entire people in order to capture a single man

As the time passed by, the mission of the kingdom deteriorated, the empire continued to war, its fortune was exhausted, and emigrants from other nations that in the beginning were like trophies conquered in their thirst for expansion, had started to become according to the watchmen of the treasury a danger for those who had control. So they thought.

CHAPTER 2

— The lush grove of the central park moved stealthily, cooling the high temperature of the city. It was July 3rd, the eve of national independence and the two o'clock sun began to soothe its cutting rays.

Paradise felt calm the urban area looked clear And Jefri Hamilton, swallowed a beef roast that a few minutes before, was cooked on the grill that they poked out in the heart of the flower. A wide shade from the tree line allowed him to share and taste with his family, however, something worried him in his role as a police commissioner, surrounded by back guards, to whom he had delegated orders for the preparations of the commemorative parade of independence, in the corner of time.

You should never have fired more than three bullets, if you thought that black represented a danger, you could have resorted to another mechanism. Even common criminals don't shoot 50 times at a defenseless man, don't forget that you are police, and you weren't supposed to leave the city in such a bad light as you have up to now," said the commissioner.

---- Don't worry, Commissioner, the Department of Internal Affairs is already taking action on this matter and we will try to clarify what happened," responded Captain Rick Salgado.

---- Well, try to speed up the investigation to determine what we are going to do, Judge Rock is waiting for the report before sentencing, there is a lot of pressure and after the sentence we are thinking of sending him to England to do anti-violence training. ---Commissioner Jefri Hamilton said.

Commissioner Hamilton, the blood test done on your nephew determined that he was drugged at the time of the shooting, public opinion is revolting and we are trying to ensure that none of this information leaks out to the press, especially the fact that your nephew is training in England instead of prison," added Captain Rick.

Commissioner Hamilton cleared the area before specifying to the captain what the minors are:

--- Captain Rick, it's not because he's my nephew, it's because he's an intelligence veteran with honors,

Consider that the order comes from above, it is above me why do you think they are making conceptions ... if not, perhaps all members of that brigade would be prisoners and you who commanded it degraded, from here on we must be more careful.

Talk to the lieutenants in your area, so that they in turn do it with the sergeants so that they do not continue to commit stupid things, every mistake they make is equivalent to reducing the treasury of the city's coffers, the mayor is very upset with everything that happened --- said Commissioner Jefri Hamilton.

--- We'll keep that in mind, sir ---Captain Rick argued.

It began to thunder and a fine drizzle began to fall, the stove began to smoke when the rain

He put out the fire. The commissioner and the captain stood under the canvas tent they had erected for this purpose.

A year before that, great tensions had been generated in the city, because of racial interdictions, a member of the minorities had been sodomized in a police   precinct

Afro, and the resentment had not yet been forgotten when they used police brutality force on another minority member, on that occasion a Latino accompanied by his family and who

He had been shot with a service weapon by one of the officers heading a checkpoint in the presence of his children, while waiting for the traffic light to change at 187th and Western Streets in one of the city's counties.

Two police officers had approached with the gun in their hands, tapping on the window on the driver's side, while the other was wandering around on the passenger's side, when El mar, attracted by curiosity, lowered the glass and questioned:

--- Is something wrong, how can I help you? ...

--- Give me the car registration and driver's license---Ordered by the officer, Kate Haque.

--- Of course, at one point, El mar responded

The officer, with a certain impatience, waited for El mar to locate the document in his wallet, illuminated by the dim light coming from the interior lamp of the car, making it difficult for him to satisfy the demands of the agent, who insisted on speed with a certain nervousness, and which El mar could not supply because he had a number of documents in his wallet that he had to verify until he identified the driver's license.

Suddenly, Officer Kate Haque, in a fit of exasperation, opened the door of the vehicle and grabbed the neck of El Mar, forcing it out before it could locate the required document.

He applied a failed trick whose sudden turn led him to the ground as El mar fell on him. --- So you are trained. --- He said, as El mar was silent.

Other agents appeared out of nowhere, who did not hesitate to throw themselves at him, while twisting his legs with the intention of breaking them without any success, at the same time that they beat him inconsiderately, stamping on him, flashlighting and hitting him, to the point of causing hematomas and lacerations with their regulation weapons, on his arms, legs and one of his ankles, until he was knocked out.

They handcuffed him, to keep on hitting him, and dragging him, while Barbarita, an eyewitness, witnessed.

That Barbarita, was the pregnant girlfriend, who that night accompanied him and who still remained inside the car, in El mart on the passenger side, following closely the conversation, realizing the beating that they were giving to El mar, with eyes moistened by the consternation crying and shouting uncontrollably, outside:

=--- Why do they do it, if he is not resisting, why do they beat him? ---... He said. While El mar was still kissing the defiant floor outside:

--- Oh! Police brutality, you love to create violence, don't you? --- He said as the officers

In silence, they remained focused on their torture. It had started to rain and the uniforms took the opportunity to drag him to one of the patrol cars that had arrived, they introduced him to the back seat that looked like a box of

Pandora, and in pain and discomfort, El mar was driven to the 46th precinct, while the Lincoln car he was driving, and where Barbarita was still with the children, had been directed to the

San Barnabas Hospital, where upon arrival, the children had been attended to, as a way of verifying the levels of accumulated trauma, in view of what had happened that night.

While Barbarita, who still remained in her trance, was applied some devices, the

They examined her with the greatest care and then, having no alternative, they impregnated her with therapies and massages, causing her to give birth.

CHAPTER 3

— When they arrived at the 46th precinct it was 12:25 am   , El mar had been taken out of the patrol car and left in the waiting room, where he kept crawling on the floor unable to get up, beset by the pain generated by the bruises, by the traumatic discomforts of life, while pressing to be taken to the hospital, officer Kate Haque claimed that his supervisor was not there and El mar told him:

--- I don't understand what you are trying to tell me, your supervisor wasn't there when your cliques beat me up, so it shouldn't matter if he isn't there either, so they can take me to the hospital, please take me and don't worry, I won't cause you any trouble, and it can be worse if you don't take me, besides I don't know why? I'm here, I haven't done anything and so this is a false arrest. --- Expressed El mar.

Kate Haque remained silent, but at that moment other prisoners who were listening to the conversation in the reception cells began to interfere by pressuring him so that El mar would be taken to the hospital, which the officer took advantage of to remove his handcuffs and take his fingerprints.

Kate Haque, had begun the process of typing the footprints of El mar Valenilla, but not before having his frustrations, and struggling in his attempt discovered that even to record it was difficult, and then several difficulties arose, the computer screen was presenting the deformed prints, causing an exasperation that led him to blame El mar of what happened:

--- why are you preventing your fingerprints from being taken? --- He said.

--- I'm not doing anything, it seems that God is preventing you. --- El mar replied.

Officer Kate Haque was silent again as he insisted on rethinking the format for fingerprinting, taking more than forty minutes that day, before he succeeded.

That lapse of time seemed like an eternity to him, so it occurred to him to think that El mar was possessed by a force beyond his understanding and he regretted having found himself involved in an encounter of that nature in front of him, however it was somewhat late and he had to continue with the processing of the footprints, while he thought about how to justify that arrest.

He needed to impress his superiors and at the time of the action against El mar he thought that this arrest would be an opportunity in his career as a henchman.

Officer Kate Haque, because of her Hindu origins, had not fully identified with the pattern of violence in the West and even her knowledge of her ancestral history had brought her the great sacrifices of Mahatma Gandhi in the face of the violence of the

The English imperial police, and those memories of his ancestral history tended to confuse him more and more rigorously, so he thought that perhaps El mar was the living reincarnation of Gandhi.

Meanwhile, looking for a way to advance in the reproduction of those finger marks, he tried to distract his thoughts, diverting his restlessness, reciting in the silence of the night a verse he learned from his Jewish father:

"Only by seeing you smile can I understand the melancholy expression, for your sadness you exhibit with nobility, and my joy quickens my soul, my heart cannot tolerate that your sadness should lead you to failure.

With my harmony I sing you my life, so that my soul inspires you with joy, I thank you for refreshing my peace, thank you eternal Lord Jehovah, thank you father that happiness, thank you eternal Lord Jehovah.

Our Father who is in heaven, it is glorious to attain your peace.

How glorious it is to experience your goodness! How happy! Come we must all praise, what joy Father Jehovah!

Jesus came to demonstrate the love he could give, with his blood he vindicated us, what joy I now feel! Is it true that Jehovah sent him? That by his blood the world was saved! What joy I now feel!

As he thought about the refrains of the poem he felt that something had begun to calm him down and he began to understand that life would always be an experiment where what was called to happen would always happen, that this was a world where the majority of the poor were manipulated and abused by a small minority, of the rich where laws were desecrated to justify the unjustifiable.

Then he became convinced that his conscience had been severed since he chose to serve oppression, those who, by violating the system, never regretted their dirty tricks, coming to the conclusion that he would either go ahead or be punished, He knew that in that nation of opportunities and danger at the same time, everything was lost for nothing, there mistakes were paid with jail or money, and other times even with life, there men could not always understand that the true justice lay in not doing to their fellow men what they did not want them to do to them.

In Paradise the most surprising events used to be generated, which sometimes originated the great good things but also the most terrible evils, because also enclosed in the walls of silence inhabited the intellect of terror, followed by the attitude and quality of discernment, of glory or abyss.

Twenty minutes had passed before the ambulance that would take El Mar to the hospital arrived. The paramedics helped him to get up and put him on a stretcher, and after ten minutes, the emergency room of San Barnabas Hospital had arrived, supported by two paramedics and escorted by officer Kate Haque, who was received by Dr. Merchant, who then subjected El Mar to a brief interrogation:

--- What happened? - Dr. Merchant inquired, heading to El mar.

--- This guy fought with someone. -- Officer Haque responded, anticipating El mar's response.--- Bullshit, I haven't fought with anyone, you beat me up. Replied El mar, denying the version of officer Kate Haque who, not expecting such a reaction, opted for

Keep silent, while Dr. Merchant led El mar to a check-up cubicle.

The handcuffs were removed again until the diagnosis was completed,

Being installed in a bed in the room, they applied a serum, and then some pain killers, later after the checkup, had determined the need for

To practice a cascanic exploration and some x-rays in the affected parts. Once the diagnosis was concluded, he was handcuffed again. It turned out that in a nearby room there were the children Mark, procreated with Celeste Capellán, the partner before the relationship at that time, and May, the firstborn of Barbarita and El mar and because they could not stand the unbridled screams of little May, who had been separated from the mother because of her possible childbirth condition, and led him to the corridor where El mar was waiting, so that they would be with him until other officers came to pick them up to be transferred to the child protection agency, which at that time called him (A C S)

Mark who was five years old understood better what had happened, but on the other hand May, who was only two years old, was not very clear about what had happened and her screams were more out of fear than loneliness, that's why the presence of El mar was like a tranquilizer for him and her reaction was one of serenity and love in front of her father, and at once she landed on his back, hugging and kissing him, while El mar caressed his hair.Half an hour later, the officers who were to drive them to the hospital boarded them, prompting May to resume his initial crying, when he felt again distant from him, he could be heard exclaiming under the strain of the crying:

--- Dad, I don't want to go, Dad, come on, Dad.

He kept repeating the expression until the officer who was holding him on his shoulders disappeared behind the exit door followed by Mark who was walking holding the hand of the other officer who was accompanying him,

Sunday morning, El mar had been moved to a private room where he was kept in custody, handcuffed and under the surveillance of an officer, in the early hours of the morning he received a visit from two junior officers from another precinct, who gave him a heartfelt apology for everything that had happened, and spread the word among the officers that El mar was a good person.

That recommendation was convenient, because that day he needed to communicate with Celeste Chaplain, to notify him what had happened and explain why he would not be returning Mark in the agreed time, achieving

The cooperation of the officer on duty in the custody, who had decided to lend him his personal cell phone for that purpose.

Because Celeste Capellán was having an affair with another man, she had decided that El Mar would check her out at the boyfriend's number, for any emergencies involving Mark, and he could not be found.

Just as he thought, El Mar did, telling him that he was in the hospital and that because there was no one to pick up the children in time, the police had taken him to the child protection agency.

El mar thought that apparently the boyfriend of the Celeste had not provided the message in time, if not, until the other day, taking pitiless advantage of the occasion to report to the police of Yonkers the inconvenience that crossed El mar, precisely at a time when she was fighting a custody for Mark.

The Celeste believed that the confrontation between El Mar and the city's police officers was a good opportunity to "kill two birds with one stone" as a way of getting revenge, and at the same time to retain custody of Mark. So when she went to pick up the child with the help of the Yonkers henchmen and the emissaries of the Department of Social Services, she wanted to convince herself of what she had been told, and "make firewood out of the fallen tree: El mar fought with the police.

Without inquiring with anyone, without knowing more reasons, I take advantage of the absence of your controversial

Rival, and with the agreement of Miss Frolinger, the public defender assigned to El Mar, who had gone over to the side that Celeste Capellán represented, issued an order of protection to Mark, and another to her.

During his stay in San Barnabas, he had been rigorously examined, x-rayed and medicated until Tuesday, October 23, when he was to come face to face with a Bronx Supreme Court judge, and another public defender from "the County Defenders" would come in to represent him, and where he would learn for the first time what he was being accused of.

A community organization that sought to guide the defense of the inhabitants of the community within the framework of justice. It was there that he found the one who would put his greatest effort into proving his innocence, she was Jocelyn Simp, who, approaching the

Court cells accompanied by an assistant reviewing the list of defendants, with some insight appointed:

--- El mar valenilla --- Pronounced.

--- Here. --- El mar answered.

--- ! Hello, my name is Jocelyn Simp, I am your defense attorney. --- He said approaching him.

--- Thank you, I am El Mar Valenilla, I seek and hope for justice. --- He affirmed.

--- All right, this is Sandra my assistant, we'll do our best to get you out of here.

--- Hello! --- The assistant came forward to answer.

--- El mar corresponded as he held out his hand.

--- Do you know what you are accused of? --- Jocelyn interrupted.

---No. Of what? --- Asked El mar with some curiosity.

Jocelyn, looked at the document he was carrying in his hands and quoted:

--- Resistance to arrest, disorderly conduct and obstruction of government administrative work --- He indicated.

--- I'm innocent, I didn't do anything for them to arrest me, they were the ones who hit me, not me, besides, I'm not a terrorist so they can say I'm obstructing the administrative work of the government, this is supposed to be a country

"democratic". --- Alleged El mar.

--- All right, let's go see the judge. --- Said Attorney Simp.

Jocelyn and Sandra went out the door they came in, while El mar was waiting to be called to appear in front of the judge.

Two or three of the detainees called, before El mar was brought before Judge Patricio who had merely called the name of the accused and read the charges against him, Jocelyn, took notes of what he said, to request the release of his defendant:

--- My client pleads not guilty, and I ask that he be released until the case is investigated.

--- Well, let's leave it to come back on December 15th. --- Said the patrician judge.

The clerk took notes, Jocelyn imitated the clerk, and the court officer extended the summons she picked up by handing it to El mar, who thanked her effusively.

--- Thank you. He said.

---- Okay, call me on Monday. --- Jocelyn said, as she handed him a card with her phone number on it.

El mar took her between its fingers and left the courtroom.

Upon leaving the courthouse he went to the 46th precinct to remove his property, including his car, and since he had not seen Barbarita again after the incident despite being hospitalized at the same health center, he went directly to Brooklyn.

There he learned that she had given birth to a baby girl, and that to enter the apartment he had to break the door with the help of one of the nurses who had attended her in the hospital, and who had offered to help her, because the key to the apartment had been

It was left on the property that had been held for El mar in the precinct, and which had refused to be given to her.

May, who was not yet silent and who had managed to get on the nerves of the assigned provider, had been returned by the agency on the same day that El mar had been released.

Two months later, when the problems began to worsen, the city's emissaries began to mobilize through the city's child care agency and the Yonkers Department of Social Services, first contacting the owner of the apartment Barbarita Roque was renting through a Section 8, who

He began to provoke El mar in different ways and even put pressure on Barbarita

Roque, in order that he did not receive it in his house.

Because El mar and Barbarita had children in common but literally had different directions, even though every night he would wake up in her apartment, but; for the purposes they pursued the presence of El mar, prevented him from forging his plan of manipulation.

By that time, a Yonkers social service worker had contacted her through a subpoena to question her about a child abuse complaint that Celeste Capellán had filed, alleging that Barbarita was bothered by jealousy attacks when Mark approached El Mar.At first Barbarita refused to attend the call, letting the worker know that since she was a New York City client, Yonkers Social Services did not have jurisdiction to question her about a slander fabricated by Celeste Capellán, but eventually El Mar convinced her to come forward.

In addition to Barbarita, El mar had also been questioned on that date, so they allowed him to be the first one to enter the interview, so that she would be behind, like this

It would be easier to take advantage of it and try to get it out with the aim of cornering El mar, which was still engaged in a fight in the Yonkers family court for

Custody of Mark, however he was not going to scrimp on demanding justice, especially when he knew the purpose of Celeste Chaplain, who in her whim of spite

She insisted on keeping him away from the child Mark, and although they had approached previous agreements, because of the petty condition of arrogance and blindness, she always persisted in an inexplicable and unsustainable revenge.

The Celeste was looking for an assiduous pretext to return to court, which had caused

El mar tried to grab "the bull by the horns" looking for the custody of Mark, whose reason had been generated when Celeste Capellán, took him out of the country chasing a further cause, was to leave him in charge of his maternal grandparents, in his country of origin, without setting any explanation to El mar, and making communication between them difficult.

No one knew the real reason for her decision but it was said that it was all due to a plan of oppression forged against El mar by the manipulation team of Paradise, where she, as the visible head of the family, had been chosen to complement the coup,

Whose success could only be achieved by using the family as a piece of that chess, and Celeste Capellán, a beautiful, silent and calculating woman, could be the checkmate piece, with which one could advance in the forge of the plan.

Everything happened a year after they joined, she had received a silent and prejudiced offer that would lead her to act with malice, and for this purpose she tried to take shelter in her cassock, making her brother an accomplice in the confessional; she had consulted the blessed who was advised by her mother, who with great diligence suggested her a vacation that would be her departure and her great farewell.

She, trying to leave without leaving a trace, had commented to El Mar that her older brother Rafi, who was nicknamed "blessed" because of his consecration to the priesthood, would send her a ticket for a vacation, where she would travel with the children, two from her first marriage and Mark, in order to spend a stay in the city of Tenerife, over there in the Caribbean.

El mar had noticed that not everything was going well, something he ignored was happening, his suspicion increased when at the airport he saw Pedrosa Elizondo lurking in the context without being informed.

Pedrosa, father of the children who were not his, and behind Pedrosa, the great obstacles that would attract him to communicate with Mark.

When he found out that his boy, the one with whom he had a close friendship, had been chosen for a forced farewell, it didn't seem right to El Mar, let alone when he knew that Mark would stay.

El mar felt mocked so he turned to Yonkers family court for justice, where he found "medicine worse than the disease" and where he found he was more "salt than the goat". Such action would generate the definitive separation between him and Celeste Capellán.

He had already been warned by a neighbor of the building to be careful because Celeste had said that government sectors interested in justifying themselves were looking for ways to criminalize him to make him look like "the bad guy", thus justifying a purpose they were pursuing.

Nobody understood what was happening, but the truth was that fourteen years earlier, in the year nineteen hundred and ninety-one, when El mar arrived in Paradise, two months after being in the city and having suffered an accident at work, he was taken out of the

Factory where military uniforms were manufactured, and ignoring that at that time, in some warehouses of the city, drugs were sold with the naturalness with which sugar and rice were sold, he had entered one of them on the east side of B Street, in lower Manhattan, and while talking to someone who seemed to be in charge of the business, he entered

Another emissary interrupted and said something in the ear of the one who was talking to him.

Apparently warned, the wrecker left the place in a hurry, while leaving El mar with the word kept between his mouth, and the one who seemed to be in front of the

Business followed the one who went to warn him, while suggesting El mar to wait for him for a moment.

Not two minutes had passed when the gendarmes entered the place, having been mistaken by the agents for a drug dealer who was nominated by Maxi Gómez, and

who apparently had a criminal record, and whose confusion had influenced El mar to be considerably beaten, looted, and arrested by the henchmen

Without uniforms to those who at that time were called detectives, without their aggressors feeling any interest in clarifying what had happened.

They had falsified the truth of the facts, and had fabricated a case for him to possess and sell drugs without possessing or selling, even though he had refused to testify

He did not accept an offer of probation, which the court had offered him, because he understood that if   he had done nothing, he did not have to accept any offer, adding to all that the communicational noises, because he did not understand nor speak the official language of paradise, resulting in these limitations the great difficulty of his defense.

In addition to the trauma of his own existence, you added to this the racial prejudice of the public defender assigned to him, to the extent that he came to think that this lawyer by his attitude, more than a defender of his cause, was a covert executioner in the service of those who accused him, with the mission of making El mar the scapegoat they needed.

At the time of his arrest, he tried, insisted and claimed his innocence in front of one of the agents who spoke to him in his mother tongue, explained to him that they were confused, that he could not talk to them about the unknown, and even so, he could not prevent them from arresting him.

Not caring about his pain, Officer Roman responded:

--- It's better to be calm, if you don't want things to get complicated. --- He answered with the scruple of a puppet moved by invisible threads.

By that time, and even though he was the legal one in paradise, they did not take the trouble to identify him by his fingerprints to determine that he was not Maxi Gomez, they did not take any consideration by granting him a sentence of one to three, with another name and

Sending him to jail with an illegal case.

When they realized the injustice they had committed at that time, it seemed a little late to rectify, they sanctioned the lawyer who in the name of El Mar, tried to sue the city, without achieving a successful lawsuit, and being the accusation for a drug case, Being the one involved a minority member with the distant family, a penniless, copper-skinned immigrant in a system run by men with slave mentalities, they did not have to do much research for pride, prejudice, arrogance and racism to take hold.

Apart from that macro mistake of sentencing someone without identifying him, something that perhaps never had been seen before in Paradise, and in the heterogeneous society of the kingdom, that action traumatized the essence of that being, who did not believe again in the justice of that kingdom that had abandoned its mystique to grow as an inclement paper tiger.

Everything that happened showed the fragility and vulnerability of a system that in theory was sold as the dirty Mecca of social justice, where silence was paid with money, or with death, because this was the Paradise of those days, where men progressed or died, and in whose system of free enterprises, created and solved by Enlightenment and gray men, creators of violence and social manipulation, where public opinion was conditioned by economic progress spread left and right by owners of the great capital.

A public opinion, that even knowing what it wanted, did not stop doubting the sincerity of its freedom of expression, that's why the one who paid was in charge, the masters emanated from the kingdom, and El mar by its own experience knew that the freedom of expression was promoted in a section of one of the constitutional amendments, but for him, who had to live what very few had lived, the reality was different.

Among the discomforts experienced, he had suffered a cyber attack when he was writing one of those little novels with which he wanted to do himself justice, when he had written page 156, they blocked the document so that he could not open it under the allegation that it contained illegal expressions, he tried to find who would open it without any

Successfully, he wanted to denounce the action with courage in front of the civil rights institutions, but he remembered that there freedom of expression had become a myth that the people clamored for with their cries.

Since then a kind of persecution had been unleashed that did not let him advance or grow, but above all he persisted in the fact that one day justice would come

that he so longed for and never received, it had been fifteen years before he faced the police again, but despite the illegality of the record, the city emissaries always waited for the opportunity for El mar to fail for them to take revenge and justify the mistakes they had made against him.

He had tried to sue him but because of his initial trauma, he was not successful, but above all he used to question how justice could best be served without resorting to violence, when the owners of the system, even when they were wrong, tried to impose themselves by force.

CHAPTER 4

— Mr. Jimenez, who had attempted to ascertain Barbarita Roque, insisted on persuading her to join the efforts of the Department of Social Service. He was a specially assigned case worker there, and would do everything possible to find a mechanism through which they could discredit El Mar, and pass it off as a violent and dangerous person to the community.

He was an emissary of the system and if he complied with the mandate he would surely be promoted or rewarded, since many had tried before him, without success, but involving in the attempt the two mothers of the children of El Mar, he thought, that it would be much easier without them seeming to have a personal interest, but at that time, Barbarita was still in love with her man and she was the type of woman

that when she loved she gave herself away, and at that moment she did not intend to betray the man who made her sigh, although Mr. Jimenez would not allow her to come out of his refusal unscathed.

Barbarita refused to collaborate, defying the arrogance of those concerned, and in a short time the problems with the owner of the apartment where she lived, whom they had also contacted in order to request her collaboration, became more acute, because when they intended to hit someone, if they could not do it with a stick, they used a stone.

That is, if they refused to get involved voluntarily, they implicated him by force and for that some resorted to provocations that induced the implicated to lose his temper, to justify himself, or to create false witnesses to manipulate the authenticity of the evidence in favor of the victim, they were unaccustomed to losing and when in order to win they needed to provoke the guilt of their victims, to justify their justice system in the face of

To public opinion, they resorted to whatever was necessary, always aware of leaving no trace of their illegality.

Then the owner was asked to rent to Barbarita, a patriotic collaboration making it difficult for her to one day because she did not know the language of Paradise, and therefore the rights of the tenant, the owner refused to renew her lease and taking advantage that El mar could not accompany her to the court of

Housing, guided by a public defender assigned to victimize the poor, signed an agreement with the owner that in about three months she would leave the apartment.

It turned out that being a Section 8 tenant, to find an apartment before three months, was not easy, and once the deadline to return the property was met, it was not worth crying or begging the judge, the allegation that she had no place to stay with the four boys, who without the greatest modesty had refused to extend the deadline, signing the eviction order, which with so much interest, executed the officer appointed for such a merciless mission.

Seeing that she had to leave the apartment, staying practically out in the open, section eight had become obsolete and therefore she had also lost it.

El mar got a space near where she lived to give the children time to finish the school year, but since there were four children, two from Barbarita's first relationship and two from El mar, it was not so easy to find someone to rent one

It was a very important decision for the city of Barbarita, which had a room and allowed four children and two adults to enter, because El Mar had given up its apartment to move into Barbarita's, until the pilgrimage that they were going through at that time took place.

Two weeks after getting the room, due to the number of people who occupied it, the owner, alleging the need for the space, asked to have it vacated, until they managed to get the authorization of the mother of the nurse who had attended Barbarita in the hospital, to stay overnight in her room.

They spent a few days in that condition until El mar managed to get an apartment

study, which allowed her to settle in properly and from where Barbarita would travel to drop off the children at school, because the Christmas vacation was over but the year was not yet over.

El mar also continued to fight the charges that the agents of the

Bronx 46th Precinct, until the time came when they decided to make him a confusing offer through Jocelyn simp.

It was May 25 when the sun was exhibiting its burning rays, it was eleven o'clock in the morning when Jocelyn told El mar, with the greatest naivety of her career as a lawyer:

--- They want you to stand up in front of the judge, and agree to have the case dismissed in six months. He explained.

--- ? Are you sure that's not a trap? argued El mar, with some mistrust.

--- No way. Jocelyn specified.

--- Well... it's okay --- he said El mar.

They entered the courtroom, in the center was Judge Patricio and on the left was the clerk, followed by the court officials.

Three people had called and they had sent him the appointment, El Mar felt a little uncomfortable, he did not trust the system's emissaries because he already knew the arbitrariness committed against him for so long, so he was not willing to continue to be abused, he was curious to leave the room and for that he told the lawyer that he would go to the bathroom, and once he got the authorization, he called a lawyer member of the firm who would represent him in the civil claim, and sought information:

--- How are you, sir? I have an offer, in the dispute with the gendarmes, the emissaries of the prosecutor's office want me to go before the judge, to confirm that I accept that they dismiss the case after six months --- said El mar.

--- If you are innocent in six months, then you are innocent now, tell him that you accept the proposal if they dismiss the case now, otherwise, tell him that you do not accept it. ---The lawyer consulted told him.

--- Very well thank you, I will. --- Said El mar.

He returned to the courtroom, and notified the attorney of his change of mind.

--- I'm sorry, I've thought about the proposal and I've decided to accept it, if they dismiss the case now, and not in six months, if I'm innocent in six months I'm innocent now --- he said.

--- It's okay. --- Jocelyn stated.

A few minutes later they called the name of El mar, Jocelyn responded to the patrician judge:

--- My client does not accept the offer --- he said.

To which the judge, pretending not to notice with a certain amount of courage, replied:

--- I thought he was here to make a plea, get out of my

Judge Patricio shouted at attorney Jocelyn, who was embarrassed not to be able to attend.

He was able to hold back the crying, adding to that the claim of El mar.

--- You realize, if I had accepted that, without my conditions, I would have fallen into a trap. It's just that there is no honest man here, when those who represent justice are

the first scoundrels, why did you do that? --- Replied El mar mounting a melo-drama to the lawyer simp, which sharpened his crying, reliable mind.

---- forgive me. Said Jocelyn Simp, between sobs.

--- That's fine, but don't repeat this, especially not with me, you are a young and beautiful woman you don't have to be a judge or a lawyer when it comes to your defense, the right thing to do is to be bound by the law. You have a great future if you resort to your levels of ethics and

Conscience; I understand that's the way the system is, and that it doesn't mind confronting father and son and best friends, but when you have the power of discernment, you can refuse to act like a worm, that's why minorities hunger for justice. --- Said El mar.

--- Okay, let's forget about this bad time and never talk about this again. - Jocelyn said, with some regret.

They did it as agreed, she would call him to let him know what the next court date would be.

El mar, he used to describe the expression police, as the force of coercion and repression, paid by the poor in the service of the rich, he had managed to accumulate a series of experiences that had led him to doubt the credibility of the gendarmes of the mayor's office, however, he knew that it was necessary to develop patience, exercising tolerance.

Even though he had managed to observe an officer with one of his photos drawing an arrow on it that pierced his temples, or more than one of them shooting it into his head with their regulation weapons, or trying to manipulate it when it was time to back up in the car in front of a red light, with expressions like :

-- What do you want us to do, arrest you or write you a ticket? --- for him to answer:

--- I'm not afraid of them, do what you have to do.

El mar was never violent, however, in the face of so much injustice and unbridled abuse, he once thought of taking justice into his own hands, but a ray of light radiated from him

A pattern of reflection, and he thought that "the saddest tears that wet the tombs, were for the words that were never said", and to keep the biting silence, would be like grieving his presence, then he said:

--- It is better to think before acting, in an unthinking moment if by revenge an intolerant one armed and took the justice in his hands, before they kill him he could take a few, but it would be useless, almost always the innocent fall, and nothing new would be for the system that had evolved and was maintained in the violence, "the weak would never inherit the earth because they would not know what to do with it", Martin Luther King was right, when referring to his generation he said that: "He did not lament

Both of the crimes of the wicked, and of the shocking silence of the good.

He really knew the bosses' motto: "the dead to the hole and the living to the buoy", and the best thing according to El mar was not to play along, because some of them used to think about winning or killing or declaring their opponents crazy, so violence would not be the best

Counselor, because even if a person achieves the desired purpose, the machinery would be ready to label the daring one as a terrorist, and he recalled the parody of Benedicto Jiménez, when he referred to the truth, and added:

--- "If truth depended on words, the structure of the world would have to be changed. "

He was invaded by a series of faltering expressions, which would define his philosophy of life, and so when he woke up after each dawn, he redefined the path, seeing as pleasant the possibility of always visualizing the future to protect the future, and thinking that the homeland was the land that motivated the cause of life, he understood that the light would always flash in the conscience of those who fought for the cause.

He smiled as if mocking himself, a fresh air as if it were a whirlpool blew over his face, and he continued to walk.

CHAPTER 5

— El mar, walked for a while as if without a fixed direction and stopped at a block where a party was taking place, some boys who were playing the rasperos sang animatedly

— --- Nobody complains in this place, maybe I am the exception because I am not of the bunch, if you are awake and you are not asleep, they want to whip you as a punishment.

Apparently freedom, we have it here, but if you something strange tries to denounce, the government mafia, you might want to hit yourself.

They are afraid of the truth and if it makes noise they must eliminate you.

In the dirty work they don't give the front, and they use a hitman to reprimand you.

They think they are the cream of humanity and a false prophet will create you.

They use God to justify, but their evil cannot be hidden.

The riffraff in the courtyard disgusts him, to hide they offer him a contract, but with the

Intention to break the sack.

With immigration, they seek control, and they fear losing some of the power.

When the worst anguish assails you is when faith is renewed.

And if faith is activated, and the light of truth shines in the consciousness, it seems to them a trick of science.

If man is conscious and rebe-enderesa, he is called nature's mistake.

The blue buzzards, prowling the city, trying to find someone to victimize.

They invent a ruse to justify a ticket or infraction that must be paid.

They fear criminals, they ignore their actions, and the man in the job they want to prosecute.

They do not know about justice nor do they want to rehearse, their great concern is to be able to find, who to fine, to justify the commission they intend to win.

A thunderous applause followed by a surprising joy was heard as the singers concluded.

On one of the walls that enclosed the yard where the event was held, a graffiti was read that highlighted an expression: "If there were more music schools than military men on the streets, there would be more guitars than machine guns, and more artists than killers", followed by another chorus that specified: "we are responsible for what we talk about, not for what the others understand, and that is why we are not afraid of the enemy that attacks, but of the false friend that embraces".

Just as he finished reading the graffiti, the gendarmes appeared at the venue, under the pretext that the loud speakers had to be lowered because public order was being disturbed.

El mar that still felt the effects of the trauma that had caused the disagreement with them, thought that nothing of what was happening, could be happening to him, and parodied in silence Oscar Wilde, with that "men live the novel that they have not been able to write, and write the novel that they have not been able to live" for a moment wanted to ignore what had happened, but thought that: "the whip strengthens, and who punishes makes us strong, and hummed a chorus as if reciting a verse:

---- Those who criticize you make you important, those who envy you make you valuable, and those who wish you the worst, have to endure the best.

Then he decided to set aside his scruples by acting as he saw fit, smiling at one of the agents and retiring with some caution in his mouth:

-- "my conscience is greater than your evils. -He said as if he were talking to his other self.

When he had left the place, he met an acquaintance who, without stopping, blew him a kiss in the air, to which he added:

--- If the hungry are hungry, don't waste food, she stopped smiling and greeted him with a kiss on the cheek, as she said:

--- Hi, you don't age. -To which El mar answered him:

--- I prefer to stay young to attract your attention... I sounded that El mar was burning, I sounded that the earth was burning, and for dreaming impossible, I sounded that you loved me.

--- Ha Ha Ha, you are my poet, you know I love you --- she said.

---- but you don't show me. I replicate El mar.--- Ah, you're the one who won't let yourself be seen...You took care of love, and call me. - He said as he

I kissed him on the cheek again.

--- I will call you, thank you.

--- El mar said to him, squeezing and releasing his hand. She walked away, while he watched her walk away in silence.

In a short time, he had learned that ignorance was like blindness, and he remembered those college years, when he questioned a neighborhood girl:

--- If you finished, high school, when do you plan to enter college? -he asked. To which she responded:

--- What for? My boyfriend lives in the kingdom, which is the pure little Paradise. ---She expressed a certain curiosity, while El mar insisted:

--- So, what does one have to do with the other? --- he questioned again.

--- A "Green card", that is, a residence of the kingdom, is worth more than a profession. She argued quite naturally.

El mar, on the other hand, had been somewhat disappointed with the response, and had noticed that some young people in the central Caribbean were sailing from confusion to alienation.

CHAPTER 6

— Commissioner Jefri Hamilton's phone line extension phone wouldn't stop ringing as he returned from the bathroom to his desk. He settled in properly before lifting the extension when he heard the receptionist inform him that the mayor was on the line:

--- Please pass it on... Say, Mr. Mayor... do you want me to be at the meeting tonight?...All right, I'll be there. Thank you, we'll see you later, yes sir, goodbye.

As he was about to hang up the phone, Captain Rick entered the office and immediately went through the details of the assigned tasks.

--- Mission accomplished, Mr. Commissioner, your nephew is already on the plane.

--- Well, now I'm more relaxed, thanks Captain Rick, what have you heard about El mar valenilla report?

--- Everything is defined, internal affairs found no evidence to charge him, Officer Haque is in trouble, the prosecution may drop the charges, he was with the family," he said.

--- Explain to me better, what happened to the interrogation of the bride? ---... he asked, Commissioner Jefri Hamilton. --- Barbarita Roque, her name is Barbarita Roque, everything coincided with what he said. --- Reaffirmed Captain Rick.

Commissioner Jefri Hamilton, frowned as he stated:

---- Life, life, life, how has it all changed? What a paradox, before I was commissioned, I was a civilian in the service of the then mayor, the police were unaware that I

I was a man of the mayor, one day I was caught with two kilos of cocaine, but since they belonged to the mayor and one of the judges of paradise, they reduced my sentence to possession of two passes for my use under the allegation that I was working on an undercover mission, until I finally managed to climb the ranks of police commissioner, but now everything is more difficult, none of us can escape the radicalism of an insatiable public opinion, reinforced by the press ---- he said.

--- Commissioner Hamilton, your story sounds like a police novel, but you are a lucky man. ---Captain Rick added.

--- More than lucky, Captain Rick, I would say... with very good relations. --- Said Commissioner Jefri Hamilton, emphasizing the expression on his face, and the play of his eyes.

--- Ha,Ha,Ha,Ha.---Captain Rick laughed.

At sunset a yellowish sun filled the skies, its flush light glistening through the grids of the glass windows of the skyscraper.

The day was cool and began to attract some grayish clouds that turned into rain and wind, which enervated his aspirations, but his share of power as a commissioner, set the hope for new beginnings.

That's how it was played in paradise, if the luck marked it to win, it won, and if it did it to lose, it lost.

The truth was that after the terrorist attack, where the Twin Towers fell, which turned out to be like a minority hecatomb, where thousands lost their lives, and where some experts in the field did not stop commenting, that because of the condition as it had generated everything, it could have been a conspiratorial self-coup.

Since then, life in paradise had taken a surprising turn, and this event reminded government authorities that within the

The city was a great focus of discontent, where many people had justly or unjustly suffered, and not knowing who intended to take revenge, they

They had to take great security measures, and there was no lack of those who were followed or guarded throughout the vast territory of Paradise.

 El mar, because of the conflicts that had surrounded it, surely would not escape from being a generator of suspicions.

But he knew that however great his aspirations were, they were   not always what man would have wanted to be or have, but what life brought with it, and therefore he used to think how wonderful and extraordinary every day was, if he decided to be happy no matter what.

He was rarely angry because in doing so he understood that behind the mask of another identity, the executioners wrapped their bodies in the black savannahs, in order to raise the sword of extirpation over the heads of those who carried the burden, but that by arming themselves with good will those who seemed defenseless simply blocked the attempts of evil.

Being the adhesion of his spirit the strength of his essence, his convictions became stronger than his whims, and his faith was so held on that he overcame and bent the prejudice of pride.

For him the race of life was fraught with difficulties, but what mattered most was not to give up the path to the goal, strengthening faith beyond the banner of glory. At that time, the diplomatic status of El Mar kept him happy, so much so that when he walked through the surrounding streets he often stopped to greet people he knew, showing his great popularity. That same afternoon he met again another acquaintance who also greeted him with a certain kindness:

--- To God, my heart. -She said.

--- Goodbye, beautiful, it's nice to know that I'm beating in your chest. --- He answered her with a high splendor of courtesy.

The smiling young woman continued on her way, while he watched her swimming in the silence.El mar understood life in a different way than many of his friends did, he sought to survive without being dragged into the parasitism that was so fostered in paradise, because when the individual depended on government donations, and did not make an effort to free himself, he regularly became the raw material of those in charge, he always looked for a way to report his taxes each year, and when he did not do so as a salaried employee of one of the corporations in the context, he did so as a self-employed worker.

And before the disparity of his instability in paradise, as a long time resident he had tried to obtain the citizenship of the kingdom, but due to the conflict of 1991, the city obstructed his aspirations while influencing the Immigration Service, who in turn, without great contemplation, did not spare him, alleging that he had been involved a few decades ago, in possession and sale of narcotics.

According to the immigration laws of that time, those allegations, even if illegal and without proof, were invested in him by a candidate who could be deported for "misconduct".

And although for many years El mar valenilla continued to struggle, the new approaches had become more acute, upon returning from a trip from his home country, seven years after the terrorist attack.

They continued to search for Moors where there were no costs, and at the time of a check his passport and permanent resident card were seized.

A deportation order had been issued, and although he was allowed to fight in immigration court, from that moment on he could not leave paradise or go back to his country of origin

Nor to any other place, and the few friends with whom he exchanged some point of view, came to believe him a trustworthy prisoner.He saw El mar so involved with the judicial system that when he was not going to court, he had a summons to attend another, until on one occasion he discovered himself with more assignments than any lawyer, having to comply with summonses and citations from the various courts of paradise.

Such judicial occupations led him to walk in immigration court, family court, criminal court, traffic court, child support court, among other government departments, which we refrain from citing so that readers do not get the idea that I am fantasizing or overloading the actions of El Mar.

Although those moments generated tensions, he sought ways to maintain his equanimity, even developing the belief that pain was strengthening, and betrayal made him thoughtful and cautious.

Disillusionment made him skilled and opened his understanding, while experiences made him wise. He was really able to overcome with courage all those moments of bitterness, and there were moments when he thought the system was creating the conditions to drive him to suicide, without the intervention of the henchmen.

He had moved away from social life, some missed him, or others were indifferent, he had few friends, because many of the few he had kept, were tempted by the betrayal, and for a few coins, there were those who wanted to give him as a Jew to Jesus, but his strength prevailed, his pain turned him into hope, and he discovered that faith was the best tool to overcome the conspiracies.

Sporadically he would express a contradictory paraphrase, where he would be heard and say that politics should not be confused with injustice because many used politics for injustice, while others used justice for politics.

In that moment of thoughtful dismay, he was assailed by a thought of that day when he left the house at the usual time, the air was blowing in its breeze a garland of a flower that landed on the tip of his nose, which led him to an active reflection of life, nature and God, how a black-haired man used to get gray, how flowers germinate from a seed, and how the sun with its light that hides in every evening, reappears every new day with a glow of hope.

--- Beauty --- He thought --- Beauty is like God, there is no doubt that they are seen from different angles, worshipped from different cultural perspectives.

It is true the proverbial expression, "to go after justice leads to life, but to go after evil leads to death". --- Express.

Then for a moment he experienced pity, terror and anxiety, he was unaware of the subtleties, he knew that the subtle was what induced the heart.

As far as he thought about the cultural relativity of beauty, he understood that not always what seemed beautiful to one would turn out to be the same as another.

But innocence, candor, naivety, and the grace of imagination were for him the true beauty.

He then compared religiosity and ignorance to the channels of superstition.

34

CHAPTER 7

— Celeste Capellán played nervously with her eyes concentrated on a lock of her hair emanating from her temples

His eyebrows denounced his concern, his gaze lost in the horizon tried to concentrate on the words he would say in the quote from El mar Valenilla, with whom, as he had said before, he had a son in common, and to whom he had tried to give "the life of squares", in Paradise, trying to prove it in all the facets of his aspirations.

She had just entered her forties, and felt lost in the deep waters of her aspirations. A display of frustrations invaded her soul; very few things had gone well in her life.

She was an only child among three boys, from a prosperous family in the Caribbean region, called "Tenerife", being the youngest of the brothers, she believed that she deserved to reach the whims of her aspirations.

His father was a retired police captain, his mother a longtime pythoness and card reader, until Rafi, the eldest of the male children, had been ordained a priest, who had rebuked her to abandon the practice in the name of God:

———— Mom, please, when are you going to stop that, if the Archbishop realizes this, I'm going to be very upset. And from then on he made his clientele become parishioners of the newly ordained son's parish.

All of them had concentrated on raising Celeste Capellán like a teddy bear, to whom nothing should be denied, and everything should be tolerated, and this custom had become to her a value nationalized like an ink on a piece of furniture, contributing in this way to the aberration of her formation, she instead started washing the stole of the priest, and remembered those years of her childhood, when she was reprimanded by some

Mischief, she would lock herself in the room she shared with her parents, stroking her hair with intense nervousness. She grew up infatuated, believing herself to be a key figure in distinguishing between the leadership of her region.

In high school, she integrated a group of middle class girls, more arrogant and bad-tempered than educated, who had developed the attitude of being naughty, joking and mocking, to the point of angering the teachers, who had begun to see them as anarchists.

Of that group of seven teenagers who were cutting classes to go dancing at the disco, only two graduated, the ones who had been superb and radical in front of the director of the girls' school, María Inmaculada, the registration disappeared on the campus, and it seemed as if they had never attended that high school, and among the injured, there was Celeste Capellán who neither the intervention of the clergy, who through the priest brother wanted to help her, was able to clarify the situation. A short time later, she met a man from Tenerife who had lived in Paradise for a long time, they fell in love and a few months later, she managed to get him a visa for five years, which allowed him to move to Paradise, where through an immigration fraud, she contracted a marriage for business with a police officer addicted to cocaine, known to the groom Pedrosa Elizondo, and through which she achieved permanent residence. For five years and some months he lived in free union with Pedrosa Elizondo, with whom during that time he procreated two creatures, a female and a baron, which had allowed him to remain united, under the tension of that acquired character, taking his pulse to check which one of the two wore the pants, and as it was obvious, the temperament of Celeste Capellán, would end up tracing the route to follow.

One day, when Pedrosa Elizondo felt the sulfur of his courage, deciding to take revenge, he bit another concubine with whom he had a sexual relationship, on Celeste's bed.

Cama had rolled around in his absence; Pedrosa, disturbed, felt discovered and had to admit to him his sin and all that he had done, having been sworn by Celeste Capellán, formerly such a felony, that from now on she would take revenge on men.

Taking advantage of what had happened, she told the priest about her husband's infidelity, who stayed away, and although he did not excommunicate Pedrosa for the infidelity in front of his sister, he let Celeste decide.

It was then when Celeste decided to return to Tenerife, remaining absent for more than five years, at that time it was very easy for travelers to remain absent for a long time without the residence of the kingdom, was affected, only needed to return before six months, so retain the validity of its legality.

Many neither entered nor exited just sent their passports to get a stamp in the kingdom and in their port of origin, maintaining their status without problem.

For his part, Pedrosa Elizondo kept the flame burning of what he understood by love, and continued to pursue Celeste, in love with her, as much as on the first day. Even in the distance he remained attentive to the needs of his children, so he continued to provide for them.

When the economic crisis threatened to hit Tenerife, Rafi the priest required her to use the green card, returning to work in Paradise to help the household economy, and she traveled by surprise.

At the dawn of a new millennium, at the beginning of the 21st century, one hot Wednesday in August, El mar, discovered it in the pure temperature of a hot summer.He had noticed their noble look, sprinkled with their beautiful, shy and insecure countenance, with a meekness that is typical of those who died in silence.

CHAPTER 8

— The politicians of paradise had implemented a system that financed women to control men

Some immigrants from different parts of the world who arrived in Paradise after two or three months of stay, began to lament having abandoned their traditions, jobs and properties, to readapt themselves to the new cultures and experiences of Paradise.

That place where everyone longed to arrive, despite the existing facilities in the context, induced many families to disintegrate easily, especially when they lacked a solid base of human integrity, so it was not difficult to perceive frequent divorces, separations and confrontations between parents and children, leaving clearly settled the issue that disintegrated family, victims more controlled.

The truth is that everyone placed their hopes in the apparent economic facilities that, within the framework of selfishness and individualization, the immigrants assumed they would receive from the charitable institutions of Paradise, but mainly many members of those generations of immigrants possessed a mentality conditioned to believe that the great wealth of the world's mafiosi had been raised with great ease in the criminalized democracy of Paradise.

By that time, the laws of tolerances would incriminate those who made their first "mistake", and made it easier for them to take advantage of an evidentiary program with pre-established conditions, where the person involved in the first violation, automatically

He criminalized even if he was innocent, because by accepting the probation he was admitting his guilt, giving the system the advantage of avoiding civil lawsuits.

In this way, the prisons of Paradise were kept full of "offenders" who entered and left according to the seriousness of the crime, but at the same time these offenders were becoming a source of work for the leaders of the system, giving rise to the creation of prison corporations and henchmen to care for and repress their victims.

These clans facilitated the organization and expansion and permanence of the kingdom, reimposing the impression that the system was everyone, and that there one could choose to be, what everyone wanted to be

The truth was that since its foundation, the kingdom possessed the same techniques of imposition, the essence was the same only the form had changed, and its population often lived on the laurels of alienation, victim of different types of addictions, and El mar came to think that Paradise, was an oppressed people behind the mystery of superstition and vanities.

But while Paradise was floating in abundance, other nations of the region were in poverty, being necessary to submit to policies traced by the kingdom. They had traced their parameters of operation where they emphasized that all those who sought wealth had to pay homage and adapt to the system that controlled any possibility of making fortune, that the kingdom was a capitalist nation that had grown thanks to the use of capital, and they emphasized that neither wealth nor opportunities would be within reach if organized capital had not provided those benefits.

That night, El mar, he listened to the television news, and then wrote a poem that he titled:

"Hope in the Distance, dedicated to Barbarita Roque, and said "Although you see that I am late, I have you present, and although I see you distant, your absence reinforces me, I will never be sad because I know that you exist, and even in the distance, you are of my longing, and with my voice shaped reinforcement hope, that one day we will meet, and satiate the desire. So that your countenance, turns in an instant, blushing your face, and defining the nuance, so that I interpret that it has been happy again".

That night was special, Barbarita felt flattered and in gratitude prepared her a mole dinner with guacamole, one of her favorite dishes, later they retired to bed, and she defenseless and naked admired the flabbiness of her manly sex, before immersing herself in the blanket that would cover them, at the moment of rubbing their bodies, they embraced, kissed, heated their skins exacerbated by an impudent desire, and a moment later she felt invaded by a deep ecstasy, and a warm, gelatinous liquid came out of

inside her vagina, smearing the center of her thighs and in an attack of inspiration she sighed and said:

--- You're mine, you're my man, I'm yours daddy, yours...

He hugged her tightly and said:

--- I too my love.

After the bath they went back to bed, and although Barbarita had embraced him, when he fell asleep, he had a nightmare where Celeste Capellán appeared laughing out loud, while her child Mark was crying; it was something like a scene of real life that to him in particular was unpleasant.

The laughter became a redoubled echo, and when he woke up, he discovered that he was bathed in sweat, so he wiped his forehead with the palm of his hand and said as if to himself:

--- Uh... I'll have to be patient, it's as if that woman, even in her dreams, was chasing me, I really don't know, what would I do if I found her hanging from a cliff? Or would I extend mine to her, so that she would climb up?

He made a brief silence, as if reflecting on what he had expressed. Barbarita woke up hugging him, and the children continued to sleep, but a few touches on the

Door induced him to be distracted, he got up at once, and even in his pajamas he went to the place where the touches came from:=

--- Who? --- I ask. On the other side of the door, a woman's voice was heard.

--- Good morning, I would like you to give us a few minutes to give you a message.

El mar with a courteous breath peeped out timidly, between opening the door, and showing half his face, to tell   him:v

--- I would like to let them pass but I am not dressed yet and...

They interrupted him, understanding him and giving him a magazine promoting his ministerial representation:

--- God loves you, and has a wonderful purpose for you, those tears you have shed, will be triple compensated, you don't have to worry, you are preparing for something very big, everything that has happened and what is left to happen, will happen naturally, and you are a pillar for that event, God's blessing remains, and we will see you again soon. -Said the woman.

El mar valenilla, which had been moved, responded:

--- Thank you.

Meanwhile, the women withdrew down the stairs, he rubbed his eyes with the back, and for the first time he felt them moistened, and he was left with the impression that those messengers, whom he had heard, seemed to him more like incarnated ghosts, and like a flame of light in the darkness, his heart accelerated and a little worried, he went back to bed, and slept again until eleven o'clock in the morning.

CHAPTER 9

— Shortly thereafter, El mar had been summoned to court again. It was September 5 when he was at the checkpoint where he was requisitioned by an officer on duty, before he entered the apartment where the judge would see him, and just when he was urgently dressing and putting away the strap, watch and personal belongings that he had to take out so that they wouldn't ring in the checkpoint machine, a grunting officer pressed the agile mobility of two of those in line who had stopped on the way.

--- Come on, come on, move it. --- He was saying.

As usual, the cell phone rang, it was Jocelyn Simp:

--- Hello! Where are you? -He asked.

--- Hello, Miss Simp! I'm here, I'm going up, in five minutes we'll see each other. -He answered.

He boarded the elevator, when he had gone up to the floor, entered the men's room, and immediately met Jocelyn Simp who was waiting for him in the corridor, they shook hands and she asked him to go into the room and wait for her until she returned, El mar did as she suggested.

Jocelyn left, going to the second floor, to the prosecutor's office, where he had held a brief conference with the prosecutor, who in turn had delegated his assistant to communicate the solution. Fifteen minutes later, Jocelyn was back and asked El mar to accompany him.

They returned together to the office where the assistant district attorney was waiting for him, who received him cordially.

--- He is El mar valenilla. --- Said attorney Jocelyn Simp, introducing El mar.

--- Nice to meet you, I am Ms. Watson, the assistant district attorney, please sit down --- she answered.

El mar occupied a seat in front of the assistant district attorney's desk, and she subjected him to a brief interrogation, including what had happened on October 20th. In a few words he told her in detail what had happened, to which she specified:

--- There's no contradiction, what you say is the same thing the agents said, that it happened, the only thing is that they did it wrong, because they didn't have to hit you... but you've said you're going to sue. --- You said. —

El mar was silent as she continued to expose herself:

--- Well, we're going to drop the charges anyway... Do you have a copy of your driver's license? - He questioned.

--- Yes, of course, El mar responded, as he put his left hand into the back pocket on the left side of his pants, took out his wallet, dug into it, located his driver's license, extended it to the assistant district attorney, who ipso facto put it in a photocopy machine and reproduced it, returning the original, and preserving the copy he had taken.

--- All right, go back to the room, your lawyer will explain it to Judge Patricio, good luck. ---She said, with the same courtesy she showed when she arrived.

--- Thank you. --- He answered--- El mar without looking around, walked three steps, and turned its head.

--- Go ahead, I'll be with you shortly. -Said Jocelyn Simp.

--- Well, I'll do that --- argued El mar.

The assistant district attorney shook her head as El mar left the office.

 In less than five minutes Jocelyn Sim was back, she told the judge the

Disposition of the prosecution, but the judge Patricio without being moved argued:

--- You need to tell me why you're throwing that case away.

At that moment the phone rang, the secretary picked it up without letting it ring, and after a brief pause she said

--- Judge Patricio, he's from the prosecutor's office.

The Judge lifted his extension and repeated:

--- Why, are they going to drop the case? --- He asked curiously.

--- The prosecution made an investigation, and it was determined that there was an error with the above-mentioned

El mar valenilla--the ADA answered on the other side of the line.

--- Very good. --- He said, as he hung up the phone.

He signed a few sheets, and extending them to the secretary said:

--- El mar valenilla, all your charges are dropped, your case is withdrawn. -Stated.--- Thank you, thank you --- He expressed El mar with simulated sanity but with great satisfaction.

The secretary sealed the sheets and extended them to the lawyer, who took possession of them, left the room and accompanied El Mar to the exit:

- - - I congratulate you, tell the civil claim attorney that I will fax you the case papers, it has been a pleasure representing you and I wish you luck," Jocelyn said.

- - - Thank you once again, the pleasure is mine and I hope we meet again under better circumstances, see you later.

Jocelyn smiled enormously. They shook hands and said goodbye, and he left the room with great hope.

El mar, which had parked at a certain distance from the courthouse, walked on without taking shelter in the shade so diligently offered by the trees on the road, and not even the bark of a dog could take it away from its path.

He boarded his vehicle and before he got anywhere else, he went to Larry, with whom he had signed in advance for the civil claim, and who had already defrauded him with another case, on that occasion a car accident, that had taken him for valid and good and after a year he returned it to him alleging impropriety to continue the representation.

Because of his experience, El mar questioned him about the claim for police brutality, and certainly Larry swore to him and affirmed that on that occasion it would be different, thinking that human beings could rectify their mistakes, he again believed in the possible sincerity that this representative had shown him, however, El mar was unaware that the prejudices and the incapacity and lack of ethics of certain law firms, could induce him to break his promise.

The malicious intention from the moment of H-50, which consisted of that first meeting in the civil court of the claimant and the city's lawyers, had already been defined, a new conspiratorial action had already been aired, a crude betrayal, however El mar, had not yet taken into account the attitude of its representative, and it seemed too early to be aware of it, but Larry, its civil lawyer, had taken possession of a cynicism characteristic of those chosen for a cheek. And the way he allowed the questioning was more inclined to favor the interests of the defendant.

That weekend, El mar and Mark, got together again, and they did it in Barbarita's house, they were very close and Mark, felt a great appreciation for his father, with all he had lived, the boy needed love and understanding, Barbarita had started

to show a bipolar behavior, she could not control the jealousy attacks against Mark, when she noticed that he remained very attached to his father, which incited her to yell at the boy in an inconsiderate way, whose action was unpleasant for El mar, which

He perceived as an injustice, correcting it at once, before that misunderstanding, also Mark was upset who tried to leave on their own, seeing El mar needed to avoid it, that had happened a few hours before the time that Mark would be returned to Celeste Chaplain that afternoon Mark, seemed very stressed and did not let El mar know his need to go to the bathroom, so he defecated in his pants, minutes before reaching the mother.

When Celeste learned of the incident, she took it as a pretext to counterattack El Mar, adding to the report to the Yonkers Department of Social Services that El Mar had used violence against Barbarita in front of the child, so the child had been summoned to appear in Yonkers family court on September 26.

On that date the accusation would be known, so El Mar realized that they would have to be accompanied by Barbarita as a witness, and knowing the conspiracies, that Barbarita's testimony, was going to disrupt their fallacies, conspiracy, they resubmitted the case for November 3.

The Floringer, in her capacity as an ex-officio lawyer lacking in argumentative capacity, and sold out to the conspirators, allowed anything against her defendant, without any opposition.

Previously she had tried to persuade El Mar, offering to remove the order of protection from Mark's school, if he reached an agreement with Celeste Capellán, and accepted the supervised visit, and he was forced to respond:

--- Since I started this case, I'm coming to terms with it, and it always violates it, resorting to lies, always looking for its advantage. -She said.

--- If you don't accept, your child will hate you. --- Pleaded the Frolinger, laden with pride.

--- Why?...he is aware of the plot you are preparing against me. ---El mar replied, with sereni

The Frolinger, kept silent, then when they went in front of the judge, El mar accused her that she was not representing him properly. That it seemed rather that she was working on behalf of the opposing party, to which the judge responded:

--- She is here to help you.

--- It should be, but it isn't. -Said El mar.

The judge Duchess remained silent, which Frolinger took advantage of to argue about a document that seemed to favor El mar, but with a definite intention of confusing the previous allegation of that one:

--- We received a letter from the city attorney's office, notifying us that what happened with the Paradise police has nothing to do with children, --- said Frolinger. She extended the document to the judge, who caught it between her index finger and thumb, and began to read it with thoughtful, careful silence.

When the reading was over, the judge reauthorized the visits that El mar had with Mark, which had been suspended after Celeste Capellán had made the report that El mar "had fought with the Paradise police.

All this had happened long before Barbarita Roque provoked the incident where Mark had been upset, and where she had to appear in court to deny Celeste Capellán's claim.

It was easy for Barbarita to remember this, especially since on that date, to avoid her testimony, they had moved the case to November 3.

All those memories were generated, because of what happened on September 26, when he left to see the Judge Duchess, by chance in the middle of the corridor,

El mar and Celeste, having an exchange of silent glances allowed the girls of their eyes to ravage.

Not content with this, so that El mar would not believe that women would fall like ripe fruit, she recreated the hour of despondency, and being scandalized went to her lawyer who was also wandering through the corridor of that funeral court, and although she had seen and heard nothing, she lent her ears to the Celeste who, like a little girl replied to her:

---El mar outraged me, it just told me that I am a son of a bitch.

Although El mar didn't know what was happening, because he was going with Barbarita, he went out to the street, saw that Frolinger looked into his eyes and without knowing what it meant he told her:

---- What... are you afraid of? There's no reason to be afraid, but... "If you're afraid, buy a dog".

During that time they had made preparations for the next meeting, waiting for him with a surprise garnish, he had arrived on November 3, he had gone to the family court, but at the reception they informed him that the case had been transferred to the domestic violence court.

He moved El Mar to the criminal court building, where the domestic violence section also operated, and upon his arrival was imprisoned, claiming that he had a warrant for his arrest for violating a court order.

Two weeks later he was released under the provision that he should attend some drug and violence programs, something that turned out for him to be an idiosyncratic shock, adorned with racial prejudice and conditioning, he struggled or not to have to attend the programs because he was neither violent nor had a drug problem.

However, the court seemed to be conditioned and willing to create a case for him that would justify what was to come.

One of the assigned programs was called (TASC), which stands for Alternative Treatment of Street Crimes, something that to El Mar came to seem like an act of malice and prejudice, because he, was not a street person and had not committed any crime.

He had already gotten rid of the drug and alcohol program, St. Joseph's Hospital had taken his urine test, and when he discovered that he was clean he exonerated him, but he still had not been able to get rid of the violence program, as it had to be paid for.

The program's administration sent a letter to the court exonerating him, but Judge Thomas B, who served on the domestic violence court, insisted on keeping him in the violence program, assigning him to another one they called (Sancia),

Where El mar also claimed its lack of resources to pay for it.

He also dared to question Judge B, asking if he would receive any commission from the payment for his desperate insistence that he register for the program, which hurt the pride of those involved, by sending a letter denouncing El Mar's refusal to join the program, which would condition the judge to make a drastic decision against him.

On the night of April 2, El mar had been besieged by a strange premonition, and it was difficult for him to fall asleep.

Then, on April 3rd, it was a Friday and the dawn was cloudy, the rain threatened to invade the atmosphere. El mar took a shower, said a tender goodbye to Barbarita who had been left in charge of the children, and went to the streetcar.

The streets looked little busy, and before boarding her destination she contacted Maycol K, the lawyer who had replaced Frolinger, and who had been informed of what had happened in the assigned programs, who notified her that she would have to return to prison, and although El mar wanted to plead and justify himself, he did not find a breath of hope.

Everything was planned by the conspirators, and he, Maycol K, as a public defender, would have to submit to what had been agreed.

A few minutes later, he was entering the court room, and when he came in, he provided a copy of the letter he had sent to the programs, to Maycol K, who immediately

He extended the judge, Thomas B, who read silently, and between the lines, having been a surprise to him, who was ignorant of the literary qualities of El mar, frowned and said as if he were shouting:

---Someone made this letter for you, someone made it for you.

Without allowing him to express himself, he determined to imprison him, alleging a violation of a court order.

This action had really enraged El mar, and had led it to desire to be the owner of a heavenly power, in order to do justice with its own hands.

--- You have refused to comply with the court order, we will send you to prison. -Judge Bailey said.

--- I am innocent, they are forging a conspiracy, I have not violated anything, if you were not shielded in the investiture that protects you, then you would know what it is to abuse an innocent. --- He said.=

Maycol K intervened, seeking the attention of Judge B: --- Judge, you have made your decision, but I want to tell you that here there is an economic situation, I can return in two weeks.

--- Maycol K said, with more courage to confuse, than to seek a solution, specifying his confidences after those subsequent talks sprinkled with sarcasm, which further increased the courage of El mar, which had interpreted such an intervention as a prayer of cynicism.

He accused attorney Maycol k of legal negligence and of joining in the conspiratorial act and replied and shouted, leaving those expressions from El mar, hitting the intellect of Judge Thomas B.

At the time of that decision, which he considered abusive, El mar, even being a moderate person, wanted to be the owner of a force that would allow him to make a mess of such terrible vileness. The henchmen handcuffed him and took him to a cell located on the sides of the deliberation room.

Five minutes later, lawyer Maycol K, still with a remarkable concern, approached the cell and behind the crack of the bars questioned El mar:

--- who made the letter?...

--- I made it --- El mar answered.---

Oh, now you speak English? Attorney K. continued to inquire.

--- I speak, read and write English, and I will sue all the abusers. -El mar," he emphasized, "is still battered by the vileness of discrimination.

--- You're fine, you'll be assigned another lawyer on Monday said K.

--- Does that mean I'm going to be locked up until Monday? questioned El mar.

--- Yes, --- He responded as he left followed by an interpreter.

CHAPTER 10

— That weekend he felt possessed by a certain restlessness, he did not think they would leave him imprisoned for practically anything, as he understood it, he resigned himself to contemplate the sunset, through the windows of the bedroom, where he had been lodged.

He had been taken with other prisoners to Vengala, a Westchester County prison, and had been accommodated in the J-2 dormitory, which was a frame made of cement blocks painted white, with red trimming and iron columns, painted blue, whose space of one 150 x 100, was distributed in fourteen cubicles of double beds and 26 of separate beds, one 30 x 20, where lunch was served, television was watched, card games, monopolies and dominoes were improvised.

Next to the access door to the corridor, there was a desk from which a correction officer guarded, on the roof 15 feet from the prisoners' heads, 18 glass windows were detached, which rested on a long column formed by iron and cement, and through which the sun during the day illuminated the bedroom, which did not prevent the refrigeration of the same, because a central air turned on twenty-four hours, did not stop whipping the skin of its inhabitants, who needed to be sheltered until the summer of that time.

A television was attached to the wall that communicated with the main street, which gave access to the surroundings of the building's reception, and from where they were informed of what was happening in the outside world.

That afternoon something had called the attention of the population, and sirens and whistles, had disturbed the calm, in J-3 the adjacent bedroom, the boys let escape a wave of violence, invading the inhabitants, generating a series of fights that induced the presence of the turtle squad in the corridors, armed with masks not to be Identified by the prisoners, fire extinguishers they carried on their backs, and devices to cause electric shock, which although prohibited for other institutions, were like a recreational toy for them, and what was attractive to their users to control riots.

Shortly after, a prisoner was taken hanging from the faltriquera, and in the direction of the box, a narrow and isolated room that was also called the solitary.

The campus of Véngala was a large group of buildings, civil constructions with enormous windows with wide arches on the first floor, with pointed roofs, and there, located at the back was the prison. Rectangular blocks, surrounded by hurricane gates, and in the distance a thick vegetation.

On Monday, he arrived in the cold and grey, had been made to stand early in the morning, would be returned to court, and upon arrival had been made to wait in a small room where only two were allowed.

They remained motionless due to insaculation, between disgust and morbidity, he passed his gaze along the corridor, he saw a guard penetrate in the direction of where he was, it was ten o'clock in the morning when he heard the corridor's phone ring; for a moment he got excited, he thought he would be taken out, but no, the officer answered the phone and went to the next cell and called another name that would be taken to see the judge.

A prolonged mutism invaded the room, and he figured out the cell as a torture room. Everything was scheduled for after noon. He was already standing in front of the bench when a new judge requested his authorization to assign him a new lawyer, while K continued to lurk with apparent concern. El mar believed that it would be dispatched that same Monday, the new lawyer had asked the judge to grant his release, but something strange had happened, at the same time he had been assigned, at that very moment he had been withdrawn, and the judge claimed that there would be a new date to return, really the plot was not a game and

Conspiracy had been set in motion, however, at that moment, another lawyer appeared who would lend himself to doing the dirty work of the occasion.

In two or three days, El mar had become thinner, one of the court's custody officers left the room and immediately reappeared accompanied by the prosecutor who would be hearing the case that afternoon.His seductive gaze had become confused, but his eyes had remained superbly open, and his pink skin had turned green, his language had become incomprehensible, he stumbled around justifying the unjustifiable, trying to persuade the judge about the possible option of keeping El mar imprisoned.

Then the judge took over the interrogation in front of El Mar, pressed him and in a long and unconnected peroration led him to repeat what everyone already knew, his innocence.

The room was flooded with a musky smell, the prosecutor moved from one side to the other, her hands were shaking uncontrollably, her sclera had turned jelly. The prosecutor had begun to despair, moving with a certain impatience, began to reread the file and after a brief pause added, modulating her voice with a certain intention:- - -

Once in his life, he had to sell drugs.

Elmar understood themessage, so it clarified:

- - - I have neither used nor sold drugs - - - it replied.

The prosecutor indifferently insisted on her accusation:

- - - In 1991 he did nine and a half months in a state prison.

--- he added

--- One illegal case, of which I am also still innocent, was committed by another and they wanted to pin it on me, I was imprisoned by another and now to justify their atrocities, they have been conspiring to criminalize me by force --- he said resolutely.

The prosecutor gurgled as if she wanted to clear her throat, which was blocked by the

Uncertainty:

--- It is true that he has never wanted to assume his guilt. --- He said with a feigned cynicism.

---- What faults do they talk about... or maybe they think they are free of them, to "throw the first stone"? I am innocent and do not insist that I plead guilty.

Faced with that controversy, the judge decided to send the case back to two weeks later.

At 1:45 a.m. a storm started, the same officers who had transported him in the morning were returning him to Venice.

The city of Yonkers was left behind, an explosion preceded by a ray of light invaded the atmosphere, the palm trees twisted, the trees shook. The sky darkened at once, and it seemed that the wrath of God was falling upon the earth.

The driver, stopped the van untimely, the rain did not let him advance, suddenly it seemed that a gigantic bird fell on the glass while everybody lost consciousness, El mar was kept awake, then an angel appeared to him, and spoke to him:

--- Do not be afraid, everyone will be fine, says the Lord that to give what has to be given, you're going back to prison but it will be for a short time, after you get out good things await you that he will grant you rewarding your faith, receive the strength --- He said.

The angel blew and El mar fell asleep and when he woke up he thought he had had a dream, those who were more awake, the van began to move again, the clouds had cleared, and a refreshing wind blew on the windows of the vehicle.

As the afternoon was eclipsed by the road, and travelers believed it was a privilege to contemplate a summary of the history of the universe, the sun once again appeared radiant and defiant.

In the twilight the surprised and stunned birds returned to their nests. And the prisoners arrived at nightfall.

While they were changing their clothes for prison uniforms, they waited in Brookings Center, which was the reception cell, from where they would be transferred to the dormitories, where they were confined, and there El mar met Isabel Volqué, who smiled at him from the front cell.

The prisoners who remained as if in limbo, aware of what was happening, reacted like a pack in front of a defenseless lamb.

They became competitive and the compliments were lacking, while El mar tried to reach Barbarita Roque by phone, with whom he had not been able to communicate since the day he left the house.

Elizabeth had seen him before he looked at her, and when he could not communicate with El mar, he turned around and found himself in front of her gaze that was smiling at him with affability.

--- Look at my eyes," he said.

She smiled again and called out to him:

--- I want you to write to me-- I say.

---- What? I ask El mar pretending not to understand.

---- She repeated, straining her voice, and even smiling.

---- Who? Me? --- answered one of the prisoners in the group.

---- No, the. --- She said with her index finger referring to El mar.

El mar, smiled, Isabel gave him the address that he copied on a toilet paper, with a little piece of pencil that was given to him by one of the prisoners, who had managed to smuggle it in.

From that day on, they began an exchange of correspondence, resulting in the fact that that girl and El Mar had many things in common, both had studied at university and such coincidence had contributed to a very good communication and exchange of ideas, which facilitated tolerating in peace, the stay in the prison.

Isabel Volqué, certainly was a native of Tenerife, and had studied in the area of accounting, was seven years living in Paradise, was a single mother with three children who fell in prison, were under the care of her ex-husband, and father of them, his time in prison exhausted him reading, dancing alone, walking on the court, and when he had space left, watching television.

At first he thought prison was hell, but he also thought that what didn't kill made him stronger. She had a surprising sensitivity, in her seven years in Paradise, she had been thriving and looked less old than her 33rd birthday.

But in addition, she was like a flower fertilized for love, tender, with a youthful silhouette and a naive smile. Real estate entrepreneur, with considerable profits.

Five-seven tall, light brown hair, cibio eyes, trembling lips, with a smile that showed the goodness of his soul.

Monday dawned clear and radiant, it was April 27, when spring gave way to summer, the treetops had turned green, and in the distance the rows of abandoned buildings emerged like pharaohs.

The streets seemed deserted and the spring wind beat in the faces of the few pass-ers-by who went out to wait for the bus to get to their respective places of work.

The rubble, those remains of garbage were piled up with stealth, the swastikas were slipping in thought.

He stopped a bus in front of the prison of véngalas from where a woman, who was accompanied by two children, got off, others boarded and the bus

He left, the taciturn woman headed for the reception, stirred by the rays of the morning sun. It was Barbarita Roque, who, full of uncertainty, had gone into El mar to find out the fate of El Mar, upon learning that he had been taken prisoner.

El mar, through other prisoners who had obtained their freedom, had notified her of the place where he was, and once she had tried to meet him, a week before she had left the children in the care of relatives in order to inquire about the require-ments for a visit, and because visits were granted according to the alphabetical letter of the prisoner's last name, it was not possible for him to enter that day.

A new attempt had taken her back to the place, on the day specified to be visited, being a failed attempt, she could not enter either, that day she had presented herself accompanied by the four children and in the visit they only admitted two, then the administration offered her a special conception to enter the next day.

Actually, the next day it was not her place to visit El Mar, but seeing the failed attempts that Barbarita had made, even though it was not her place, they would let her in if she only had two of the four children, so she proceeded just as the social worker from Venice had indicated.

Paradise was an eminently extreme nation, where, in spite of the structure of the system, people used to be more stressed than happy, when it was cold people trembled, when it was hot they sweated.

It was lived in a liberal democracy, where man could express himself as long as he did not overdo it, and there was so much confusion that those who confused "magnesia with gymnastics" and "freedom with debauchery" were not lacking, but many times in judicial or international policies, they used to proceed as tyrants.

Especially when a poor man was involved in a court case, he regularly assigned lawyers instead of fighting to prove the innocence of his defendants,

They insisted that they be made guilty, thus contributing to legalize the violation of human rights.

By this time something similar was happening with El mar, and so many others, that although he claimed his innocence, the court emissaries, although lacking evidence, tried to break him by holding him in prison on the grounds that he had violated an alleged court order, as claimed by the Yonkers conspirators.

CHAPTER 11

— When Barbarita Roque showed up at the reception to visit El Mar, she was given a grim, bold and flashy-faced custody:

--- What can I do for you? --- He asked.

--- I come to visit El mar Valenilla --- Barbarita answered.

--- Who are you? - He insisted on custody.

--- I'm his wife... Well, we're not married but I'm his wife and they're his children --- she said indicating to the children that they came with her.

The children were not left behind either, and nodding to their mother's words, they spread a huge smile.

Give me some ID.

Barbarita put her right hand into the front pocket of her pants, took away an ID and with a halo of shyness extended it to the custody.

The custody caught her between her fingers, scrutinized her thoroughly, while she argued:

If you were his wife, you'd bring your last name!

Barbarita didn't show any enthusiasm, but she responded:

--- I told him that I am not legally married to him, but we live in a free union, they are his children and I am the woman who bore him the children, can you understand that? She answered somewhat unmoved.

--- Yes... I can understand that. Resigned custody responded.

At that moment, the social worker was moving along the left side, through the door leading to the reception desk, so she told the custodian:

--- It's okay, she was here yesterday, her thing is fixed, I'll take care of it --- she said.

Custody moved away, leaving the space free, the worker opened the computer screen and told custody:

--- Call house J-2, tell them that number 3 Valenilla Mar has a visitor.

The custody obeyed her, while she opened the door authorizing Barbarita to pass with the children.

He took her through a corridor, led her to an anteroom where she was thoroughly searched, given a key to a safety deposit box, where she could keep her personal belongings and those of the children, such as jackets, telephone, house keys and anything else that was forbidden to enter the visiting room.

Once this process was concluded, she was introduced to a large room, where she waited for El mar to appear. At that moment, she answered a call from the parish chaplaincy, to go to the telephone to finish her shift, with the intention of checking on Barbarita, ignoring that she was waiting for him in the visiting room.

El mar in the chaplaincy made use of his shift, he tried to communicate without anyone answering, finally opting to extend the shift for another time, returning to his location, where another authorization was waiting for him to leave again.

On that second occasion, he would go to the visiting room, where even though he ignored it, Barbarita and the children were anxiously waiting for him.

When he knocked on the door to enter the room he was received by a custody officer, who subjected him to a thorough search, giving him way not without first seizing some telephone numbers from a television channel, which he had on him with the intention of putting him in

Possession of a visitor, so that he could notify the press of his arrest if he was not absorbed in the stipulated time, however, when he was seized everything went wrong.

As he entered, he felt his eyesight blurred, as he walked around the room in an optical effort to rediscover who was visiting him, he ignored him, because he had no visitor that day.

He lucubrated in the wide hall, trying to locate a familiar face, until on the right in a secluded corner, he perceived the children sitting and away from the thickness of the visitor population, and next to them Barbarita Roque.

A single glance was enough to know that she was suffering, her wet eyes said so, which produced in El mar a tender emotion, which in the same way made nostalgic tears flow that rolled down her cheek.

A strong embrace accompanied by a passionate kiss, sealed the glory of the encounter, three weeks had passed since the last time they had seen each other, and that moment of reunion, with the embrace of their attraction, confirmed the sanity of their love.

And he discovered that when the absence of the heart longs and claims, that is when one really loves.

During the day before, two weeks before he was imprisoned, she had confessed to him:

--- When you leave, your absence causes me pain in my heart.

So El mar knew about the pain that Barbarita Roque had been experiencing, alone and with four children, when she had really started to depend emotionally on him since they met.

El mar kissed the children, embraced them throughout visiting time, while he and Barbarita held hands, gave each other kisses and looks, like lovers who had just met, the children too, felt happy.

Barbarita told him how depressed she had felt about his absence, and how this had affected her even in fulfilling her daily responsibilities, he comforted her and told her:

--- Don't worry, if God wants it, we'll be together soon, I love you, I'm going to marry you --- he said still standing.

She squeezed his hands and, mocking the warlike looks of the custody officers, kissed his lips.

One of them noticed, walked in their direction and interrupted him:

--- Does your visit begin now... or end?

El mar answered him in the language he spoke:

--- I'm starting now --- He said...

--- Then sit down. --- He ordered custody.

Barbarita and El mar, obeyed him in silence, the custody returned to their observatory, and they sat there talking and planning until another officer appeared to inform them that the visit was over.

At that moment, all were saddened and even the children spread their lips with little drums showing their pain before the farewell, kissed again, and melted in a deep embrace. Barbarita, did not want to turn her back so she went away in retreat, and before her silhouette was lost behind the door she said:

--- My love, don't stop taking care of yourself

And El mar answered him:

--- Thank you, you too, see you soon.

Barbarita, had been lost of sight, El mar, stopped perceiving her when she crossed the door, while she already in the anteroom, subtracted from the box that had assigned her all her belongings, and abandoned her with the children, the female was hanging from her neck attached to her chest inside a charger that they called "kangaroo", and the baron holding her hands, until the bus appeared that would return them to the proximity of the city where they resided.

That night he dreamt that he had been invited to a party, that he and two friends had been accompanied by Barbarita, and that he had found another childhood friend, but that the latter was walking around so strangely that he looked like a homosexual, and El mar was staring at him, elucidating the change perpetuated in him, whose secret passions had accelerated the ambivalence of his spirit and the beating of his heart.

And then she saw how the first friends who kept her company played a joke on Barbarita that had caused her anger but at the same time she refused to admit a closeness to those whom she perceived as evil creatures that smeared her with malice, causing her a nervousness that induced her to a clumsy conjecture, where she withdrew from her warlike and traditional idiosyncrasy, suddenly found herself invaded by a euphoria where she realized that being at peace, was her happiness.

El mar, woke up self-interrogating, and self-questioning said:

--- I do not know why I dream that, what do you want to tell me, is that I will have a problem with Barbarita?

The next day was Friday, I had received letters from Robert and Isabel Volqué, they were two of the friends I interacted with, I had met them in vengeance and without any major obstruction, they shared their friendship, until they decided to write to each other, and it was a way to soften the time they were called to spend inside the prison.

The letters arrived every three or four days, he only wrote to them, but almost every day he tried to talk to Barbarita on the phone, who he comforted with words of encouragement and hope, and when he couldn't talk to her, he left her a recorded message,

telling her the day and time that he would try to check on her again, and she would wait for the call, that was when he would call from the chaplaincy.

Since El mar did not always have access to the telephone, he would figure out how to communicate and to do so, he would pick up the handset, when the operator said:

---- El mar took advantage of it, and instead of saying her name, as she knew his voice, he left her the message of his interest, so that even though he couldn't hear her, she heard him, so that the call went out free without the prison service charging him for the minutes.

The days advanced vertiginously, the prisoners in orange uniforms, when they went out to the esplanade, seen from afar, gave the impression of being a carrot crop.

The days were exhausted, going from the esplanade to the gym, from the parish to the clinic, or those who were interested in attending the law library, to investigate their case, if they had not yet been sentenced, attended the first two weeks of their stay in Venice.

El mar had achieved great popularity among the prison population, to the extent that they began to call it by the name of the president of the kingdom and wherever it moved they shouted it.

Something surprising had begun to happen, and it was that in the prison very few people were friendly, and almost nobody shared his properties, instead with El mar, it was the opposite, because those who at first provoked him, and wanted to cause him difficulties, had begun to donate him necessary tools for the stay and survival in the prison, that oscillated from food, and flip-flops for the bath, to detergents, pencils and papers that he consumed, for his records.

His cubicle was crowded with members of the population, who sometimes would leave him four or five extra plates of the food served in vengeance, and other times would come over to invite them to play, on other occasions he received letters from those who wrote to him asking for advice that El mar used to offer in the following manner:

--- Hello, I received your masterful letter, and I take this opportunity to answer you, and hopefully the judge, on the day of your court, will give you hope and positive disposition, so that you can leave this prison of opprobrium and discouragement, so that balance and peace, will be manifested in you and your family.

If during your stay you have a quiet house, thank the God of your being, you must avoid that no one off hurts your time and your peace. Speak to God and express your concern, ask him to forgive you, forgive anyone whom he has to forgive, and forgive yourself.

You took care, I also take care, thanks and see you soon.

That particular style of El mar, relating to those who sought its guidance, had begun to generate jealousy among some of those who self-destructed through ignorance, yet there were more who loved them than those who despised them.

He had managed to influence sectors of the population so much that they considered moving him to another dormitory.

El mar often dreamed and on that occasion he had dreamed that the president of the kingdom of paradise had gone to the county of the city where he resided, to ask him for a report on what the needs of his community were, so he and the president had taken a tour together, entering a restaurant where they had shared a dinner, but they saw the president as an artist, but then they realized that he was really the president of the nation, who was taking notes from the report that El mar provided, and once he had done that, the president had said goodbye to him with a handshake, and at that moment, he had woken up.

With El mar something strange happened, because his dreams were not simple hallucinations of fatigue, they were revelations, in an occasion in which he, in an action of community service, gathered and transported to his destiny people that he found in the streets, the angel that always spoke to him, spoke to him warning him that he was born with the purpose of serving the Lord, but that not being what he was doing, what he was calling

To realize, meant that in his free will he had begun to go astray, and that it was better to take the road that would lead him where he should go.

He had not understood what they intended to tell him, so first his car was damaged, and not as he repaired it and continued to insist on the same road, a little while later the henchmen of the city crashed into him and even reporting the car as lost, he repaired it again and continued on his way.

He had tried to raise funds by asking for donations, and one Saturday night he found a homeless couple who were afraid to sleep on the street, because the time to enter the shelter was expiring, they begged him to transport them, he explained that he only transported people who interacted in the project where he was working and that it was not prudent for him to ride strangers without authorization.

The strangers insisted to the extent that they convinced him, and he chose to take them, but he set two conditions, which consisted in that for such purpose they had to make a donation to fill up with gasoline, and furthermore, they would have to ride one forward and the other backward, the strangers accepted, when they approached the place where they were going the man began to pretext to justify not filling up with gasoline, he said:

--- this vehicle is defective, you are therefore putting our lives in danger, I will call the gendarmes.

El mar, knowing the communicative indisposition he had with the henchmen, tried to get them out of the vehicle by force, the man refused, and he understood that he was trying to create a conflict.

The woman came out but the man remained inside, refusing to come out, then El mar advanced two blocks ahead and stopped, again asked the man to get off, but he continued to refuse, the woman who had gotten off communicated with the henchmen and they found him standing around insisting that the stranger leave his vehicle.

In the presence of the henchmen, the man had no choice but to dismount from the vehicle, he exposed in his own way the reason for the situation, to El mar they did not let him speak, he thought they would write him a contravention, according to what the law provided for a circumstance of that nature, But instead, they fabricated a case against him for allegedly driving recklessly, seized his car as alleged evidence and took him before a judge in Paradise, the judge released him praising the level of education he had achieved, and added:

---We will release him for his academic efforts. We will set a new date to clarify the circumstance in which the conflict was generated.

They let him go, and although the prosecutor had arranged for the vehicle to be returned to him, the henchmen kept up their pretext, until the conflict with Celeste Capellán, who had taken El mar to Véngala, arose.

Once locked up in Venice knowing that he had to be taken to the city to clarify what had happened earlier with the car accident, they did not, so he had to wait to leave the bars, to verify what had happened in the city.

CHAPTER 12

— El mar confirmed that God lived in him, he felt the spirit moving on his shoulders, or on the scalp of his skull, and he was more convinced by the revelations that had come in the preceding weeks, where the groves were shaking and the packs were getting in the way, as the psalms coincided with him.

He saw how anger and pride had permeated the souls of the judges who had sent him to that unnecessary prison in a delirium of martyrdom, but Judge Thomas thought he heard an expression that confused him and frightened his heart:

--- The Lord said that on this earth there walks a baron, whom you will never ever be able to defile, even with your earthly power, and I add, my spirit does not conceive or accept such evil, the movement will come, society will rise, and the proud will repent.

Judge Thomas squirmed in his seat, stroked his blond hair, took off his glasses and in an automated action cleaned his windows, got up, walked to Judge Morgan's office and said:

--- Something strange is happening to me, I don't want to think that I'm starting to suffer from schizophrenia, but I feel besieged by a voice that tells me about a prisoner --- he said.

 ---- A prisoner? .... Which prisoner? --- Morgan inquired.

 ---- This is El mar valenilla. --- He answered.

 ---- It's the same one I let go and you put back in jail, it must be consciousness.

 --- Do we judges have a conscience?" Thomas replied.

 --- I do, my years have helped me to learn discernment, you are still young and you let yourself be guided by pride and appearance, I let him go because I believe him to be innocent, to justify you I added some programs that did not correspond to him, and even so, you imprisoned him again, what do you want with that? --- Morgan expressed.

 --- He is extremely stubborn, and we cannot allow a stranger to come and impose conditions on us," Thomas said.

 --- He's not a stranger, he immigrated 19 years ago and we know who he is.

 --- Morgan replied.

---- When I sent him to the program he said that I was going to send him to prison, and that God was going to imprison me, and I can't deny you Morgan, I'm a little worried... I know there hasn't been enough evidence to imprison him, but it's better to owe money than to do favors, and now I've started hearing voices and the voices are referring to him, I don't want to think that I'm going crazy. --- Said Thomas with some disappointment.

--- At that cost, it's better not to pay favors, well, let's see what can be done," Morgan emphasized.

The summer was coming back in its climatic essence, the sun was filtering through the skylight, and in his bedroom Danny Raquila, on his bed, was accommodating his body, trying to find the most comfortable position for rest, he had been sentenced to one month in prison because after seven years of having suffered a construction accident, he had tried to reach his retirement without success.

A month had passed without her being able to pay child support from her first marriage and she had ended up in jail.

Now he, between lament and reply, exposed his frustration and his enmity with God. For more than 15 years he was gathered together, and his spirit was so weak that perhaps God wanted to test him in order to strengthen him, but he could not assimilate this barbarism as he understood it, and his depression was so great that as many times as he spoke of his case, he smeared himself with tears.

His new wife was about to give birth, and he did not want his son to be born while he was in prison, when El mar first saw him, and it seemed to him that he needed to be treated, because he could not control his desperate distress.

El mar needed to speak to him, giving him a breath of hope, and letting him know that it was better for him to control himself, since he would not be locked up for long, and that his wife needed him healthy especially when she was about to give him a new child.

All this had happened after he had introduced himself.

--- Hello, are you Caribbean? --- I question, Danny.

--- Yes, how do you know? --- replied El mar...

--- I've worked with your countrymen, and you are very different from the others. --- He said.

---- Oh yeah, in what way? I question El mar.

---- They are friendly, hardworking and above all very dynamic," added Danny.

---- Thank you for what is due to me... What is your name?

--- Said El mar smiling.

--- Danny, they call me Danny Raquila, and you?

---- El mar answered, holding out its hands.

---- Like this, just like this? ---- Danny replied.

---- Thus, El mar valenilla. --- El mar responded emphasizing the name, while Danny shook its hand.

From that day on a great friendship began between them, and through him he met Gary Wess, an Anglo, originally from paradise, and to whom Danny Raquila told his sorrows before the arrival of El mar, which could be said to be like his teardrop.

In fact, in the short time that they had a relationship, because on April 15 when El mar was returning to court, Danny was serving his sentence, and he was very excited because he would have the opportunity to meet his newly born wife, and above all, to meet his newborn son.

However, he did not cease to blame God for his difficulties, ignoring that he blamed himself, and was heard to say:

---- Don't talk to me about God that I'm an atheist. God did not help me when I needed it most. -He said.

---- Even in the moments of most terrible anguish, you should not doubt yourself, doubting God is blaspheming against you, because that spiritual force that rules the destiny of man is within us.

Since you always give yourself what you have to give yourself even when we try to avoid it, it is good to specify that before you are born, we choose the path we are going to travel, that force that dwells in you allows you to act according to that free will, but if you were really an atheist, you would still bring in the depths of your soul the intention to kneel down and say thank God that I am an atheist.--- El mar told him.

Then, Danny smiled, trying to clear up his confusion, motivated by that slightly calmer speech he said:

--- El mar, I admire you, you are a teacher, it gives me peace, when you leave you will have to go to my house to stay even for two days, my wife will be happy, it is unfortunate that you did not arrive earlier, I only have three days left, but we agreed on that since you leave call me, I will be waiting for you. He said Danny, reaffirming the invitation.

---Thank you, whenever I can contribute to your peace, count on me. El mar answered.

Danny was very grateful, and in the following days, El Mar helped him to fill out some requirement forms that would help Danny after his freedom, to get financial aid, medical insurance for the treatment of his back, and some letter requesting his retirement that so many times he had been denied because he considered himself young, even though he lacked stability and strength, to continue that kind of work he was doing in the construction area.

When the day arrived, they said goodbye very effusively, El mar would return to the court, and he was leaving freedom, however, because the judge sent back the case of El mar, for the 5th of May, El mar had to return again, and on his return Danny had already left, it seems that on the way the phones were lost and they did not see each other again, however even after being free one and another remembered each other.

CHAPTER 13

— The next day, early in the morning, Gary appeared in front of El mar, as a reiterative sign of their friendship, he took with him a book that he would give him to intensify his reading, he was still lying down when he was moved by it.

---- Oh! How's Gary, are we getting up early?

--- That's right El mar, it seems that way but it's going to be ten o'clock, that's why I decided to bring you this book to read, I just finished it and I thought you might be interested --- Gary said.

El mar took hold of the book, explored its pages and said

---- The Rebellion of the Masses, by Ortega y Gasset, interests me, I'm going to read it, thanks Gary, sit down.

---- Thank you, El mar, I have to get to the bookstore, I'll be back later," Gary said.

---- All right, I'll wait for you. --- El mar nodded.

Gary Wess, nodding in a dense, sad manner, nevertheless did not stop sketching his neatest smile.

Under his populated eyebrows lay his eyes that were of a silent blue, his physiognomy itself showed him with a peaceful figure and languid attention, he was not so communicative, but El mar had awakened in him, a lovely sympathy induced by his persuasive charisma, since Danny Raquila introduced him in that unfathomable June sunset, his

The relationship expanded to such a degree that he spared no effort in his exchange of friendship and solidarity.

Gary arrived to offer his wife's services, in case El mar needed her to communicate with Barbarita, in order to help her with the children when she went to visit him, so she would go in her vehicle driving her to Vengala and facilitating the visit.

And so through the days they became more and more friends, and whenever El mar needed papers or pencils, to write his little novels, or answer some of the letters received, there he was providing these facilities, as he had a better chance of getting them, because he was attending school.

So all the handfuls of pencils that El mar had used for his writings, he would supply them, and when the tips ran out, he would take them to school and take them out again, returning them to him with a handful of leaves so that he could continue writing.

Gary Wess, had completed a master's degree in business administration, but had been working for a manufacturing company, and on the day of his arrest, he was driving back with a few gulps down, and when he was pulled over, he was tested for alcohol, and tested positive, so he had been referred to thumb six months in prison, and now he was waiting for the judge to release him, or assign him to a program.

Despite his languid attention, he was always willing to collaborate with those in need. One day he had come across El mar in the law library of one of the blocks, and El mar needed to collect some legal information to support the defense of his case, but the time they gave him had run out, so Gary told him:

--- Note that you took the magazine to the bedroom, then returned it. --- He said.

When another of the prisoners who had been struggling to know what they were talking about, and who was in charge of the library, wanted to move it, he stepped in:

--- I'm sorry, this is my job and you can't take this magazine out of here --- he said.

---- Not even leaving an ID?

---- No. --- Said the manager dryly.

To avoid being reported, they did not insist, but removed the advertising page of the legal magazine, with the aim of making contact and buying it.

All these guidelines of solidarity had increased their friendship and Gary always tried to contribute to El mar, part of the acquired ration, and he used to reciprocate by giving them a knife or an apple, which they received at breakfast, which sometimes he used to keep, and it accumulated.

Although El Mar never bought "comisaria", which was the name given to the provisions that in addition to the daily food, they used to buy the inmates who had money in their accounts, from the prison suppliers, either because the family put him in, or because they worked inside, he always had his pantry crammed.

El mar thought that God provided it, or that he made those who had to give it or negotiate with it, that's why the chicken ration he received on Sundays, because he was not a carnivore, he sold it for about two dollars and fifty cents, which was equivalent to five soups, and each soup was valued at fifty cents, which meant that each transaction was executed through the process of barter, which was the exchange currency, since they could not handle cash, even if they had it accumulated.

As you should know at that time in the prisons of the Kingdom states and specifically in Paradise, they used to automatically open an account for the prisoners with the money they carried in the bag, at the moment of entering the prison, where they were deposited the gifts in money that their relatives and friends wanted to leave them when they went to visit.

Some supported her with the money sent by her relatives, and others through what they produced by working in the different lines of "Vengeance", some worked in the laundry, others in the kitchen, in the library, or cleaning the floor, or in the dressing room

where the clothes worn by the prisoners were kept at the time of their admission.

But there were also those who were self-employed selling protection to inmates, so some felt safer protected by other inmates than under the care of the gendarmes.

Others worked making flowers or drawings, crucifixes from threads and fabrics, pretending to scare off their own demons, or cutting hair like barbers, paid by Vengala, but encouraged by the population.

Or like El mar, which wrote novels by the page, and rented the reading of every five handwritten pages, for an envelope of soup, the equivalent of fifty cents, and also wrote and sold poetry and romantic letters for the brides and the prisoners' lovers, at five soups a copy, so that being separated by the bars some prisoners found it difficult to keep the fidelity of their loves from prison, and sought to persuade the lovers with the verses of El mar

Every day his popularity increased, to the extent that even those who had received him with hostility had changed their minds and began to respect him, and El mar saw the change in their positive attitude toward him, especially when he managed to make a prisoner smeared with sadness smile again.

Everything happened with the arrival of Jeremías Arietas, a native of the heart of the neighborhood, before his entrance to Vengala he had fallen madly in love with Chari Moncada, a young woman of the neighborhood, who was also enthusiastic with him, but who was well seen by the Mole, a little boy of not very pleasant attributes, but who ran a gang of facinerosos in the sector, and who believed that with a little insistence, the women could fall like fruit of good taste, in the arms of a consecrated lover.

With a certain mischievousness accompanied by excessive sarcasm, he set his eyes on Chari, and proposed to hold further plastic with it, and tried to make her confident of his confidences, so when she was on her way to school, seeing that she had to pass in front of the block where he distributed his drugs, for a moment of contemplation, the Mole was paralyzed with emotion, but coming to his senses, he harassed her, pitied her,

Always looking for a way to make her look at him, and although Chari did not pay attention to him, there were days when she, in order not to seem abrupt, would fake   a discreet smile, but after the smile, came the speeding up of her steps to leave the scene.

Who would have thought that an unrequited love could generate such an unfortunate situation! Because in view of the evident rejection, the Mole with his spirit in convalescence, encouraged by his leisure time, forged a costly triviality, and one day using one of his clients, paid her to threaten Chari, warning her that if she did not get away from Jeremiah she would have difficulties, and Chari, confused, thought that Jeremiah, was betraying her with her, and sad and crying, fled in a halo of motionless dust.

The Mole had taken his first step, the trap was set, then coming out of hiding to supervise Ursula Glas' dirty work, he walked up to her, kissed her cheek and said:

---- The intimacy of your brilliance will reverberate my hope, good work Ursula, you see this package of bills... they are a thousand dollars that will be yours when I complete the work, with this that happened today, for sure Chari will get away from Jeremiah, let's wait until tomorrow to see how we are going to do it.--- He proposed Ursula seemed thoroughly informed, the Mole felt her smile, and smiled at her as well. She spoke after a brief silence:

--- What do you want, for tomorrow? --- I question her.

---- Don't worry, I'll let you know:

----- You take these two hundred dollars, I'll wait for you tomorrow morning... Ah, take this little stone with you so you can treat yourself.--- She said, stretching out her short, chubby arm, holding between her fingers a little bag of cocaine that she diligently caught.

---- very well Topo, "for the money the monkey dances" in the circus of life, it will be done as you say, I look at you, I see you, bye-bye cocoa. -Ursula said to him with feigned joy, as she placed a kiss on his cheek, zigzagging through the noise of the cars, crossed to the other side of the avenue and left.

 The Mole saw her walk away unrepentant, at the end of the street her silhouette was lost, he smiled, aware of the risks.

June wandered in the atmosphere and was confused in time, the sun's rays filtered through the atmosphere in a lethargic manner, a fine drizzle wetted the pavement.

From the mole's neck, a giant medallion was detached, showing the face carved in gold of an Eastern idol, and on his black T-shirt written in white letters, a slogan stood out saying: "Better dead than poor".

The next day was Friday, the asphalt was still wet from the rain of the previous night. The Mole appeared on the block earlier than ever, he had planned everything with malice.

It was 7:35 a.m., and in ten minutes he was waiting for Chari on the road, and just after the expected time, on his way to the school that was nearby, at 7:45 a.m., the Mole, who was talking to two of his subordinates at that moment, had ordered him to leave in disguise:--- Water, water, wake up, here comes what I am waiting for --- He said, as those disappeared, gurgling, before blocking Chari's way, telling her in all the splendor of his purpose:

---- Hello, diva, it's good to see you again, I want you to keep in mind, that among all the aspirants, I'm the one you become, with me you won't miss anything, and if a star can come down from the sky, I won't hesitate to extend my arm to reach it for you.--- He expressed with an exorbitant paraphrase.

That enormity sounded to her ears like a copla of diaphanous notes, but between smiling and shyness she resorted to diplomacy:

---- Thank you... Can I have permission to go to school and be late?

---- Of course, my queen, whatever you order, my beauty," answered the Mole with exaggerated sympathy, as he unlocked the path where Chari was walking, which continued on its way while the Mole watched her leave with a morbid expression.

Five minutes later Ursula appeared, brought by a certain cadence in her walk, with the intention of following up on the Mole's proposal, she greeted him, while he proceeded to instruct her in the final guidelines:

--- Listen well Ursula, I'm waiting for someone who comes to pick something up, at nine o'clock, at that hour as always Jeremiah, will pass by here, to go to his work, when he comes I will give a little something to someone who is waiting for him, when that happens go to the rockrose.

---- What? interrupted Ursula.

---- With the gendarme on the corner, with the officer, and tell him that you saw someone selling drugs, to whom I will hand over the bags, nothing more, you sneaked a look and then you acted.--- He said, with all the splendor of his evil.

And since the devil never walks alone, it turns out that as I plan it. So it happened; that day Jeremiah was depressed, head down and almost dragging his feet, because he had not been able to communicate with Chari, because the evil forged had impacted so that she would hide, without him knowing the reason.

In the naivety of his innocence, he never imagined that the Mole, a wizard of malice who made him believe a false friendship, was behind this conspiracy with the clear intention of ruining his life.

Everything had started in the previous winter when a sports vereta that guided the Mole, after a heavy snowfall, had refused to light, seeing Jeremiah for his reputation as a good mechanic, needed to go to a call that the Mole had sent him, and since then he continued doing the mechanical services that the Mole deserved.

Everything went very well until the Mole found out that Chari, the girl he used to court, ignoring her condition, was Jeremiah's girlfriend, which turned out to be a hard blow that he had refused to accept because the Mole felt for Chari, a kind of platonic love, long before he decided to propose to her.

It was then when he couldn't control something like, an attack of envy when he heard the news, so he didn't take care to comment where his buddies heard it:

---- Chari is a lot of woman for that "mechanicucho" full of grease.

CHAPTER 14

— Then the Mole swore not to rest until he conquered it; he had heard that intuitive imagination was the secret of geniuses, and from that moment he began to forge what would be the best way to get out of it.

First he dispensed with the services of mechanics that Jeremiah offered him, because he thought that if he discovered that he had feelings for his girlfriend, he could kill him by cutting the brakes of the car, taking advantage of one of those days when he requested it for a repair or revision of the car, and precisely on that morning he was determined to consummate his macabre intention.

When Jeremiah approached where he was before the mechanic noticed, he made his arm around his neck, and with the greatest caution placed two little bags of cocaine that he held between his thumb and ring finger, while with malicious cunning he patted him on the back, mockingly, with a comradeship of pride and cynicism, while Ursula followed the instructions received.

A woman previously noted by the mole approached him receiving another bag just like the ones the mole had put in Jeremiah's pocket, and trapping it between her bony fingers she walked behind the mechanic, and upon reaching the intersection where the officer was on duty, she approached Jeremiah with the intention of being seen by the policeman while talking to him, and seeing that she achieved her goal, she saw that Ursula on her undercover duty, as planned, approached the officer and whispered to him with a double intention:

---- As you could see, the officer does not respect you, they just made a drug transaction in your eyes and you didn't even realize it, look at you where you are going," he commented, like a snake that induces sin, motivating the mobilization of the officer.

---- Hey, you two, stand there," he said, straining his voice.

The woman, with a certain perspicacity, avoiding being seen by the gendarme in her action, threw the bag of cocaine she was carrying on the asphalt, and since Jeremiah was unaware of the plot being set up, he felt surprised and incredulous at what was happening.The officer used the radio and at one point the street was crowded with henchmen, five patrol cars had arrived and found no opposition when they arrested Jeremiah and the woman, who was taken to the gendarmerie and dispatched, because the officer did not notice when she had thrown the evidence on the asphalt, and since it was a woman, in the absence of evidence it was preferable to let her go, and so they did.

On the other hand, Jeremiah, who had found the two bags that the Mole had placed in his bag, had been retained because he could not prove the contrary, since he had been taken by the infraganti.

Thus began Jeremiah's awakening, and he had begun to realize that "trust was the shortest way to make a mistake," and that "good intentions were full of the ways of hell" and malice and thorns that damaged his life.

Ursula knew that he was innocent and so did the henchmen, who even when checking his identity, finding out what kind of person he was because they had drug tested him and found him clean, had held him until the situation was clarified.

Jeremiah thought that "to err was human, that what was not human was to blame the errors on the shoulders of others". And for a long time he believed that evil was a demonic tool to deactivate the human being.

For his part, the Mole had been left with the field free, Chari had noticed the absence of Jeremiah, and although he had decided to go looking for him at the place of work, he did not find answers because he had not had the opportunity to warn anyone of his retention, so as Jeremiah lived with his cousins, he tried to investigate with them, but he also did not manage to find out anything, because they also ignored what had happened.

Chari felt devastated, and even blamed herself for Jeremiah's disappearance, but she also thought that he had abandoned her for Ursula, and that she was questioning herself and did not understand how if she loved him, he had left in silence and without saying goodbye.

The mole instead continued in his plan. Whenever she went to school, he insisted on conquering her and helping her forget about Jeremiah, and one day he blocked herway:

--- You don't have to shed any more tears for someone who left without saying goodbye, don't suffer anymore, you threw the dead in the river, the dead in the hole and the living in the bun, it's been two weeks without him looking for you. He said with all the integrity of his pride.

Chari, feeling blushing, did not think possible what the Mole had just said, so he questioned with some curiosity:

--- How do you know, that two weeks ago --- she questioned intrigued. However, the Mole who was ready for her answer assumed an evasive stance and resorted to poetry:

--- My soul despairs in the absence of your love, and I wait for you, my darling, I wait for you, who like a seagull takes flight and comes flying to me, that's what

I want from you. But I will also tell you, that two weeks ago I accidentally heard, that someone was asking you to get away from him --- he answered.

---- What do you know about it? Because when she told me that, I didn't see any witnesses around. She said she was even more intrigued. --- My love, the walls have ears, and a little bird told me so," argued the Mole with some sarcasm.

---- Don't call me your love, I'm not your love. --- Chari answered abruptly.

----Since I met you, you have been my platonic love, but you could become my real love... Of course, if you want to, a nail takes out another nail, and you don't have to die in vain.

-- I don't want you to talk to me. Chari replied sharply.

--- That's how I like them, brave to tame her --- replied the Mole always with his sarcasm. Chari kept silent, and the Mole saw that his eyes got wet, which he took advantage of for a re-attack:

---- Jeremiah, it's not worth your tears, maybe he went with someone else, but it doesn't matter, you know that I love you well and you can count on me.

Chari kept silent, which he took the opportunity to touch her, took her by the shoulders, carried her to his lap and caressed her hair.

--- I don't want to go to school --- Said Chari, drowned in tears, almost gurgling, stuck in tears.

--- You're to eat with me, I'll study with you --- insisted the Mole.

He believed he had the skill to vent his anger at the oppressive desire, without giving it any hint that would induce him to personalize the fight. He knew the trick of manipulation, and relied on the power of guile, making the innocent appear guilty, when in fact the fault was his.

Since that day and by then, the Mole had started dating Chari, ignoring her, the truth of what happened.

Two months had passed since the terrible maneuver that the Mole had forged, and which had led Jeremiah to prison, and Chari to take refuge in his arms, until one day in

That she cut classes and surprisingly without warning appeared where the Mole lived, and found him "foyando", or rather wallowing, with another of the admirers he used to frequent, and then she chose to wake up instantly, not before suffering a terrible disappointment:

--- Why are you doing this to me? --- Don't be irritated my love, she gives me what you deny me, but you remain still that even so, you are the cathedral and the parishes more. He said with a sardonic laugh.

The girl who accompanied him smiled with disbelief, while Chari started to run, besieged by tears, without stopping until she reached the confines of her house, where she reflected on what had happened that morning, as she found the house alone, she chose to go to bed and slept until the early hours of the morning.

It was two o'clock the next morning when she got up, she felt rested and took the opportunity to review her grades, knowing that the next day the general exams in high school were starting, and although she felt prepared, she needed to feed back her knowledge, she felt with enough energy for that purpose, since she had rested without being bothered by her mother, who had found her deeply asleep when she returned from work.

That day seemed to be a success, Tuesday dawned with a bright sun, and her grades would be interesting, but on the way back to the house she managed to hear a scene with sound, where Ursula was arguing heatedly with the Mole, and whose discussion revolved around a claim that she extended to him:

---- Listen, Mole, I want you to hand over the remaining eight hundred dollars of the thousand you offered me for my unjust participation in the conspiracy against the mechanic Jeremiah.

---- Ha, ha, ha, and did you think that I was going to pay you a thousand dollars for something planned and executed by me?

---- Okay, if you don't pay me I'm going to start by telling Chari the whole truth, and then we'll see how you leave after she knows that Jeremiah never cheated on her, and that he's in jail because of you.

Chari, who had been following the conversation without them noticing, burst in unexpectedly:

---- You don't have to tell me anything, I heard everything.

The Mole, unaccustomed to receiving surprises, had to make an effort to fake the rudeness, and with the most thunderous irony he extended his arms to try to distract her.

---- Oh my love, you had missed, you were waiting, you lost me, what's wrong with you? He said trying to attract her to him.

However, Chari with an almost violent reaction, extended his open hand and with the palm blocked the displacement.

---- Stop it, cynic, don't come near me. She said to him in anger and trying to make her way away in a hurry.

The Mole wanted to stop her:

---- My love, don't leave me, don't listen to this tasting..." he said, referring to Ursula and he still hadn't finished expressing himself when he received a slap on his left cheek from her.

- - - - Respect me, dwarf, "but your grandmother will be the one who tastes you, you dirty, stupid". - - -He said looking to provoke him.

At that moment, one of his henchmen approached him, saying almost in his ear.

- - - - Go away, the gendarmes are coming. - - -He said.

The blushing mole moved his face and inopportunely as if he were fleeing he made a mistake by taking the opposite path to the one where the gendarmes warned him.

By the time the officers arrived, everyone had left.

CHAPTER15

— Among the population of prisoners there was usually something that could be called bad time, because although some of them seemed normal and serene, they did not always inspire the best motivation to trust them, because if that was the case, at a certain moment they used to suffer a setback that revealed their authentic personality, letting the jealousy, the delusions, the selfishness, the frustrations and the anger among other barbarities and adjectives come out.

Something had happened that came to justify the expressions of friction and tension generated between Afro-Saxons and Hispanics, who, cornered between walls, sought to show their power by trying the strongest and most brazen to subdue those who seemed weaker, so when someone exhibited something with a certain exchange value and another wanted it, they asked for it first, and if the one who possessed it was weak and refused to give it up, but didn't hide his fear, then the one who wanted it took it by force.

Charlie Colombo had received his commissary articles, provisions that had generated unrest, and David, induced by hunger or curiosity, had demanded that Charlie Colombo share it with him, but despite the fact that black David was a skilled boxer, Charlie Colombo refused to share it, signing his uneasiness, because from that day on, black David dedicated himself to   instilling terror in him.

Threatening to strip him of everything, and even attacking him, in a moment of carelessness.

Already the population distinguished him, because of his cheekiness, he was not afraid to create temptation, and he used to pass it from cubicle to cubicle promoting garbage, so I often heard him say:

- - - - Do you want to smell? - - -He would say.

Everyone used to look at him as a clown until the clash with Charlie Colombo, who, driven by fear, had been intimidated by his demand for an emergency transfer to

Another bedroom, fearing being beaten and stripped, or attacked while sleeping, in the J-2 bedroom, used to cluster by community, with whites targeting whites, African Americans targeting African Americans, and Hispanics targeting Hispanics.

It was a form of self-protection by unifying in its different versions, the case was that sporadically when the prisoners had been together for a long time in the same residence, they ended up becoming friends and each one sought to be close to the group that exerted a certain influence, to avoid being abused by the stronger ones.

Two days after Charlie Colombo's transfer, someone arrived who, upon realizing that he would have to live with one of his enemies in the dormitory where he had been taken, refused to stay in the same place. He insisted that for his safety he should be transferred, but he was unable to influence the administration to make his transfer happen.

Then he felt possessed, took over the phone used by the custody on duty to make reports and began to bang it against the wall, until he managed to get the attention of those who did not hear him, and had himself moved from that place, first he was punished in the box, accused of attempting to destroy minor state property, and then to another bedroom as he wished.

He preferred to be alone and not in the population; he knew that when one was in the population, one did not know when one would be attacked, or when one would have to assume a defensive posture.

He was never far from the truth because precisely when they went looking for him, the turtles, the Venice riot squad, arrived by surprise turning and dragging everything in their path, the prisoners upside down with their hands tied around their necks, it was their strategy to refuse to be recognized by the prisoners to avoid revenge, if any of the abused ever met them, outside the prison.

 He felt the pressure on his back when two of the turtles lifted him by his shoulders in retaliation for trying to break the phone used by the guards.

He would be led to the box, the solitary cell, and with restless serenity resigned to wait for his verdict, he preferred an extension of time to have a corpse made from his body. There was no shortage of those who predicted the sentence:

----They built a new charge against him, accusing him of conspiring to destroy government property. - They commented as a group.

Everyone knew and no one was unaware that prison was another world where violence lurked, with no one knowing where it would erupt or who it would affect, because there it was ignored

When a criminal would emerge to execute the criminals.

Whoever had a lesser sentence had to simulate it, spreading it was a challenge that induced jealousy, and violence, which caused the extension of time inside the prison.

Some hated the officers who arrested them and the judges who sentenced them, wanting to have them in their hands to vent their anger, and when they used to talk about them, they would name them in a derogatory tone.Sometimes, when they wanted to bother someone, they would enter that person's cubicle and start insulting the custodian on duty with the crudest insults, giving him space to write down the number of the cubicle where the insults came from, so that the resident of that space would be punished.

The cubicle of El mar, was frequently visited by a considerable group of prisoners who were going to request services of cards, novels or poems, and in their free time they also used to invite him to play cards, dominoes, patché or chess, and among them were also some of those who, upon his arrival, had tried to manipulate him or instill terror in him, without achieving anything of what was intended because he was condescending and tolerant, but firm and unwavering at the moment of making a decision.

Sporadically, to avoid a fight among the population, the custodians used to organize the schedule for watching television, specifically in the J-2 bedroom, Hispanics watched it from ten to two in the afternoon, the rest of the time was assigned to African Americans and Anglo-Saxons, and those who were not very fond of watching television used to invest their free time in reading or playing.

On Saturday afternoon, El mar and Gary, had met, to discuss a literary topic and an hour later when Gary felt exhausted he got up to retire, but as El mar had not had time to clean his space, he had been willing to sweep and map it and when he thought he would have some time to rest, Jeremiah appeared to propose a business, whose offer was tentative, so when they called the gym, El mar and he chose to stay in order to discuss the offer:

How are you doing, teacher? --- He greeted Jeremiah with a solicitous voice.

El mar, which was finishing its work, placed the mop in the bucket of muddy water, then responded with effusiveness:

----- I'm very good, thanks, and you?" he said as he held out his hand.

---- I'm going to pay him to write something that will convince my girlfriend to come back with me.

---- And what happened? I question El mar.

---- Before I was imprisoned, a misunderstanding arose that I didn't have time to clear up, and here it's been difficult for me, my calls don't come through. --- He clarified.

---- You're fine, what do you want?

---- A letter with a poem... How much is that, five dollars? --- Asked and affirmed Jeremiah.

---- Yes, I think it's a good offer.

After agreeing on the true purpose of the letter and how he would like the poem, he turned to the following text:

"Far from you, I feel on the cross, like a dark crucified man without light.

I still don't know how I caused that pain, which sowed doubt in your heart.

Behind the Moorish shadow, distant and without you, I want your presence to be happy.

If, for me, you came back, I would know that it is you, the silhouette of your body brings me the light.

Your impulsive love, serves me as a shelter, I want your presence to be with you".

Then he addressed it to Chari, explaining in detail what had happened, signed it and sent it to the post office.

It was not difficult for Chari to understand the details, it was the midday of Saturday June 20th, and because of those circumstances of life by the letter of Jeremiah's last name, the assigned visit would be the other day, and she, just as Barbarita had done with El mar, so Chari was induced to do it with Jeremiah.

On Sunday, Chari got up early and went to Vengala, where he managed to find Jeremiah, at first an aura of confusion and mistrust surrounded him but as the day progressed, joy assailed them again, he had told them everything, they forgave each other swearing eternal love, Jeremiah took the opportunity to ask Chari to request El mar in his visit, and he did.

When El mar entered the room Jeremiah introduced him with Chari and explained that El mar had been the author of the letter and the poem that had motivated her to clarify her confusion, Chari thanked El mar confirming the strength of his verses, confessing

That destiny had conspired for the events to be generated in the way they were, and when they were about to say goodbye Chari said to Jeremiah: ---- Love, when you go out take him home to the party," he said, referring to El mar.

---- Of course, honey, he will be there.

---- Thank you, sir, for helping to make everything clear.

---- Thanks to you, for allowing me to participate, you are young people with the right to be happy.

---- Jeremiah told me that you guys do Bible studies---Chari Express.

----Yes, we do it in the prison parish, but we continue it in the dormitory," said El mar.

---- I see it as a way to kill time...Said Jeremiah.

---- Don't read the bible to kill time, don't go creating a murder case, Ha-ha-ha. It's a joke. Anyway you have to read it as the word of God who created the heavens and the earth --- said El mar.

--- He looks like a shepherd. --- Said Chari.

– – – – I would rather say a prophet. I affirm Jeremiah, with complicity.

– – – – Thank you, the important thing is to have the capacity to love and forgive, when I think of telling my enemy I love you, and I remember the wrongs he did to me, then I say I love God, which is the same as forgiving and loving myself, to forgive and love my enemy.

– – – – Everything sounds beautiful, but I don't know if I can forgive the Mole, the author of all the evil that almost led us to the breakup.

– – – – Don't worry my love, what goes around comes around, and life takes care of everything.

Their lively conversation had been interrupted by the custodian who approached them to tell them: – – – – Time, the visit is over. He said dryly.

Chari with wet eyes embraced and kissed Jeremiah tenderly:

– – – – See you soon my love, I'll be back on Wednesday, everything will be fine, the lawyer told me that the judge is reviewing your case, and that possibly on Thursday they will let you go.

Chari – – – Turning to El mar, he added:

– – – Lord, thank you for everything and do not forget that in us you have a new family – – – He said.

– – – – Thank you for considering me one of your family, I will see you as such," he said as he kissed her hand.

Chari, felt assaulted by the emotion, and withdrew without being able to prevent the tears from flooding her eyes. El mar and Jeremiah returned to the J- 2 dormitory.

That afternoon the cubicle of El mar was crowded again, the population had been informed that he had convinced Chari, Jeremiah's girlfriend, to forgive him, to go back to him and to visit him, because before that letter poem, Jeremiah was under the uncertainty of a desperate depression.

In fact, the clientele of El mar, had increased, since by the condition of prisoners they felt abandoned, but the letters poems of El mar, with a payment of

Five soups per copyright, equivalent to two dollars and fifty cents, helped to boost their hopes.

The voice had spread about the feats he was producing with his pen, and the new prisoners had also begun to consult him, to listen to his advice and suggestions, and they commissioned from him letters, poems and little novels, which after they read, they sent to their mothers, wives, girlfriends and friends. El mar was highly regarded by the prisoners, because when one of them had many visitors, the others had a certain respect for him and kept a distance when they wanted to go over, because they used to understand the message that the individual was not alone, so they started to consider him at the level of a leader.

CHAPTER 16

— In those days, a new visitor named Lazaro Osorio had started frequenting El mar, and one could say that they became collaborators of the cause, because he started illustrating letters and poems that El mar wrote. He went to prison with a file of sixteen convictions and several sentences, so he tried to take away by force the rich people's money, and to go around violating the surveillance and trespassing without permission on the houses of millionaires.

He was thin, five-eleven in height, had big eyes, a hooked nose, and was always ready to hit anyone who threatened him, and next to him were some who had fallen for petty crimes like Bernardo, who was walking the streets drunk and hugging a beer.

There was also another one called Arturo who had stopped in front of a shoe store and because of those coincidences in life he greeted an acquaintance who was leaving the store at that moment and had   stolen some shoes he was carrying inside a backpack that was hanging from his back, having noticed the safety of the theft, going after him, surprising him underhand, believing that Arturo was an accomplice of him, and without being able to prove the contrary and without the perpetrator denying it, they were both handed over to the public prosecutor.

Now everyone was either serving time, or waiting to be sentenced, or waiting to be exonerated.

The leadership of El mar had increased so much that even the officials had begun to nickname it after the president of the kingdom at that time.

Later, the church services had been called, and when it was time to pick up the pass to go to the chapel, Officer Williams who was covering the shift that day said:

---- El mar and Gary, I hope you will pray for me. -He said with some conviction.

----Officer William, because of your faith you are now saved, we will pray for you.

---- Thank you," added Officer Williams. Another prisoner, who was taking a shower at the time, poked his head out and shouted:

---- Pray for me too.

---- His name is Kent," said Officer Williams.

---- Yes, I know, thank you. --- El mar answered, as it came out.

Gary made his way to the gymnasium, while El mar, followed by Arthur, Lazarus and Jeremiah made their way to the chapel. On the way, an officer who seemed in a very good mood greeted him:

--- Goodbye president. He said.

El mar nodded its head and continued to walk to the parish and when it arrived it was placed in the first row by the protocol commission, chosen for this purpose.

That afternoon the preaching had touched the hearts of the participants in the service, and from the organ emanated a music of praise followed by a song of adoration, where the crowded participation could not control the crying, and among them was El mar, who also felt that his eyes were crying without being able to prevent two tears from flooding the skin of his face, while Lazarus applied comforting pats.

The shepherd prayed to the Lord asking for mercy for the prisoners who in the next few days were to be presented in court, mainly those who were not common criminals, but like El mar had arrived there because of that circumstance of fate.

When he arrived at the house, it began to be said that the Holy Spirit had ministered over El mar, while he sat in front of the aluminum table to conclude a poem he had been commissioned to write, one they called Mary because of her long hair and little girl's face.

Maria was throwing balls of dented paper at him, trying to provoke him, in order to get him out of concentration, so Lazarus who was watching was induced to admonish him: --- You hear, stop joking, can't you see that El mar is busy, and not for play? --- He said.

El mar, which was still on its back, without realizing what was happening, turned around and with a framed calm, indicated it with its index finger and said:

---- Stop Mary, don't keep letting the demons minister to you and that's not good.

At that moment Mary, who was a few meters away, followed by others, approached the cubicle of El mar, feeling   that it was somewhat invaded, she stood up and asked with the greatest courtesy:

---- Don't you understand that I'm busy, please, I want you to clear my space, now.

---- Why?

---- Don't be problematic, you've already said that I'm busy and I have to conclude what I'm doing. -El mar reaffirmed.

Hearing again the plea of El mar, Mary and her followers went away in silence.

At night El mar had fallen asleep late, and he dreamed in sequence, first that he was in a museum with a group of children, and then that he was walking down one of the streets of paradise accompanied by his little girl, and that she was carrying her hands smeared with white, and that he had come to a flat and extensive space where a shower spilled a jet of water, having asked for permission under the pretext of washing the girl's hands, he had been allowed to do so.

Entering the place instead of taking care of the girl, she walked a little further into a square where there were many goods, including purses and hats, and continued walking, arriving at an apartment with two rooms where one of them had damaged pipes, causing the floor to be flooded with fecal matter.

He then settled down to continue dreaming, but was awakened by loud shouts from prisoners in beds 37 and 38, who had started a sharp argument.

--- Stop moving, and let me sleep, "bastard" --- I shout with all the splendor of a greengrocer the number 37 ---.

Don't be quarrelsome and be quiet, "you piece of ass"," answered the number 38 rudely.

--- Go to the dirty bathroom and don't do that on me, I'm going to call you to the custody, you'll see that if you keep on we're going to have problems, satyr...---I answer the 37 any.

---- Espeeerateeeee, ah.--- I'll finish the 38.

It happened that the number 38, who occupied the second floor of the bed, had been immersed in a sinful act by fornicating with his body.

The scandal had woken up the others, and the officer who had silently followed the event, immediately communicated with the sergeant who spared no effort in ordering him to be "packed up", as they said in the prison slang, to refer to being moved from his home, however such action had led him to be isolated, locked in

A solitary cell.

It was the eve of the third day that El Mar was due to appear in court, and where he was expected to be released, and that day he had been summoned to the prison system clinic where they had begun treating him for a diabetes that had been announced five years earlier and to which he had never paid any attention, but knowing that in three days he would be going to court, the doctor from Venice summoned him to provide him with information on how he should cope with the impending illness.

They punctured his finger to measure his sugar levels, that day he had it at 139, so they gave him a pill for that purpose, gave him a phone number to call to follow up on the treatment, in case the judge let him go.

Anyway, El mar thought that God had him alive with a purpose, he did not believe in diseases and thought that he had the internal mechanisms to heal himself, and used to believe that many of the diseases were manufactured in the laboratories of the kingdom, and dissolved to keep the health system active, and to expand the trade of drugs and medicines, always called to strengthen the finances of investors.

Later, after a game of cards with Lazarus, they had called for a Bible study, where he had attended in the company of Arthur, and where he had also met again with Robert, and together with the pastor of that evening, after they had praised the Lord, they prayed in faith for the success of those who would be taken to court again the next day.

The prayer had been raised with such faith that El mar said it felt the presence of the spirit again because it experienced a movement in the scalp, while seeing its skin blush with goose bumps.

CHAPTER 17

— The next day was Mars and he had been woken up early in the morning, it was four o'clock when the custody of that day approached his bed to remind him to prepare for his court day. After showering, they took him to medication, and from there to the reception, where they would exchange his prison uniforms for clothes to wear to the Street.

Before his departure an immigration agent had come to pick him up under the pretext of deporting him to the European continent, so El Mar was forced to show him that although he was not naturalized from the kingdom, he belonged to the American continent not to the European one, he had been subjected to an interrogation regime, which El Mar was able to answer with wisdom, showing that he had been legal in the country since the first day of his arrival in paradise and that from then until the moment he was facing, 17 years had passed with his status.

The Immigration agent before the explicit exposure dialed the phone and notified his superior, that there was a great confusion with El mar because he was not of European origin, but a Caribbean American. A few minutes after the verification, which seemed more like a mockery of manipulation, they boarded the transportation and headed to the courthouse where all the prisoners who came had been called to see the judge.

Confused and enigmatic he walked back and forth, until a thought illuminated his mind, and rather when El mar heard it, it seemed to him like a prayer with rhythm:

– – – – You're getting out today, and the trial will be on July 1st," he said. – – – It's okay, I'm still waiting – – – argued El mar.

Attorney Dino J, who seemed to have urgent business to attend to, chose to return to the courtroom, moved along the path he had already walked, and with a certain amount of stealth advanced along the way.

He had assumed an enigmatic expression that had him disturbed in some way, so he said as if he wanted to be heard:

– – – I lied to you Valenilla Mar, today you are not going to leave here. He said as his silhouette was lost behind the cement frame.

As Dino J had said, it happened that day, they had left him without calling him in front of the judge, returned him to revenge without any explanation, but then he found out that they had referred his case for a week later.

In the evening they called the religious service but since El mar had gone to a new dormitory, even he was not authorized to attend from block F 251 to the Chaplaincy because he was not yet listed in that block, it was being somewhat more difficult for him to mobilize.

In that new bedroom everyone had a little more privacy, because the rooms were separated; they had a toilet and a hand washer inside, besides, there they had more time to think better.

El mar came forward to the custody and asked for a form to request an appointment with the social worker to discuss the problems he was facing with the lawyer who had not called him in front of the judge. And another for the chaplain to include him in the list of Catholic service, not because he was too interested in religion, but because in that return he got free use of the phone to call Barbarita Roque.

With the intention of leaving, El Mar attended all the religious services, and on one occasion a custodian who wanted to question his idiosyncrasy suggested that he attend one of the branch of

Services, and tried to make him understand that if he attended the Catholic service, he should not attend the evangelical one, to which he specified:

---- To my God is one, there is no reason to deviate religion, I am imprisoned and I do not see anything wrong in talking about God from the different conceptions in which he is expressed to the believers, the right thing is that religion unites men, not divide them. God is a whole for everyone, and is not a political candidate, so, please sir

If it's not too much to ask, include me in the list of all church services, if it's not too much to ask, thank you.

The next day was Wednesday and, as usual, he woke up early. His new room had a view of the plain where some prisoners used to gather at recess time, and from the window one could see the dim lights of the cars that used to move in that direction, the grass splashed with the night spray, the green of the meadows and the chlorophyllated groves; surrounded by the green of the grass, which, seen from a distance, were perceived as serene as the calm waters of a summer lake. The birds' song suggested the impression of a national park.El mar continued to gaze in absorption from the window, watching the minutes escape in the panoramic distance that disappeared in the visibility of that strange presence. Something strange had happened that induced him to act vertiginously, with unexpected actions, letting a panoramic shine escape from his pupils.

An exciting movement produced a whistle that competed with the air, then a memory of what happened in court came to him while he was waiting to be taken to the judge.

It turned out that someone coming back from the hearing room, in a fit of provocation, went directly to El mar, to ask him to stand up for a seat, he looked at him silently and said:

– – – Why are you doing this, were these seats bought by you so that the rest of us would have to get up to make you sit down?

– – – – No, but I was there before I was called to see the judge.

– – – – Okay, I'm going to give up my seat because I don't want to get into any more trouble than I am, but you need to start developing your levels of consciousness, because

Maybe you wouldn't like to be in my place and have me come in and ask you to stand up for me to sit down, would you?

Black kept replicating between his teeth:

– – – – Give it to me and let's not argue.

El mar was incorporated by giving El mart.

– – – – You are right, there is no need to argue. I affirm El mar.

– – – – Yes, because we're going back together to revenge," he said. On hearing the confession, El mar questioned itself and mumbled as if thinking aloud:

– – – Vengeance, as he knows that we are going to return to Vengeance together, would it be that he was sent to provoke me to justify my imprisonment? They kept silent and as the black man had said a few minutes later, the guards appeared and handcuffed them again, to return to Vengala. During the trip the black man had withdrawn, assuming a submissive, humble attitude, and finally they returned speaking amicably. El mar continued to reflect on the reasons for why? The judge had not called him to discuss again the conditions of his freedom, he knew that many men in paradise used to occupy public positions, and many times they were worse than some common criminals, because they used to show themselves as tyrants accustomed to hypocrisy, deceit, exploitation, and varnished themselves with limited knowledge that, infatuated by ignorance, they exhibited as trophies of pride and vanity.

Sometimes they hurt with their decisions those who, far from the opulences, used to lie down where they were surprised at night, waking up the next day early in the morning, that minority hit by the competitive circumstances that paradise used to offer, but that many times were not always able to become self-sufficient in the evolutionary survival, between the offer and the demand.

It was approximately three o'clock in the afternoon when he made those reflections, the day had developed in apparent tranquility, and he thought that Barbarita Roque, would show up to visit him, but it was not so.

That day he discovered that the sugar had balanced when the meter showed it at 109, since they started measuring it was the most balanced of all the measurements the tests had reported.Suddenly, the guards implemented the action of the day, blocked the stairs leading to the second floor, and closed the doors of the rooms.

It happened that a prisoner had suffered a heart attack falling in one of the corridors on the second floor and the guards came to pick him up to transfer him to the hospital.

Half an hour after everything had happened when they unblocked access to the different sections, El mar went to the dining room, and found that in the television section someone was commenting on the abusive actions of the group of turtles, or black cat, as they were called in prison slang, referring to the officers who specialized in breaking up riots or fights between prisoners, so it was commented that when they appeared in scenes they appeared masked and with a little camera that only recorded what the prisoners were doing, not what they were doing to them.

It was also said that they possessed a testar on the forearm, which when activated produced a strong electric shock to the body of the prisoners they touched, and whose discharge could cause heart attacks in their victims that they later attributed to damage suffered in the fights held by the prisoners, so they did not

He liked to be seen in the face by the prisoners because they were afraid of being recognized when they hit someone involved in a prison fight.

Later, El mar returned to the room where he proceeded to review the day's press, by then there was talk of a swine epidemic that was ravaging the world, adding to this concern the problem of the economic crisis that was also a general concern.

The guard appeared and took him out of his moment of reflection, asking him if he had received the tray, letting it be understood that someone had taken over his diet, without the guards noticing it, so El mar asked him to get one of the trays that existed because it was worse to go to bed hungry.

The custodian taking into consideration the suggestion called the kitchen, and a few minutes later they had uploaded a tray of spaghetti with meatball and salad of lettuce, carrots and green beans.

Later, two hungry people who lacked food took precautions to try to get some rations, while one of the wealthy who had received their supply of commissary, was ecstatic watching television distracted by the programming.

They had planned to take away from him some of what he had received, and for this purpose one stayed to watch the movements of the potentate, while another took away the amount due, which they would later share among themselves.

When the owner realized it was too late, he protested, insulted, but nobody said anything, because even those who saw kept silent.

It was useless to persuade the custody that as an advertising "cliché" repeated the expression:

– – – – "If you see something, say something" El mar retired early to his rooms and while he was sleeping he saw in a vision that the prison bars were opening wide, so he thought that soon God would set him free, and he waited for the day in faith.

He took advantage of the silence of the night, then wrote letters to Isabel Volqué, and to Robert Mazara.

One of the prisoners in the adjoining room brought him an orange and soon after that the guard appeared to close the door to the rooms, which although they were usually done by remote control he checked to make sure that no prisoner would leave it open.

The next day was Thursday, some prisoners were commenting on the achievements of the new president-elect at that time in the nation, who, according to public opinion, in a short time had developed the economy and created jobs, and it was said that he had signed a law that favored undocumented immigrants, since some of them in the past served their time in prison and many times for being undocumented, before being deported they left him locked up for one and two additional years serving illegal and unnecessary sentences.

During this time, these victims were subjected to great psychological suffering, even though at the same time, these prisoners were a great source of income for prison management, since the state had to pay for the sustenance of those it wanted to keep.

Many times these prisoners felt used, because even though they were innocent, they held him longer than the law warranted, which meant a fragrant violation of human rights, which very few had the courage to denounce.

CHAPTER 18

— In Paradise, the government did not always make decisions directly, but used agencies and corporations, where the responsibilities of the

Actions did not always have a visible face, so conspiracies were facilitated that almost always arose from groups of people with aberrant mentalities and

Unconscious.

From the first moment they took El mar to court and returned him to prison without seeing the judge and without giving him any kind of explanation, he thought that behind the action there was a malice, which led to an injustice and therefore to the violation of his human rights.

He noticed that some details had begun to change, the letter he sent to Isabel had been returned, they were even hindering him from going to church, he had lost communication with Barbarita Roque, because whenever he tried to dial the number where he always dialed, the operator had begun to notify him that that number was invalid.

The same thing happened when he tried to call the legal services office to inquire about Dino J, the lawyer assigned to him by the court, and he also failed to get adequate information, or was told that the lawyer did not belong to that office, or that they did not know who he was, until El Mar once told the receptionist that he had answered the phone:

---- Enough, they are violating my rights, they have me locked up for nothing, from the first opportunity I have I will be forced to denounce this crime," said El mar, almost alarmed.

---- It's okay," she said, "I can't comment on her case, and we're not currently representing her.

---- If those are the instructions you were given, fine, I have no objection, you are free while I am in jail.

It was raining like crazy, the rain lashed the trees and flooded the grass, softening the earth so that it will adhere to the shoes as a muddy residue.

At lunchtime, the prison warden unexpectedly showed up in the company of Captain Rick and a sergeant, who wanted to supervise the area inhabited by the prisoners, seizing on their way all the additional belongings to the pre-established ones.

They carried two large transparent plastic bags where they made the collections that would go straight into the garbage.

Obviously, on that occasion they took the measure to ensure that no prisoner would show his nose while they were searching and searching.

In addition, they also sought to ensure that the prisoners did not have in their possession drugs or weapons that could be used in some of the fights that used to take place there.

El mar, he used to ask himself, how could prisoners get drugs and knives in prison? Then one of the inmates diligently answered him:

– – – – The jailers themselves enter it and sometimes distribute it in many ways.

– – – He said so convinced that he looked like a priest preaching.

– – – – – And what do they gain from that?.... He questioned El mar with a naivety that seemed different.

– – – – Master, I don't even have to explain to you, you are an intelligent man, you surely have noticed that in prison they make exchanges, a favor is paid with another favor, when they do that they pretend to preserve the control of the power, the more

Time we're in prison, more money they get for us," he said with a mischievous smile, and before El mar questioned him again, he added:

– – – – – Yesterday I saw that one of the barbers was distributing it, and I have to go because that is a compromising issue, take care teacher.– – – – He added and headed south, along the corridor.

El mar saw through the glass window that the sun was appearing in the distance and thought – – – – how beautiful and romantic the evening looks!

He went to his room, sat down at the night table and, as he had done many times before, visualized again the splendorous panorama from his window, thought about Barbarita and recited the verses of a poem while he was capturing the ideas on a blank page: "My dear Barbarita, beautiful and funny little life.

Beautiful and beautiful rose.

Hope to love you ostentatious flower of the sun.

Heart of my passion, radiant and glorious love

Tenderness of heart. I shine with your splendor.

I fertilize you like my flower".

Then he got up, went to the bathroom and took a shower, and when he left the bathroom he went to the TV room where the film "The Ten Commandments" was being shown, that inspirational film induced him to reflect.

He withdrew to his room and through prayer he spoke with God, as if thinking aloud as a Moses who deserved some answers, monologuing a refrain he expressed:

– – – – Lord, I know that for you nothing is true or false, that everything is framed according to the glass with which it is looked at, and I also know that in you and for your purpose, what seems bad you do well, and without the intention of blaspheming, perhaps because of your condition as God, you cannot always be understood.

How is it, Lord, that you, despising sin and yet respecting free will, allow the wicked to exceed in their wickedness?

Why, are those who are just so misunderstood, and what is the reason that the rich get richer and the poor get poorer?

Why is there no balance in the rationalization of wealth? Why do earthly judges tend to play God by absorbing the guilty and condemning the innocent? Do they lack vision?

Forgive my blasphemy if in questioning you I have committed one, but no one on this earth has an answer for a hungry spirit thirsting for justice, so why do lawyers pressure the poor to become guilty even if they are innocent?

Why do a high percentage of the earth's politicians, in the name of their personal ambition, plunder the public treasury and destroy society, requires the evolution of involution? How is it that you, lacking any limit to curb the potentates of earthly power, allow them to misuse the quota assigned to them? – – – He questioned El mar in such a way that it seemed to experience a trance where he could no longer prevent the exacerbation of that spirit thirsting for justice.

It turned out that that night he received the clarification of his questions, the answers to which made it clear that knowledge was what saved, and that ignorance would continue to be the mother of all evil, specifying how good it would be if man learned to identify the balance of justice and truth, and the limit of lie and evil.

God had revealed to him that, if there was no limit for the time in the exercise of the eternity, he would find the answers in the process of his expansion, because nothing was before or after, everything was stipulated and defined, and what had to be known was known when the veil of ignorance was broken. El mar recalled that this is why Christ said "you will know the truth and the truth will set you free".

And he thought about the history of mankind and the laws of Drakon, because salvation has always been engraved in the soul and has manifested itself in the heart.

What has gone has always come, and when you sow in the vineyard of good, you reap good fruit.

In addition, he also remembered that he who killed with the sword died, because the balance of justice consisted in "not doing to others what you did not want done to you.

At the conclusion of the reflection where he reached the revelation, I question him God:

– – – – Do you understand now why not everyone on this plane is yet prepared to know the truth?

The next day he woke up later than ever, he was possessed of a great peace in his heart, he completed the day's assignments and later returned to the room, looking out the window he discovered that on the front esplanade the residents of J-2 were playing, he saw Gary walking, while Arturo Bernardo and the others were playing "soccer". Lazaro Osorio and the Mole were sitting under the shade of a tree.

El Topo had recently been captured in a raid where Ursula, that young generation he treated on the streets for a long time, after so much running around, turned out to be an undercover agent of the gendarmerie of paradise.

He had played a leading role in clarifying the case of Jeremiah, who the next day after the capture of the Mole, would be released.

That same afternoon the block where El mar was staying in Véngala, had been taken out to the esplanade where the residents of J-2 were still staying, since they entered the esplanade, El mar started a warm up exercise, a kind of prolonged walk, with which he tried to keep in shape, while he was exercising, he discovered the presence of the black David that still lived in J-2 and that because he had been working outside he was enjoying his break coincidentally.

He shared a watery conversation with another member of his congregation, from the very moment he discovered the presence of El mar he was glad to have seen it:

– – – El mar!..... That's my friend... I shout with pride.

El mar that had noticed his joy approached him serenely, and extended its hand to him with effusiveness:

– – – – – How are you David, what are you doing here?

– – – – Oh, my friend! Vacationing in revenge– – –she said in an intentional joke.

– – – – Uh, this is the only place where only by force can I be, here I would never want to vacation again.

– – – – – SSSSShh, ha, ha, keep your voice down, I don't want my stay prolonged.
– – – Said the black David, with a gesture of comradeship, implying that he had been absent from work and was walking clandestinely.

El mar took the opportunity to send a message to the J-2 population, mainly Gary, who suddenly felt the need to use the urinal, his bladder asking him to replace fluid,

However, from the esplanade it was not so easy to access the bathroom, and if he did it in front of others he ran the risk of being written.

Black David gave him the solution:

--- El mar, my great friend, I know you are quite scrupulous, but in times of cyclones and earthquakes you have to leave the label, so be sure to pout to distract the custody, that you have an emergency that you have to solve, so you know what you have to do, and I am not telling you more because now I am leaving.

--- Said the black David, holding out his hand as at first and withdrawing at the call of an officer.

El mar lay face down on the grass, lowered its zipper and pretended to pout. This action satisfied the intention, to the point of satiating this physiological need, without the guards noticing.

An hour later they returned to the block, and at 2:30 they were locked in their respective rooms, it was time for a nap.

El mar dreamed of Barbarita again, she could not be seen, but while he was eating with David and another stranger at a rustic wooden table located under a leafy tree, you could hear her voice coming out of a wooden house painted white with light green trim:

----- Is this a restaurant?

---- You could hear him say, among other not very clear expressions, while David and El mar looked at each other tasting some glasses of rice pudding.

He woke up just when he was called for the diabetes test, that afternoon he had it at one hundred and eight, close to balance, because the real control was between 72 and 105.

He returned from the clinic and consumed his assigned diet, which on that occasion was a fish sandwich on whole wheat bread, and white rice with new bean shells and applesauce.While eating the evening news he reported on bankruptcies and the unbalanced economy, and on an arrest by the Bureau of Investigation of a corrupt police officer who was forcing a crack addict to sell drugs in order to get his money.

 At night El mar had dreamt again, but this time he dreamt that he was in a restaurant where he was buying food for his child Mark, and in another picture he saw himself going with Barbarita to a supermarket to get some clothes that he had left in the store, he had taken some suits wrapped in transparent plastic, they took him to the house where they resided, and he discovered that both of the pockets on the back of one of the pants, there was money, in the right pocket twenty dollars, and in the left one a five dollar bill.

He wanted to analyze the meaning and thought that the Lord was revealing to him that after five years he would relate to Mark again, and that he would receive money due after twenty years.

The day had come when Jeremiah would be released from the very prison of Vengala, and in the living room Chari was waiting for him.

The day was overwhelmed and fog covered the treetops, the traces of the sun's rays had vanished, and in the distance the visibility disappeared.

A door of the antechamber opened and there at the threshold was Jeremiah accompanied by a custody without uniform that provoked Chari's distrust, who stood heavily from her seat, contemplating with disbelief Jeremiah beside the new custody, looked at him with a confused look, and for a moment thought that Jeremiah wanted to m r, looked for an explanation in the depth of her pupils.

Then Ursula Irrigan, being a woman aware of what she had caused, went ahead to clarify what seemed obvious:

---- Calm down girl, you look flushed but it is not what you think nor is it what it seems.--- She said to him. She suddenly proceeded--- I am a police officer who served undercover, and things happened in a way that I was forced to continue with the plan, if I backed down in addition to putting their lives in danger the operation could fall, so I owe an apology to both of them, but I also want to tell them that their sacrifices and cooperation, will be compensated and recognized, there is a compensation that will serve them for their plans

Futuros, since I was the officer assigned to that mission, and given the circumstances in which it all came about, it was my duty to come and apologize.

Chari smiled for the first time, Ursula did not seem to understand the rapid change in Chari, but she embraced her anyway:

----- Forgive me. --- He said to her as he kissed her cheek --- He pulled out his detective card and handed it to her as he inquired --- Here is your man, anything call me, however they will soon be checked for recognition.

------ Thank you," mumbled Chari.Ursula expressed her assent by a nod, and she returned through the same door where she had gone before with Jeremiah.

Chari continued to be ecstatic as she watched her go away until she disappeared on the threshold, turned to Jeremiah, wrapped her arms around the neck of her beloved and exclaimed:

--- I got it, I got it! ---- She repeated enthusiastically, kissed him again, intertwined her arm in his, and they went out to the parking lot.

Chari and Jeremiah were a model couple, young, enthusiastic and full of optimism, had met the day of a severe storm when she leading the family car had been stranded by flooding in the vicinity of the service station where Jeremiah worked, she following the advice of a driver who had given the number to send a crane or a mechanic, had marked She was in emergency mode from her cell phone, and Jeremiah answered the call and came to her rescue; however, she did not imagine that that encounter would mark her life forever.

That time she felt so protected and so grateful that she could not fake her interest, something that was not indifferent to Jeremiah and when the time came ,three weeks later when she requested it again, he broke the silence, and declared himself as a blessed or a clergyman would do by skewering: - - - - - Forgive the confidence, Miss I hope and do not consider me clumsy, I am not a person of much talk, with all my respect, I would not want to offend you, nor would I like to lose you as a client, but whenever I see you my heart is scared.

- - - - - Oops, how gallant, what if he's shy, what if he's not?

- - - - I am simply declaring my feelings to you, not to be mocked - - - Jeremiah said to you with some suspicion. - - - - No my love, I'm not making fun, since that first day you called my attention, I have not been indifferent, I'm glad you took the first step, so that later I won't go around saying that I was the one who proposed to you.

- - - - Miss, if you love me, I will make you an altar to worship you.

- - - - You don't have to do that, because I'm not a saint... Adoring God loves me, besides, call me by my name and tutor me because when you treat me as a lady and you, I think you are addressing the director of the kindergarten school... come hold me tightly to my love, seal and confirm our commitment...

Jeremiah brought her to his lap, and ipso facto they caressed each other, and kissed passionately;

It was Saturday afternoon, sitting in front of a gazebo in a park in Paradise, where between kisses and hugs they had consummated their love.

A leafy tree covered their heads and on the right side of the street there was a beautiful gothic building made of marble, where one of the many religious temples of Paradise was located.From that day on, they were like lovebirds from a nest of affection, she was a native of Paradise, and he was an immigrant of those who assiduously attracted that land of opportunity.

Although she had not had the opportunity to meet Jeremiah's relatives living across the border in the surroundings of the Pacific, in the land of the grouper, and understanding that very few know their destiny, she felt that this stranger was the love of her life, and did not hesitate to make possible that happiness that her heart denounced.

When they checked the clock, they discovered that it was going to be ten o'clock at night, Jeremiah was riding in a car that a client had left him for a check-up, they went to where the vehicle was parked, in the vicinity of where they had sat, first he took her home, then he parked the car at the gas station, and walked two blocks to his house.

CHAPTER 19

— Sunday was bright, the rays of the May sun were prevailing, in the afternoon something had happened in F-2 that had closed the doors that gave access to the rooms, and the door to the dining room, and certainly a terrible and nauseating smell, was circulating through the corridor.

Someone had managed to circumvent the surveillance by bringing in a marijuana cigarette, which he had smoked carelessly, and due to this type of incident, the most rigorous measures had been taken with respect to maintaining better control of visitors, since some visitors took the risk of introducing, for some prisoners, controlled substances.

Regularly the mentioned action used to be put in practice by some women who, carrying it in their mouths, tended to kiss the recipient by passing it into their mouths.

On some occasions, they managed to evade the surveillance, but on other occasions when they were discovered, the prisoner would swallow it and the guards would end his visit, and they would take him hanging to a clinic, where they would tie him up in a straitjacket on a bed with a hole attached to his buttocks.

Everything happened in such a way that he was supplied with a specialized laxative to make him defecate on a container placed under the hole of the bed, in order to be able to rescue the substance ingested by the prisoner, which regularly were plastic bags whose content was then submitted without any damage, to a rigorous analysis.

If it was found to be a prohibited substance, the prisoner would be given a new charge, and his previous sentence would be extended, meaning that he would serve more time in prison.

At that time, the prison population in paradise oscillated between 62,577 inmates and the women who historically, due to their sedentary condition, had been in charge of

families, either because the husbands went off to war, or because they were in prison serving time, by then some single women or mothers of families had begun to populate the prisons and most of the time the children were left in the care of government agencies.

The women of Paradise who were then imprisoned were classified as follows:

Twenty-one percent were Latino, forty-six percent were African-American, and thirty-one percent were white, some of them, and most of them, were for violent crimes, indicating that the justice system in Paradise, was generating harsh consequences for the relatives of many of those prisoners who, being innocent, were sporadically sent to prison, looking for ways to soften them up, so that when the court made the proposal to make them guilty, the prisoner would think twice before refusing to accept it.

Thus, many, knowing how difficult it was to stay in jail for a crime the prisoner did not commit, preferred to blame themselves in order to get out faster, and the city and state with such action ended up saving time and money.

The majority of the officials of paradise had an arbitrary mentality, because they had developed a cultural historical idiosyncrasy, which made them feel superior to others, the fact that their society at the time of its creation had exploited the line of slavery by subjecting a minority to the humiliation of exploitation;

He had helped to cement in his new generations a slave mentality, which induced him to use racism for discrimination, and violence for expansion and consolidation in the pursuit of power.

A large part of the population was still resting on its laurels, and Vivian was immersed in the past of its history, trying to impose what they believed had to be done over the feelings and safety of those in excess, refusing to change the values and beliefs of the plantations' ancestors.

For this lineage, democracy consisted of the population having the opportunity to choose by good means what the ruling class understood should be done, because if they refused, they risked being discreetly persecuted, manipulated and blackmailed, often having to obey by bad means.

Before the Mole entered the prison, he was unaware that his days of street crime were numbered. Ursula had already submitted her management report and only needed to confirm the whereabouts of her accomplices to define the location of the, and once the objective was defined, Ursula approached him in apparent peace, sending the same woman he had used as a decoy in the capture of Jeremiah to act as he did this time, introducing another undercover agent with the mole, who ended up buying half a pound of cocaine, which the mole happily authorized him to sell.

---- I don't know you, but since she's recommending you, I'm going to see if I can get it for you.   She dialed her cell phone and spoke to one of her accomplices: --- Hey, get off half a pound, tell the chicken to come with you.

When he authorized the sale over the phone, the undercover agent took out a wad of tickets and handed it to him: – – – – Does that cover the price? – – – – the agent asked him.

– – – – Wait, wait... Don't pass me that money like that, where people are looking at it.

He grabbed the bunch of bills, stood in front of the wall of one of the buildings and counted the amount.

– – – – Very good, I like business with white people, you do, who know how to pay.

A few minutes later, the two men appeared, carrying a package wrapped in their hands, which they extended to the agent, after a gesture of authorization made by the Mole.

The undercover agent silently caught the package, only when it was being removed he argued: – – – – Thank you very much, "your house is still my house" – – – he said in a more sarcastic than joking tone.

He left, and with him, the young woman who had introduced him to the Mole, when it seemed that they were lost in the corner, other agents appeared shouting with loud speakers:

– – – – Don't move, we're police and you're surrounded.

There was a moment of confusion, the two who had delivered the package began to shoot.

The others threw themselves face down on the sidewalks, others ran through the streets on the defensive and aimlessly, there was a moment of screaming and confusion that facilitated the escape of the two men, however, when the Mole tried to vanish, he felt a cold cannon over his temples, five agents in total had him surrounded:

– – – – – You are arrested for possession and sale of drugs, you have the right to remain silent, anything you say can be used against you, you have the right to an attorney, if you cannot afford one, one will be appointed to you.

Three of them stopped pointing their guns at him and began to subject him to a softening punishment. Already handcuffed, they kicked and punched him, landing him on the sidewalk in a halo of violence, while the Mole cried out in defiance:

– – – – Stop, criminals, if I'm already arrested, why do you keep hitting me?

He kept screaming until one of them silenced him:

---- Shut up," he said, punching him in the mouth with his open hand, which made him bleed.

The Mole was on the verge of rebellion, perhaps, if he had not been handcuffed he would have starred in a punching match.

Even with a bloody mouth he said:

---- Aggressive animals, do not understand any other language than violence, hypocrites, persecute those who are supposed to be violent, and are the first to provoke violence.

---- He exclaimed.

---- Shut that louse up or I'll shoot him," said one of the agents, irritated by the effort.

---- He demanded another one while a handkerchief rolled up in his mouth.

They dragged him to one of the patrol units waiting for them, and started the march.

El Topo was a native of Paradise but whose father was Italian and whose mother was Puerto Rican, with whom he had spent most of his life. He identified more with the culture of the Latinos in Paradise than with the feelings and thoughts of the Europeans.

He had finished high school but refused to go to college, he thought that in the environment where he was moving and with the offers he was receiving, it would be better for him to have a career in crime, however life itself was teaching him how wrong he was.

In a short time, the mole realized that he was acting as the bait in the sandwich. On one side were the police and on the other the narcos, to whom, without a doubt, some would have to answer perhaps with their lives, for the slightest mistake.

It was in this way that he had been captured and had come to replace Jeremiah.

Coincidentally, one day before his departure, Jeremiah had warned El Mar that he would be leaving the next day, leaving him the information of where he could be found in case he needed something during his stay in prison, or if he was offered to check it at the time of his departure.

An aura of coincidence, or causality, was being generated and the day after the departure, right in the F-2 block, in the vicinity of 220, the Mole made his act of presence, he was there, they had taken him to wait for his sentence, or the offer, because he did not want to plead guilty alleging that he was not the one who sold the drug.

And since no drugs were found on him, they could not prove possession or sale, he had been left fighting the case from inside the prison, since they had made a case of conspiracy and complicity.

That day he had met El mar in the dining room and introduced himself by asking El mar if he could sit at the table where he was, but so that you won't be confused, let me make room for you to be the direct participants in that conversation:

– – – – They call me the Mole, thank you for allowing me to share your table," said the one with the air of playfulness.

– – – – Don't worry, the tables are for everyone's use... So you're the famous Mole?

The Mole grasped his chin with his left hand, and responding with another question he questioned with suspicion and interest:

– – – – So, you know me?

– – – – Knowing you, as I know you not, but I have heard of you.

– – – – Really, am I that famous? ... Ha, ha, ha, – – – He continued to question the mole, while he expressed a laugh.

= = – – It seems that yes. – – – stated El mar.

– – – – – To the point, to the point... Tell me, who told you about me? – – – Asked the Mole with insistence and with an uneasy attitude.

– – – – No one in particular, but I heard that someone who recently left was here because you cheated him. – – – – – El mar responded with surprising conviction.

– – – – So that I say to you that not, if you know the truth, but I must specify to you, of anything it is necessary to lament in the war and the love all the impossible thing is born, he stayed with the woman who I wanted for something well intentioned, Jeremiah is a good boy, he was my mechanic, but it is that the devil ministers to you when of by means there is a so pretty woman... Good, if you get to know it you will see how pretty she is. – – – – – He said with the impression of never regretting it.

– – – – I'm looking for a way to understand you," said El mar, keeping silent as the mole stood up:

– – – – I feel satisfied to know you, enjoy your food – – – Said El Topo.

 El mar said goodbye by shaking his hand, but without saying anything, the Mole came out while he saw him go away.

At that moment one of the prisoners who was waiting for El mar to be released, and who seemed to be watching for the Mole to leave, went over to him, to tell him something that

gave the impression that he could not keep, because the prison accelerated the conscience of the man, activating his adrenaline in such a way that nothing was indifferent to him.

I can't deny that this comment fell on him like a dart that accelerated his spirit.

El mar was not of men loving injustice, he, did not sponsor it, and it seemed that the exponents of the paradise had made a business of all lines of human existence, it turned out that he who wanted to talk to it, needed to vent:

He said a refrain that seemed more like a gossip in the hallway, it was that an undocumented prisoner, who had been held beyond his day of departure in flagrant violation of his rights, everything was because the law at that time considered that if the immigration department was interested in a prisoner who had served his sentence, if after 72 hours they were not going to pick him up, the facility should let him go, however some officials promoting the failures of the system, one day, said one thing and the next day did another.

Certainly when a prisoner was told or offered something, and it was not fulfilled, they spent much of the time stressed out, looking for ways to rebel, or looking for someone to take it out on.

In this way, things that seemed terrible were generated inside the prison, so that the officers who served as custodians, often for fear of being killed, saw things that they preferred to keep quiet, and it happened that sometimes the custodians knew who was selling or smoking the drugs inside the prison, and before being the dead they preferred to be "the grave", they thought that the silence should be "more eloquent than their own words".

There was a lighter punishment for prisoners who violated the rules of accommodation, which was usually called "Key Lock", which consisted of locking the prisoner in his electronic door room, by remote control, for the time that the violation of the rules of accommodation warranted, which could be from one to two weeks

No access to the dining room, telephone, or television, among other privileges, and no going out on the esplanade or receiving visitors.

This used to be generated regularly when they performed a routine search and found an iron or a knife or some tool, or when they fought among the prisoners, who in addition to writing a contravention or "Ticket", seized the contraband

found, and the fighters were locked in the box, and another time in a room where he was kept naked, standing and with his arms open forming one here.

That day in the afternoon, El Mar received the answer to the letter that he had sent so insistently to Isabel Volqué from the F-2 mailbox, which by the way had already had several failed attempts, because it had been returned to him on more than three occasions.

It was then that he thought of confusing the collector of the letters, abbreviated the name of the sender, and taking advantage of a visit to the J-2 clinic, sent it from the mailbox of a block where he was no longer there, managing to have it delivered that way; thus, the survival tactic had begun to work.

In the response to that letter she confessed to him what he feared, they were already conspiring with their correspondence, she let him know that three letters she had written and sent to him had been returned, she reiterated her unconditional friendship, among other details, something that El Mar found pleasant. So he decided to wait to answer that heroic letter, because both had coincided touching the same day to go to court, in addition to that letter had received another from the director of chaplaincy.

CHAPTER 20

— Stiff Blend, veteran of the air force of paradise, was satisfied to have flown high returning alive from foreign land, his beard was identified as a red Anglo origin, also had the reference on El mar, Gary had already spoken of him, El mar was outlined as a leader who all felt attracted, Mr. Blend also wanted to talk to him, so when the other finished Stiff was shown.

He wanted information from the central Caribbean, he wanted to know more about the Republic because he saw that island as a possible option in his pilgrimage, so they had agreed on that block pulled by the threads of fate.

----- How are you? Had we introduced ourselves? he said to El mar in a questioning tone.

---- I had not had the honor.

----- My name is Stiff Blend, are you Caribbean?

---- Yes, why? El mar corresponded.

---- I want to move to your country as soon as I get out of here.

----- Oh, that's interesting, there's only one problem... I am not the consul or the ambassador, if you thought I would give you a visa. ---- Said El mar Joking.

----- Oh, no, no, no. All that I know is no, Gary mentioned you," said Stiff, seeking to substantiate the colloquium.

----- Oh, yes! Now I remember, you must be the same one Gary told me about, nice to meet you, I am El Mar Valenilla, I know the condition of the area will please you---- He said with some foundation as he extended his hand to greet him.

----- Yes, it's me." Stiff answered, extending his hand and added, "It's a pleasure to meet you, we'll talk tomorrow because now I have to go somewhere else, see you later. They said goodbye, squeezed their hands again.

El mar rose from that interview table, went to the clinic of J-2, in his turn of waiting saw pass Maria and Cruz, those since they saw it stopped in admiration, greeted him with hugs and asked where they were, asked him to write a letter, he promised that he would do his best, but that they were returning the letters.

Mary and Cruz listened to him in silence, hugged him again and continued their journey to J-2, El mar watched them enter.

As the days went by, El mar and Stiff continued talking, Stiff revealed to him that his interest in going to the Caribbean was due to a mandate from God, which had indicated that he should move to the area, specifically to the Island where El mar was originally from. This information was very well received by El mar, who promised to provide him with all the help he could get, had provided him with the phone numbers and address so that when he left, he could contact him to make the offer.

In addition, they had also agreed that they were both in prison because of the erroneous testimonies of the mothers of their children, who had tried to claim custody that they had tried to avoid with spurs and swords.

---- God is with us, so much so that I wanted to talk to you without knowing you, the holy spirit dwells in us, look at your eyes, they have the same color and the same brightness as mine.

---- That's right, nothing is casual, everything is defined, God traces the path for us.

---- Exactly like that, I add Stiff.

The next day had been scheduled as May 13, the day when precisely El mar would return to court.

Everything is perfect, we will be in communication - Said El mar standing up.

---- Okay El mar, good luck tomorrow, tonight I'm going to pray for you.----- Stiff said.

---- Thank you.

An anachronistic vision in the wake of humanity, was the pattern for the great awakening, those remote times lost in the mists of the centuries, were experiences that forged life and opened the way.

So much pain and suffering had conditioned the thought of El mar, to the levels of thinking that the laws of Paradise had become like a funnel, where the wide was for the potentates and the narrow for the needy minority, who in fact, suffered the most.

There were so many qualifiers that many thought that that environment was comparable to "a drop of snake urine in an ocean of excrement" or something like a school where the "evildoers played terrorists", because the mystique of the constitution by which the nation was founded had been lost. The evil began to shine like gold in the mouth of a dragon, some even thought and commented that a conspiracy was being forged to criminalize sectors of the needy minority, so that once the footprints were damaged, they could not become citizens, thus maintaining political control, managing and manipulating the sectors that had traditionally been subjected.

On May 13 the prisoners had been woken up at half past five in the morning, the trip from the prison to the court was less than an hour long, however, El Mar had not slept all night, he thought he could be reunited with his family that day.

It was eleven o'clock in the morning when they were transferred to the court in Yonkers, something was happening, that day the lawyer assigned to him on April 5th did not appear, it was precisely Dino J, the one who interpreting the plan forged against El mar, from the first moment, had dedicated himself to a cruel harassment, with the purpose of having him plead guilty.

- - - - Guilty of what, said El mar, forced guilt to justify a false case?

For his part, Dino J insisted:

- - - - - Your Honor, I told him that if he became guilty, you would close the case and he would be given time to serve.

- - - - - Judge, that lawyer does not know the case so that he goes around making that dishonest proposal, I see that "it is better to be honest than a lawyer"- - - expressed El mar.

Judge Morgan smiled and asked him:

- - - - If we let you go, are you going to do the program?

- - - - - Of course, absolutely.

- - - - Let's save it for May 5," he said.

Life often reaffirms the evidence of existence. When a prisoner was brought to court without being seen by a judge, those abusers would want to use their hands to bring about justice. The Paradise enclosed its own reality, many lived their lives without any mishap, but others had become slaves of their circumstances, the 21st century could be the best excuse to have overcome cannibalism in modern societies, especially those that advocated the ideal of freedom, however one thing was said and another was practiced. By then, some social sectors that had not overcome psychological torture and conditioned evil satisfied their egos by imposing manipulation through arbitrary methods.

El mar thought that many sectors without being God, believed themselves owners of the sky and the land, and many times without reason, used to violate their own laws to criminalize by force people of the minority.

Then El mar used to suggest that they should resist with patience, since the cynicism with which they executed their actions was a clear sign of human rights violations, because their idiosyncrasy had led them to evolve into violence, but even so they sold themselves as peaceful, vindicators, and lovers of peace.It was not always like that, sometimes they were overbearing; but hypocrisy was being unveiled, the Psychosatrapists could not go on pretending their eagerness for power, and their apparent hatred for Humanity was so visible that in the corridors of skyscrapers they used to comment the details.Dino J had been motivated and promoted by Maycol K, for his replacement in the dirty work, which consisted simply in achieving the guilt of El mar.

His personal conduct was a reflection of his social conditioning, emanating from a temperamental, extravagant, superfluous, cynical society, and above all and despite its technological glory, and its scientific advances, very superstitious, so that contextual ceremony was lent, to show an unfaithful, self-serving loyalty.

Conditioning his skinny body with blue eyes and eagle nose forges a motivation plan, aimed at exercising the practice of psychological violence typical of abusers conditioned to intimidation:

He had gone up to the cell that served as a waiting room before the judge was seen in the Yonkers courthouse.

---- How have you been?" questioned Dino J.

---- Very good thanks.

---- El mar responded with some suspicion.

A play on words took hold of Dino J in his eagerness to confuse and manipulate

El mar, ignoring that it never adhered to any cause out of fanaticism, and that whenever it acted it did so to learn, he thought that experimentation strengthened the spirit and the experiences of each experience expanded the soul, and ignoring what would follow such action, and beset by his own fears, he said:

----- You're going out today, aren't you going to make yourself guilty? I question Dino J, looking for a way to find out about his client's claims. ----- No. --- El mar answered dryly.

----- We'll have a trial on July 1st, if you lose you'll get two years," said Dino J., seeking to intimidate El mar.

----- Oh yeah? ... I don't care, I'm innocent, besides, I have a witness.

That expression had sounded like an unexpected blow to the ears of Dino J, whose eyes had sprouted   at the height of the eagle's nose he was carrying.

---- Witness...what's his name? Dino J inquired with interest.

---- Barbarita Roque. She's the mother of my other children, she was with me that day when Celeste Capellán made the accusation, which means that if that had been true, Barbarita would have heard it and...

Dino J interrupted in exasperation.

----- But did she go with you to the family court, then?

----- Yes, that's what I'm telling you, I took her as a witness because Celeste Chaplain tried to involve her, alleging atrocities with the frolinger's consent, and involving the boy Mark as well. So they put the supervised visits back on, because

I didn't want to accept the supervised visits either. The Frolinger threatened me that my son would hate me, and I told her that Mark knew everything that could happen, anticipating that they would want to manipulate the case.

El mar told him in great detail what had happened, including that he had taken Barbarita as a witness on September 26 of the previous year, the date the conflict had started, but that they had moved the case to November 3, the date when Judge Thomas B had sent him to prison under the allegation of two alleged guarantors, told him that even though he had shown him the papers with the court dates, and that the judge had filed them as evidence, they had still been remanded in custody, then lawyer Dino J, moved by curiosity, questioned:

− − − − − − So that day, Barbarita was walking with the kids?

− − − − Yes, the children stayed in child care on the third floor. Dino J kept a reflexive silence and El mar made it clear that prejudiced in the interest of incriminating him, they had conspired to create false evidence, turning him into an unnecessary protection order with the objective of evidencing the file, because the indisposition that the city's henchmen tried to create, had nothing to do with the dispute between him and the Chaplain in the Yonkers family court, when in reality everything was due to the conspiracy where Celeste was like a pilot of the stove where would light the fire that would justify his planned imprisonment, precisely when she had already commented in the building where they resided, that the court had an interest in criminalizing him, but that she was unaware of the motive.

Dino J could not manage to hear the last word when El mar saw him walk away bewildered.

El mar continued to wait in hope of being called to the presence of the judge, however nothing happened. A few minutes later someone appeared who had been taken to show cause, and he arrived so conditioned that he went directly to dispute El mart of El mar, because before he left for the cause room, he was occupying it.

That day the sun filtered its shady rays into the sky, the heat began to besiege the bodies of the prisoners, in the cell opposite, a female over nine months old without embracing a man, openly provoked those who came and went.

The guards withdrew the first group that had seen the judge to return to prison, those, returned discouraged and unanswered that they would be released, El mar, felt more confident, he thought that what they stayed would be exonerated to return home, but nothing was so, he was waiting and not called. At that moment a secretary came in who was friendly, she had gone to the cell to verify the date of birth of another inmate who was also waiting to be seen by the judge.

− − − − They didn't take me to see the judge. Have you seen attorney Dino J.?− − − That lawyer didn't come today," said the secretary reading the information on Dino J.'s business card.

- - - - - What do you mean you didn't come; he was here, where did he go?

- - - - - I can't answer you, I haven't seen him," said the secretary, cutting off the conversation with El Mar, and calling out the name of the prisoner he went to question.

- - - - It's incredible, twice now they've brought me to court and they won't let me see the judge," he said and added, "Dino J is working against me," he replied.

The secretary was silent, and left.

El marts in the cell were occupied, the prisoners who commented among themselves kept a sepulchral silence, just when one of the guards heading to El mar questioned:

- - - - Where were you born?

- - - - - What's the point of asking? I am Caribbean and to much honor, I was born in the Republic, but what does that have to do with what is being dealt with, I have twenty years living in this country, I pay my taxes and my children were born here, then what is the problem, someone has to influence so that those who bring a racist stance change their mind, it is time to overcome the slave mentality, if I am innocent because they have to pressure me to become guilty. - - - He said.

The case was that he referred to the times of Kunta kinte and roots, implying the assumption that those times had been overcome, he questioned himself about who was criminal? And he answered himself:

- - - - I don't think an innocent person is a criminal unless those in power do.

An officer who had just left the Judge's office told him:

- - - - - Let me know when he comes back to court," he said.

- - - - Look at the calendar. - - - - - El mar said something irritated.

- - - - On June 15, she added after reviewing a list she was holding in her hands.

- - - A month later, how brazen they are! What manipulators and blackmailers, that is, looking for ways to make me desperate to force me to plead guilty when I am innocent, when it comes to a member of the minority, they are always ready to ignore ethical principles. The prisoners watched in awe and silence, after all had been brought to the presence of the judge except El mar, were handcuffed and returned to the prison.

CHAPTER 21

— That same day when they arrived at the prison, El Mar was already assigned to another dormitory, they moved it to J-1, next to J-2, and J-3.

The next day when El mar tried to leave the traditional telephone message for Barbarita, he discovered that she responded with a cry of despair and pain, crying like an inconsolable child, her hopes had been dashed.

She had been waiting for him on May 13 and when she noticed that he did not show up by that date she thought she would go a long time without seeing him.

A move of fate cemented the possibility that she would be disappointed and lose faith, the Department of Social Service took advantage of this vacuum to counterattack, this time using the collaboration of her ex-husband, Esteve, the one with whom she had procreated the first children. Before that torrent of tears, El mar began to worry, the heart told him that something had happened or was about to happen, that crying was like a break of pain, a restlessness of conscience.

He knew Barbarita's sensitivity, and could understand her pain, so in the following days he tried to comfort her through small telephone messages recorded in the space where the operator spoke asking her to say his name, as she knew his voice, he instead of saying his name, expressed what he wanted her to hear.

He practiced this technique for a long time until the operator noticed it and blocked it; from then on, El mar became resigned to that emptiness that caused the lack of communication. Anyway, he knew that the size of a house had nothing to do with the size of a home; he understood that at the beginning it meant a lot to her but he did not know how great her love for him would be, in the absence and the distance.While they shared their concubinage, she used to express some jealousy attacks that were solved under the savannah, until she understood that if she led her life in peace, she would never lose the war. She also knew that for El mar she was someone indescribably special. El mar was looking for a way to give him his merits because he knew that of all the mothers of his children, she was the one with him, and he knew that when the future was shorter than the past, dreams were only memories.

Barbarita was someone fragile that he had to protect, so he thought that the greatness of an elephant was in the way he understood a mouse.

One, and another were facing the greatest test of their lives, but the strength of faith made him understand that the brighter the stars were on the darker nights, and yet their lights simply caressed the human's pupils. Barbarita was the column that supported the children's appreciation, especially when

El mar was absent for whatever reason, he really missed them, especially when he remembered their kisses, their hugs, their graces, he thought about the universe and understood that a child's smile was like the footprints of God, and receiving their kisses was like kissing the future and he thought about the need to be patient because for him patience was something like the melody of time.

Barbarita continued to worry him, those cries of anguish that denounced pain, had made the essence of his being vulnerable, he didn't want to twist his arms, but that cry of a suffering woman softened his heart and made him weaken, even though he didn't want to let himself be manipulated or corrupted by the system.

Self-comforting, he thought of the crucifixion of Jesus, of how he had sacrificed his innocence for the salvation of those who in the times of his generation believed in the existing truth, and thought that since then for the model of existence

limited and besieged by the competitiveness that was lived on earth, almost always to save one, another would have to be sacrificed. This way of thinking used to satisfy the system, which often, in its ignorance, resorted to religion to soften the rebels and confuse the slaves, but nothing was good or bad because that free will was used by the wise as well as by the ignorant masses.

El mar continued its reflection and understood that tears melted sadness and healed the heart.

He felt that when bodies became distant, souls became closer.

He kept silent while waiting for one of the prisoners to call his wife, who in turn called him and told Barbarita that he was waiting for her.

This entire ceremony was in keeping with what we had said in one passage of this story, that in order for a prisoner to speak on the phone at that time, it was necessary to have a pre-paid bill in addition to the phone connection, a business that only benefited the intermediary company, and the facility managers.He believed he was aware that the cynics and the half-hearted were like snakes that slithered silently and quietly, avoiding being hit on the head and never succumbing.

All this understanding was the basis of his caution; he was a follower of the feminist cause while understanding that behind the silence of the living there were many punishments, and he admitted that certainly the winds were blowing continuously and without pause.

El mar did not usually deny credit to loneliness, which as a bad counselor questioned its consequences, so it was alarmed by its voice:

- - - - What does a woman keep quiet that a man would like to know? - - - In philosophical epithets she elucidated within herself answers, which made her own trick and

Soliloquy in her voice, old age as she defined it, and naive youth as she named it.

Referring to her father's words, she remembered a refrain that she named: - - - Love is pain and inertia is friendship, Barbarita induces me to give in, not without first making me understand.

Enemies strengthen man, in the light of reason they justify him, the shadow of the heart inflames passion, maturity induces you to think and youth to act... That, that is what I will do. - - - - He said, concluding the action of the monologue.

He then wrote a letter to Barbarita suggesting that she pressurize attorney Dino J to file a motion to expedite the process, and to visit her relatives to request a loan covering ten or 20 percent of a five thousand dollar bond to see if she would get out early.

For a long period he was still in a heated reflection, thinking that passion was bodily and love spiritual, considering that it was better to save the soul than to live in agony. He took advantage of it and thought that if he had time to write poems that saved the relationships of others, even if they were paid with soups, why should not he take it out to save his own? if beauty was certified in the soul.

He began to write lightly without knowing what subject he would be dealing with, he made a paragraph in the orange blossom:"I have kept silent about the torment and torture, about that infamous executioner, from my heart comes a great consolation, which transmutes the strength of the tyrant". Then he read the paper and tore it up.

Seeking to concentrate he wanted to do another paragraph and wrote:

"There is no reason to be sad, when the spirit exists, living marks its hope and the soul records the dance, simply be happy, so that it is like that.

Unsatisfied, he tore the paper again and let himself be led by the stimulation.

My dear Barbarita, beautiful rose and gorgeous.

Your kisses sowed love on my lips.

Your summery tears stamped my winter soul.

Your being is melody and your soul is poetry.

Through your eyes I saw the light.

The sphinx of your face filled my loneliness with hope

To love you ostentatious flower of the sun.

Radiant and glorious love, tenderness of heart,

I shine with your splendor.

I am inspired by your wonder

Barbarita dear flower.

I am touched by your love, I am touched by your passion.

Your body your honor I fertilize you as my flower.

I carry you in my heart.

My love, without speaking or touching anything remains the same,

 But in particular, I will not stop loving you.

Because not even with distance can my love be stopped. These verses seemed to him suitable, so he sent it to Barbarita by mail as a letter, and taking advantage of the occasion, he wrote to the lawyer Dino J.

In his letter he let you know of his outrage at the malicious tactics taken in his

Conspiratorial purpose, in the following terms:

– – – – – Mr. Dino J, my wish is that you always go well so that sometime in your life you will never have to regret it, but don't forget it is much better "to be honest than a lawyer" because to be honest with another you need to be honest with yourself.

Maybe because I'm incarcerated you think I can't ask you for an explanation:

I want you to tell me in detail, what happened, why didn't you show up in court on May 5 and 13? Why, if I had a court assignment, did they not take me to see the judge?

After the conclusion of that warlike missive, he remembered that one could not always say everything one thought, and that it was also necessary to think about everything that was said.

In addition, El mar in that letter warned him of the possibility of denouncing him at the bureau of complaints if he did not bring forward his court date. El mar would complain that Dino J was not representing him adequately.

In the evening they attended a concert of praise in the church, the races combined in the context had filled that place with a capacity for 102 people and restricted to a greater number, there sounded the various instruments such as piano, drums and the choirs that made up the voices of prisoners, who in that

At that moment they experienced the most exalted sensation of peace, hope and the integral harmony of the whole defined in the songs of praise to Jesus and Jehovah, and although traditionally the murmurs surpassed the sound of music, there it was the opposite, the sound buried the murmur. It was 9:30 when, still in a trance, they said goodbye with hugs and handshakes, the voices of the preachers were heard expressing themselves:

- - - - Good night brothers, go well. At that time the conflictive ones who often played wolves, had become lambs, and all seemed to be one, so "white, brown, copper, crossed and serene", seemed not to distinguish themselves at all.

El mar competing with the noise with the intention of being heard, he said: - - - -When your enemies remember your faults, God does not forget your virtues, how great was today's meeting," he said.

- - - - That's how El mar is, we feel in victory," answered Lazaro Osorio.

They retired in spirit and slept in the greatest harmony.

Monday dawned serene until a rumble woke the dormitory, a fire drill brought the still sleepy prisoners to their feet as they fled in histrionic panic, only to realize that nothing was happening. It was a simple drill by the prison authorities, seeking to realize what the mass reaction would be if something happened.

Those irritated by the surprise came back mumbling market insults, discovering that it was all a poorly planned ruse.

Shortly after they had cleaned up, they had breakfast and when the distribution commission came in, they were the people who every week went to the dormitories to replace the dirty uniforms with clean ones, however on that occasion they had not gone to distribute, but to seize the extra pieces, because according to their regulations, no prisoner was supposed to have more than two uniforms, so at the time of the requisition they were seized of everything that was in excess.

That morning he had been grouped together in the room where the television was watched, while the guards raised, turned and folded the mattresses.

One of the entourage had asked El mar about his bed, and after El marrch, he realized that his bed was still intact and that he had not been subjected to El marrch, so he felt confused by such distinction.

After the revision work was concluded, they called those who had sent requests to see the doctor, among which was also El mar.

When he went to the clinic he was received by a nurse who explained to him the need to have blood tests done, to know for sure, which was the real diagnosis of his health, because he had been treated without asking the origin of his ailments, sporadically he had felt some stomach pains, and on another occasion in the back, however the nurse specified that only the doctor could authorize the tests, he did not remain calm and tried to talk to the doctor, but the doctor had let him know that he was still attending other patients.One of the guards who was aware of the conversation approached him and said.

---- El mar, which you only want to live by questioning, by asking questions, is out and about," he said with a certain sarcasm.

El mar looking at him in silence smiled at him and came out.

He knew that none of those officers assigned to guard the place where he stayed with the other prisoners were indifferent to him, especially since the high-ranking officers, from a sergeant to a captain, used to stroll happily around the cubicle where he stayed, trying to notice everything that might happen.

El mar never forgot that forgiveness overshadows revenge, and that compassion overcomes anger, he used to think frequently of Barbarita and her children, and although they were certainly distant, he was invaded by a tender inner peace.

He understood that a woman's past was the seed of her present, when she stole a kiss she stole her heart, he was worried that in a situation of that nature Barbarita would stay away from the phone or keep it off, and he said

---- I feel sorry for her but I'm the one who's locked up, she's the one who has to let me know how everything is out there, because I know how it is in here, blessed be God --- I express and keep silent.

He chose not to despair, and to let God take control of his destiny.

That night he slept with more intensity, the other day he was similar to the others, with a marked difference, that night he had dreamt that he was visiting someone related to the care of Barbarita and the children, but it gave the impression that he had seen that person on another occasion, he saw in that person the face of a famous actor, And then he immediately perceived a woman who, approaching him, offered him facilities that would motivate him to relate in erotic actions, showing him the torso in a splendorous nudity, invaded by three beautiful breasts, distributed on the left side, in the center and on the right side.

Those three florets, raised in the wide expression of a Venus, induced wonder, so she sadly complained:MARIANO ----- Nobody loves me, they just strip me and go to bed. She undressed, El mar, was delighted, took her in his arms, caressed her tenderly in silence, kissed her and before the act of copulation was consum-mated, she woke up.

A few minutes later, an officer who was in custody at J-1 approached him and asked him about an application he had sent for legal papers from the court.

They were pretexting, they did not want to give him the documentation he had requested, that's when the custody told him in the next term:

----You talk to your lawyer, we have nothing official about your case, you are not sentenced.

----I had indicated custody to him.

- - - - - I've tried to do that, but he won't accept a collect call," answered El Mar.
- - - - - Then write to the chaplaincy to be allowed to take a phone call - - - he suggested custody.

- - - - Okay, I'll keep trying, but if some people don't have any papers, why am I being locked up? Even when they understand that they're violating the law against me. Said El mar.

- - - - - I don't know, we are the house, we don't influence the court's decisions, he insists with the lawyer. -He affirmed.

The custodian went away from where El mar was, went to the desk he was occupying, searched the drawer until he found a pre-drafted form of letter, went back to the cubicle where El mar was still kept, and handed him the form so that he could write to the chaplain requesting the facilities the church granted, to try to communicate with the lawyer Dino j, and also, he took the opportunity to call Barbarita, with whom he had once again lost communication.

Later, some prisoners approached him trying to get some explanation, which certainly revolved around why he had refused to accept the time served that had been offered to him in exchange for voluntary guilt, before his executioners abusing the power they held, did so by force.

Those wild hordes tried to find the reason that motivated him to accede to their whims, so they told him:

- - - - Blaming you wouldn't be in jail, and I would be by your family's side.

El mar thought they were expressing themselves as if they had been commanded, and explained to him that Jesus had died for all in order to atone for the sins of the human race, but that his spirit had not allowed him, being the innocent one, to accept the burden that a group of ill-intentioned people were trying to impose on him, and then to manipulate the cause of reality, "making medicine more expensive than illness. To satisfy their curiosity, he explained to them in detail what had happened, so that they, though not judges, would expand their levels of consciousness in the face of a real event.

- - - - I want you to understand that the rottenness is in the easy, the easy is like the mark of the beast that foresees to be implanted after the manipulation and blackmail, to facilitate the disposition of those who will have to be marked.

It's like how cheap it often gets, when you accept a guilt or "Please guilty", if you are innocent you are expressing to the system that you want to commit a crime, and the system can use that provision that seems the easiest way out, for something worse.

If I were not right, I would not fight, but since I am right, sooner or later, no matter how stubborn the masters of paradise may be, they will end up recognizing that I am right, above all possible arbitrariness, this is a society of law. Even if the powers that be are sustained by criminals, if someone alleges his reason, to deactivate that

reason, they have to prove with proof that the one who alleges the reason lacks it. --- He told them with integrity.

Those who listened to him with open mouths, the dissertation of El mar was like a chair from which learning flowed. The inhabitants of Vengala seemed to be a defenseless people, but of great value, they were like a taciturn people who hoped to break their chains.

---- I agree with you, if you're not guilty, keep fighting your case.

---- I am satisfied that you are thinking this way, in my case, they have not shown me the opposite of what I am claiming. ---- Well, if that's the case, there's a good chance I'll win the case.

That voice had called the attention of El mar, feeling certain that before that moment he had already heard it, he turned parsimoniously and discovered a jocular figure showing a smile where he exhibited some rabbit teeth.

---- Top! What are you doing here? --- questioned El mar, a little surprised.

---- I've just moved in, which means we're all going to be together for a while," he replied with a humorous expression.

---- That's what it looks like.

---- For me it is a gratitude to meet you again to share a house.

---- It is clear that one ignores his destiny, welcome to our bedroom. --- Said El mar.

That expression could not have been indifferent to the Mole, who laughed out loud.

---- He had a good one, he said.

---- Okay Mole, I'll see you later, I'm going to the law library now.

---- He studies a lot, so that I can orient myself.

--- We'll try." -----said El Mar, as he walked through the exit door, followed by Orlando, who seemed to be his escort.

Orlando had fallen countless times for the crime of drug possession, and had been offered to El mar to write on the computer the manuscript of the letter that

He was planning to send Dino J, however, upon arrival, Orlando was unaware of the keyboard and punctuation of a machine kept in the library to be used by prisoners, as obsolete as its manufacturer.

One of those who had been assigned to the unit, had also been willing to assist him in his worthy purpose, so he wrote to him to go and see him and change the court date, and left it in the bookstore with an authorization for two photocopies, and in the evening an officer appeared distributing the stationery, giving El mar the receipt of whoever had copied the letter, The officer on duty had promised to correct this mistake, since operations of this nature were deducted from the prisoner's account, and to avoid having one of the prisoners' accounts deducted from the expenses of another, it was necessary to clarify everything.

The tranquility had begun to be threatened, that day El mar had risen early, he had prayed to the Lord and before breakfast he was called to the clinic where they would check his blood sugar levels, then the nurse had given him a portion of water to take one of the treatment pills, He then gave him additional medication which induced him to pour another ration of water from a blue plastic jug, which he ignored was assigned to the consumption of the officers, and Charlie Carroso, the clinic's custodian, who in previous days had defied him, seeing him pouring, approached him with the force of his authority:

----- What are you doing? El mar, don't you realize that this water is not for you? Give me your identification card.--- He demanded.--- I'm sorry, I didn't know that this water was forbidden for us, however I have taken it by authorization of the nurse, I'm sorry.--- He clarified El mar.

------ Garbage, that water is for the officials," he argued.

----- I'm telling you my reasons, I'm sorry.

----- Give me your ID card.

El mar looked at him in silence, without saying anything, and briefly reflected on what was happening as he pleaded:

----- I don't know, what do you want with me?

---- Give him the ID and leave. Another custodian claimed he was following the conversation without intervening.

El mar handed him the card with a photograph and he went out, the other prisoners were in line waiting for their turn to take their medication.

When El Mar arrived at the dormitory he complained   to the custody officer assigned to the service that afternoon, requesting a form with the intention of reporting the abuse of Officer Charlie Carroso.

The duty officer slowly worked his way up to talk to Officer Carroso.

----- El mar, I thought we had that shape here, but there isn't one, let me go see if I can get it in the other bedroom --- he said as he walked out.

El mar was trying to prevent officer Charlie Carroso from writing a contravention without reason, he was tired of paying for alleged crimes while he was innocent.

Five minutes after the custody went out in search of the form, he returned accompanied by Carroso and four other officers who were shouting at El mar.

----- El mar, come here. ---- shouted one of them.

El mar, which was lying down at that very moment, immediately rose to the custody desk.

---- I heard them calling me, what is it about? ---- He questioned   El mar.

---- I heard that you are asking my name and looking for a way to make a report, if you report me I will write you a ticket.----- Said Officer Carroso.

---- I have nothing against you, even though you've been chasing me since yesterday, the power is to help, not to harm, what do you intend to do, extend my time here?

---- El mar, I have nothing against you either, but it is said that you are very patient and I wanted to measure your tolerance. --- Said the officer carroso with impudence.

--- We don't have to argue, you are the boss, and as a boss you don't bother, from your trench you can do whatever you want, in the end I love you as a human being. -He said.

---- I love him? ---- mumbled   Charlie Carroso.

In the face of that sympathetic expression, the officer let out an old fox smile, which helped him eliminate the tension that marked a wrinkled line on his face.

Carroso, feeling like a lieutenant, chose to retire, followed by the four officers who accompanied him.

A few minutes later, J-1's custody appeared with El mar ID card in his hand.

---- Here you go--- He said, extending it to El mar---- What there was was a misunderstanding He clarified.

----- Did he write the ticket?

---- No, you said there was a misunderstanding.

CHAPTER 22

— Such was the face of Paradise, a frequent and constant struggle where the strongest used to explore the Achilles' heel of the one who seemed most helpless, in order to impose his conditions without losing control of the impending manipulation. It was the context where the big fish tried to swallow the small one, where those who had nothing, continued to be abused and manipulated by the owners of everything, where people did not know when they loved and felt divided, because lacking a solid capital they had to accept that the economically opulent, dictated the rules of the game.

These privileged minorities, who played the solvent servants of the potentates, moved stealthily, jealous of the considerable benefits reaped from the exercise of power.

The system exhibited in the decisions of its servants that corporate vision of neo-fascism and neoliberalism, which induced them to abominate with the greatest contempt for their being, those malicious vilification, that overwhelming state of numbness in its inhabitants where the son did not always recognize the father, where the interests divided the families.

The Paradise had been constituted on a strong financial base, overwhelming, paraphernalia that perceived and controlled the propaganda and the levels of social consciousness, taking care not to fall into totalitarianism, which would end up generating a collective awakening in the form of indignation, whose arrogance would sometimes induce rebellion.

So now their ideologists had focused on locating where the violent were hiding, those who in a certain moment of bitterness could give their lives in the martyrdom of a fictitious cause of salvation.

All this was a great concern for the owners of the money who had already thought of a form of general control, the microchip the size of a grain of

Rice as a document of identity, in that mark of the beast that the religious feared so much, and where humanity would be infallibly led. This would fulfill the prophecy of Revelation14:9.

Cheekiness, immorality and dehumanization were the identity card in the criminalization industry, especially directed to that hungry and profit-seeking minority whose ambition allowed it to give in to gambling like zombies or puppets moved by a thread.

In this way, those emissaries took advantage of the situation, looking for a way to fabricate a dark past for that ignorant mass, manipulating it, creating an incriminating trap, damaging its tracks in such a way that it could not advance beyond where those who controlled the power allowed it to go.

They strove to manipulate the history of their victims by imposing the burden of their mistakes on their resumes as something that could not be changed, as a chain of slavery that should not be broken, thus preventing them from advancing into positions of power and hegemony, keeping them statified, in the same place simply depending on that sovereign will that they had tried to expand throughout the world.

All this was happening when the population, politically and demographically speaking, was growing exorbitantly in numbers.

The hegemonic sectors insisted that anyone involved in any accusation should become guilty voluntarily, for them to continue selling themselves before the eyes of the world and their public opinion, as the magicians of democracy, as the essential model, as the earthly paradise

The reality was different, in the first years of the 20th century1 a terrible witch-hunt had been unleashed against the immigrants who were reproducing every day like swarms of bees.

Paradise was something like a honeycomb attracting large portions of the world's population, yet many natives of Paradise had misjudged the course of their compass, many of those who entered the prisons which by then were called << correction facilities>> often came out worse than they had entered.

During his stay in Véngala, El Mar had noticed the malicious methods that the prisoners implemented in their eagerness to survive in a hostile environment, many of them with addictions to cocaine or marijuana, the latter being used more frequently by some of the prisoners, mainly in the dormitories, which were often combined with an oversight by the guards, While one was watching the guard, the others were inhaling it by passing it from hand to hand, and when they finished their round, the guard was replaced until their turn to inhale was over, and thus groups of three and six were formed to exercise their "happy" temptation to inhale.

Something strangely surprising had happened to El mar, which as the day progressed had gone to the esplanade and on his return managed to establish communication with Edward Robert's brother, who informed him that he had been taken to another place and although he did not say where, he assured him that he would look for a way to find out about Barbarita Roque, so that he would call him again to inform him about her.

An hour after that conversation, El mar had been called for a surprise visit, it was her, Barbarita had come back to visit him, she had taken the children.

He told her about the errands he had done for him, that he was not taking the phone because he had lost it, and after an hour of talking they said goodbye.

El mar returned to the dormitory and then went to the church where for a long time it eluded the attendees, trying to identify Robert in one of them, without being able to see anyone who could be him.

From among the population a prisoner emerged who confidentially asked him if he was Robert's friend, that Robert had already told him about him, that he knew him by reference, but that he wanted to meet him in person, that Robert spoke of him proudly as someone who could be pondered because he always had the right answer for different circumstances, so he was interested in asking him some questions.

That afternoon a singer-songwriter arrived at the church who had sensitized the souls of the parishioners, had sung various songs of worship and praise music, the service had just concluded when a voice behind him exclaimed:

- - - - - How are you, sir, I'm Alvaro Montoya, you must be El mar Valenilla?- - - He said

El mar heard his name and tilted to identify the body that carried the voice:

- - - - - How do you know my name?

- - - - - I am a friend of Robert and he has told me a lot and very well about you, I would like to consult him, I know he can give me some advice and I would like you to confirm it.

El mar realized that his fame was running, smiling he said:

- - - - - All right, take down my address and write me at J-1 # 16 at the Penh - - - he said and added:

- - - What happened with Robert?

- - - - Robert was taken away by immigration. Montoya responded.

- - - - Ah, now I understand why they are returning the letters I have sent you.

- - - - - Yes sir, that must be why... Now everything is fine, I already have your address and I will write to you. -Alvaro Montoya said.

- - - - - Yes, do it, I'll answer all your questions.

Alvaro Montoya came out and El mar entered the Deacon's office, begging for authorization to call Barbarita.

CHAPTER 23

— A week had passed since the details occurred, the presence of a man with a certain degree of distinction had altered the tranquility of the residents of Vengala, and it was even commented that this strange character could be infiltrated.

He was the professor Makrowki, an old world scientist, who had refused to make experiments with human, he had discovered a formula that applied to animals produced and prolonged the catalepsy for a month, the rulers of the kingdom were notified and assigned the managements to the paradise, the professor makrowki and his formula, had been contemplated as an objective of control and expansion, they had plans with him.

Professor Makrowki, had rejected more than once the proposal emanating from the representatives of the kingdom, his refusal kept him imprisoned taking the risk of spending a year behind bars because his pet that he used to call "baby dog" had committed a heresy causing great lacerations in the hands and legs and in the vicinity of the scrotums to a special agent of paradise who had the mission of guarding the residence of Professor Makrowki, Moved by curiosity, he wanted to get closer to the place without an order to do so, being out of control when he was discovered and caught by the "baby dog".

Although the incident did not cause the death of that curious agent, it had left him in very bad conditions, which caused the separation of the teacher and his pet, the former going to jail and the latter to "canino home", or dog's home, where he would be subjected to specialized tests until they realized that he was not in possession of any sign of rabies. Anyway, when "baby dog" had been taken to "canino home", the service personnel commented among themselves as if they had caught a dangerous criminal, someone was heard asking:

- - - - What is that dwarf doing here?

Receiving by answer of your interlocutor the following expression:

- - - - - The little one is a bravo, he just bit a government special agent to death, they say he left him in very bad shape around his zipper - - - he said.

- - - - Oh! if so, even the wife will be angry.

- - - - - Well, no, error, cold, cold, there is no need to worry, they say he is a faggot - - - clarified the interlocutor.

– – – – – Let's go to work. – – – The supervisor's voice was heard and everyone dispersed to return to their work, the speaker and "baby dog" entered through a door and the conversation remained stuck.

Now they were taking advantage of the circumstance to make Professor Makrowki understand that in Paradise one did not beg, there it was demanded and when someone requested the services of someone the only excuse accepted was "I am willing", that is how the kingdom had established it.

Something adverse could generate difficulties, they had already tried to declare it as a highly dangerous element, precisely because of the silence created around it.

Mr. Makrowki was a quiet man, with very little to say, with few friends, when he shut himself up in his deep readings, he isolated himself from others, he had his particular world and tried to develop it in his own way, without imposition and with his self-freedom.

He was a white, gray-haired man hanging over his shoulders and covering his entire neck.

He was approximately 65 years old, but his health conditions favored him to the degree that he appeared to be about 55, a month ago he had entered the prison, and although he was not yet sentenced, nobody doubted that the bites given by "baby dog", would be charged to him, however, the authorities of paradise had other plans, they knew

That he had developed a formula that could cause catalepsy and prolong it by

One month keeping the body of the target tested intact for as long as it was exposed to the condition.

He was waiting for the decision of a high court, because he had received a visit from a government envoy, where they proposed him to apply the formula for the first time in a human being, to verify the results he had achieved in dogs and cats, he did not respond but they gave him time to think about it.

The government emissary would return and he had to have an answer by that time, although Professor Makrowki in that month of his stay in the prison, had not managed to make friends, the charisma of El mar attracted him, he thought that of all the prisoners, El mar was one of the ones that inspired him the most, Anyway was his closest neighbor because he lived in the cubicle 14 and El mar on 15, had spent a week watching each other, looked at each other without saying anything, the first day of the second week Professor Makrowki who always observed El mar writing, approached the door of his cubicle and breaking the ice asked him:

– – – – Too busy, sir?

When El mar heard that he was going to him, he stopped   what he was doing, stood up and extended his hand to him:

--- How are you, sir? There's time for a chat. Said El mar

--- Thank you," Makrowki replied.

El mar arranged the aluminum table and improvised it as a seat, he said:

----- Please sit down.

Makrowki was gentle too, extended his hand and sat down in response to the invitation.

----- Nice to meet you Mr. Makrowko... I was trying to greet El mar.

---- Makrowki, my family is Russian but I grew up in Austria. -The teacher interrupted.

---- thank you Mr. Makrow... Ki, did I say it right? ---Questioned El mar.

---- Not at all, it's a matter of practice.

---- Okay sir, I've been watching you for a week now, but since I always saw you quietly I thought you weren't talking.----- Said El mar.

----- If I speak... as you can see, because the environment seemed hostile to me, I had to observe a little before I started to relate.

--- That's very good, I also study contextual idiosyncrasies in detail.----- El mar answered as it sat on the bed.

While they were meeting they touched on various topics, so that a certain confidential inclination was generated in mutual directions, they exchanged motives and circumstances, makrowki confessed to El mar and he corresponded to such a degree that by the end of the conversation both had told each other their realities, and the reasons that had led him to prison.

----- So now they are trying to get me to experiment with a human being, and even though my experiments with dogs and cats have not failed me, I am still not sure if it would be the same with a human, but they are still pressuring me, they say they are going to supply everything necessary until I can reach and verify the results, and without further prerogatives, I am thinking of agreeing to it.

--- There being no other alternative, realize that you will do it for the big country, science and your stomach, here you have to survive, moreover, so you can verify the results,

And if he succeeds, he will be honored as a scientist of the realm in paradise, and may all be for the good and expansion of science.

At that moment the custodian who had approached them said

----- Mr. Makrowki, you have a visitor.

---- He nodded as he turned to El mar:

----- El mar, it's been nice talking to you, maybe it's the man --- he said as he received a handshake from El mar:

----Good luck, professor," said El mar.

The professor ran to the desk where the custodian was waiting for him. When he saw him arrive, he gave him a red card where he had registered the professor's data and that would serve as authorization before the checkpoints as he walked along the corridors that he would have to go through before arriving at the visitors' room.

At that moment the government emissary was waiting for him, as Professor Makrowki had told El Mar, he had gone to look for an answer, and certainly the professor was forced to give in to what they were asking for, and he let them understand that the next day they would go for him as a free man to transfer him to the central Caribbean, so that in his mission he could start his first great experiment in Isla Dorada.

The central Caribbean and the original countries of the continent, specifically Isla Dorada, had begun to become a threat to the principles and ideals of the kingdom.

Those had begun to resurface with socialist ideals, and the kingdom and the Paradise that for more than a century were supplied with raw materials and cheap labor, began to see their interests endangered, so they had decided to forge a plan to prevent the rise of an adverse ideology in the area.

For this purpose, they contacted an opposition lawyer named Roger Vitine, who would record some evidence that would directly involve the President of Isla Dorada, so that the pressure of public opinion would force him to resign.

Cataleptic and to a surgery of change of face and identity, in exchange for a bundle of millions that would move his life in another direction.

There, in the depths of a carpeted room, where the walls smeared with sky blue paint stood out, preparations, arrangements and adjustments were made for the recording of the controversial video, which no artist has ever recorded; for this purpose the artist was made up as if he were going to record his last soap opera, where millions of spectators would sigh, and at that moment the presence of Royer Vitine was essential.

Lawyer by profession and former Minister of Legal Affairs of the Chancellery of Isla Dorada.

The cameraman had squared off while adjusting the camera, looked at it through the viewfinder at different angles to determine its most sensitive side for the video graphic shot, while asking it:

----- Ready to record?

Before Royer Vitine answered, he carefully cleared his throat and responded:

------ Prepared.----

Once the layout was affirmed, the cameraman focused from a wide shot to a medium frame, and started the camera with the ring finger of his right hand.

Although only a select group had been called to witness the recording, the room looked crowded, it was the full executive of the liberal governing party, Royer Vitine, had begun his function.

---- Fellow citizens of Isla Dorada, special guests from the central Caribbean, before today I had addressed you to notify you of the danger that the rise to power of the so-called socialist culture represented for the region, which lately the sectors involved have been using to confuse and gain the support of the

The population, which ignores the consequences and is blinded by curiosity, has decided, in its democratic will, to put itself in their hands.

However, the fruit of my denunciations is already beginning to be seen, and it is precisely now, when I feel threatened with death by those satraps who are part of the executive power in our beloved Golden Island, that I feel the need for this ceremonious farewell, in case something should happen to me.

If anything should happen to me, gentlemen, I want to publicly hold President Ezequiel Conrado and his comrade, wife and first lady, responsible, and with them the new Secretary of the Presidency, Minister Frankely Buendía:

Well, as you have heard me so well, I reiterate that if something should happen to me, do not forget that I have already been the object of an ambush by government groups, at the service of the executive power, I leave you with this concern, not out of pessimism, but so that we can stay awake and in no way confuse us, thank you very much, see you soon, fellow citizens.

When the applause sounded again, those who were in the first row appeared to bow and squeeze their hands; Royer Vitine was a persuasive entity, owner of a fiery verb able to drive mad and manipulate the multitudinous behaviors inducing it to the disaster of unconsciousness of the blinded masses.

---- Very good," shouted the ambassador of the kingdom, who, by the way, was a native of paradise. "I congratulate you, you have done a good job, and now I want to introduce you to Professor Makrowki, the scientist who has developed the formula for success, which you will follow to the letter.

Professor Makrowki and lawyer Roger Vitine greeted each other, and began to leave the room where the video had been recorded.

They passed by a large room furnished with picturesque paintings hanging from the walls, headed for the street and boarded a black, armored van waiting for them. They left for the outskirts of the city through a mountainous area and arrived at a hacienda that looked more like a stable or something like a horse farm, The van was parked next to a gray car and two black Yipetas. Three men came out of the van, including Professor Makrowki, lawyer Royer Vitine and the government emissary.

The van returned by the same route it had arrived, driven by a blond man who kept his eyes at all times, behind dark glasses; next to him was Mr. Johnson, the kingdom's ambassador to Isla Dorada, they advanced, leaving behind a huge dust bowl that covered the van, which had turned black with an ash color.

While in the room the three men pushed a wide, arched door, which looked like the door of a monastery, they entered a large room with colorful furniture, paintings, wall to wall banners, and two huge wall-to-wall shelves of books in English, French and Spanish, there was a freshly placed jar of yellow flowers.

They walked to the left along the corridor, arriving at another door carved in mahogany painted to the sten, so that it would match the sand-cream color of the walls, comforting the spirit of the tea-lovers.

Behind the door there was another long and wide room painted in sky blue, with white strips, it was decorated with a set of red wine furniture of six pieces that included a small elongated mahogany table with a glass on top, and in the more lateral stretchers, microscopes, operating rooms, among other utensils, it was clear that it was a private clinic with its internal laboratory, to another one the wall was located two desks, a scientific bookcase and two showcases with diverse medicines.

From inside another of the doors that were displayed in the room, two women appeared, one with blond hair and blue eyes wearing a white uniform, and another with black hair wearing a navy blue jacket and pants and a white robe open, superimposed by

On top of the jacket, and a stethoscope hanging around her neck, the first was Carol Makwinsy, the assistant to the second, who from her outfit would not be hard to guess was Dr. Colin.

---- Professor Makrowki, Mr. Vitine we were waiting for you, you are welcome, make yourself comfortable that from today, what we have is time to be together. Dr. Colin said with a youthful air to the newcomers, while extending her hand to one and the other as a courtesy gesture, the government emissary, before they started a major conversation, left the room, settling in the living room where he went ahead to check the television channels as if looking for a particular program until he found the news where he stopped to find out the news, while in the room that the newcomer was leaving, the aforementioned characters were looking for a way to come to an agreement.

---- Thank you very much. ----- Professor Makrowki responded

----- Mr. Vitine, this is our assistant Carol Makwinsy. --- Dr. Colin explained, introducing the newcomers.

---- It's a great pleasure, Miss Makwinsy," said attorney Roger Vitine.

----- Thank you very much, Mr. Vitine.

They sat down in front of a circular table located in the center of the room, Royer Vitine would be subjected to a preparatory test before being put to sleep to channel him into his mission, the distribution of the video was still missing, and the prudent thing was for him to do it personally before he disappeared from the sight of public opinion, the local press and the political world, the plan was for them to see him distribute the video in person, before his disappearance, so that at the moment his death was announced it would create a greater impact before the nation.

It was done as planned, and three hours later attorney Royer Vitine, who often recited a particular expression when referring to money matters, did it,

was prepared for the final experiment, he would be the first human being to be subjected to such a test, who would be provoked to catalepsy for a month, which would be a challenge for science, especially when that experiment would be directed to a work of preservation of the system, which could no longer fake its decadences and its true intentions.

The masses of the world had begun to awaken to such a degree that even their own artists used to influence with their words personalities like Royer vitine who used to parody Clin Eastwood when he said "Intelligence without love makes you perverse, money without love makes you greedy, power without love makes you a tyrant", and that was what the heart of those who had everything but happiness experienced.

However, the hungry and desperate people, without finding an answer from their traditional rulers, used to plagiarize authors in order to express themselves in the alternative press, using charcoal and thick brush paint on improvised and sometimes poorly written banners, denouncing offenses such as "the patience of Christ led him to death, and patience being a tree with bitter roots, it is only fair that its fruits be sweet, even knowing that" the government steals, the henchmen kill and violence grows, crime lurks, the people sleep and the press lies.

Lawyer Vitine was aware of all this and perhaps because he was one of those few politicians who had not had the opportunity to "steal", he believed that the best thing would be to become a millionaire by acting as a "guinea pig" and not defalcate the public purse, unless in an action where the people seized power, then they wanted to take it by force.

He was an ambitious young lawyer, had graduated at the age of twenty-five and had managed to rise to great positions in the national political world of Isla Dorada in the central Caribbean.

Before his country changed course he was a great representative of the neoliberal democracy with the natural support of the kingdom in the times when they were still visible his imperial tentacles, he was Minister of Legal Affairs at the Foreign Ministry, a member of Congress, a Senator of the Republic, and before his ambition he agreed to play

"guinea pig", as a possible partner on the ballot of a citizen of Isla Dorada who had graduated from one of the best universities in paradise, and who had been elicited to be the next candidate of the liberal party, as a form of indirect intervention to stop the consolidated rise of socialism in the region.

Now the lawyer Royer Vitine had been chosen by the embassy of the Kingdom by suggestion of the government of the Paradise, for the realization of that dirty work, and of which he would be built if the experiment was successful.

The offer had come with an advance of five million dollars prepaid, deposited in a bank account in Switzerland, from where he could enjoy it without any difficulties, along with his family who integrated it in addition to him, his wife and two children residing in Paradise with whom he communicated sporadically and who for security reasons the embassy of the kingdom, had granted him permanent residence, so that Royer Vitine worked without worry.

That night he had called for a private dinner for the press and some sectors of national politics, in one of the restaurants located in the center of the colonial monuments.

After the diners had tasted that night's delicacies together with the leaders of the Liberal Party and special guests including Ambassador Johnson, Professor Makrowki, Dr. Colin and Miss Carol Makwinsy, among others, they began the distribution of the video that had been edited with pre-agreed cuts, and a shocking ceremony had been prepared, so that the video was being delivered accompanied by a red carnation and a souvenir from the Liberal Party with the following message: "from Royer and us with you forever".

At the conclusion of the ceremony, when everyone had retired again, Royer Vitine and his personal guests returned to the hacienda where they would finish painting the final touches of the plan.

CHAPTER 24

— Again seated at the circular table whose formation gave it a bluish-gray aspect, and where Roger Vitine exposed his last will:

- - - - I don't want to have surgery, I must warn you not to do it before you wake up, with my current face 15 years later, I could appear as a candidate if everything goes well, and don't forget to put enough oxygen in the coffin, after everyone has left the funeral home, so we can avoid suffocating me when I am buried - - - said Roger Vitine, in all the ceremonial splendor.

- - - - - Don't worry Vitine, you mean a lot to us and we will take care of you beyond the possibilities, what you are doing today for the cause, is more than a vote of confidence.

- - - - Thank you very much Mr. Johnson, I know, you are like a father to me," answered Royer Vitine as he held him in his arms.

- - - - - All right, I appreciate it kid, tonight was great, the plan is going to be perfect. Said Mr. Johnson.

Lawyer Royer Vitine corroborating Ambassador Johnson's words, hugged him as if it was the last time he would ever see them again, tenderly hugged Miss Makwinsy and kissed her on the cheek, he did the same with Dr. Colin, and finally hugged the professor tightly while whispering the following expression in his ear

- - - - I trust you and I know that everything will be fine.

He withdrew from it and lay lengthwise on the bed that had been arranged for that purpose; first they applied an oxygen mask, took his blood pressure, measured his heart rate and wrote down the hour and minutes he would be tested, and finally they injected him with the substance whose initial reaction caused him to convalesce

Onírica before it entered the cataleptic lethargy, and later as it was experiencing the effects, it was seen as a scorpion in a gestational process, of whose

Belly sprouted the torso with everything and head, whose metamorphic action terrified a family that accidentally observed the change that had led to the condition of half man and half scorpion.

Then he had moved on to another painting where President Ezequiel Conrado appeared arriving at a room where he was waiting with his wife, President Conrado was holding something in his hands that looked like a document, but he was naked and he had seen his sex, something like a penis so small that it made him laugh, it was a mocking laugh and he was pointing at it and saying:

– – – – Then he would ask his wife if President Ezequiel Conrado was related to the first boyfriend she had, at which point she woke up but had already fallen under the effects of catalepsy.

The professor took his pulse, Dr. Colin listened to his heart, and although he appeared dead, he discovered that the experiment had begun to be successful.

– – – – It turned out that Dr. Colin called, and everyone hugged Professor Makrowki at the same time:

– – – – Congratulations, Professor, I knew you wouldn't fail us.

– – – – – Thank you Mr. Ambassador – – – Makrowki responded.

– – – – All right, Dr. Colin, Ms. Makwinsy, we'll drink to everything," added Ambassador Johnson.

Miss Makwinsy understood the comment as an order, went to the inner room and returned with a tray containing four glasses and a bottle of wine.

Ambassador Johnson taking the initiative opened the wine bottle and poured the contents between the glasses, while Ms. Makwinsy held the tray; the ambassador began the toast by raising the glass to eye level, while expressing:

– – – – Because our mission will be more successful.

Everyone imitated it by following the rhythm of the tonality, raising the vessels to a similar level.

Dr. Colin took the floor to respond with an air of triumph:

– – – So be it, Mr. Ambassador, I would also like to take this opportunity to toast and thank Professor Makrowki for understanding that any sacrifice for democracy and the free world is vital.

– – – Thank you very much for your kind consideration, my business is science, my political business is your business," said Professor Makrowki with a certain naivety.

I also want to express my sincere thanks to you, my country will be very grateful to you," said Ambassador Johnson as he left the room for the living room where the government emissary and the embassy driver were waiting.

Dr. Colin and Ms. Makwinsy made preparations for the transfer of Royer Vitine's body to the city, where it would be left in plain view until the alleged decline was made public. Party members would claim the body to be displayed to acquaintances, friends and relatives at a funeral home in downtown

The city, previously verified, and whose arrangements were already arranged by the embassy and the party.

Roger Vitine listened to everything that was happening, however, he could not move or express himself, he just listened and thought, the driver and the government emissary,

They exposed all their skills and care for the clandestine transfer of Roger Vitine to the capital of Isla Dorada, making sure that the body was made up with bruises on the face, neck and arms, and they watched the body until a police patrol passed by, which ipso facto discovered it, because they had taken it out of the van with the greatest naturalness, and had laid it out in the surroundings of the colonial promenade, which had access to four central streets, with leafy trees, to the center the statue of a liberator, and several stores and the national bank because some foreign banks in the socialist administration, had been nationalized.

The black van had been parked two blocks away from where the body had been deposited, and through some ultraviolet binoculars, they were aware of everything that was happening around where the body was.

Precisely, a few minutes after he was left, a motorized patrol discovered the body and ipso facto the high leadership of the party made an act of presence taking possession of the body of the lawyer Royer Vitine, before the police deepened the investigation, The forensic doctor had declared death by asphyxiation and bruising, which the press took advantage of to photograph the bruises and hematomas, giving the impression that Roger Vitine had been made up for a big theatrical show, the news of the alleged death of the lawyer Royer vitine, ran like wildfire.

For his part, Roger Vitine could not control an internal laugh, because he listened to everything that was happening.

The farce was so real that no one doubted the descent of the expired one, especially since both the captain in charge of the investigation and the coroner were accomplices of the

They did not insist on anything other than handing over the alleged body to the Liberal Party, and without much preamble, that is what they did, and the Party, as planned, placed the body in the "Hail Mary" funeral home that was in the vicinity of where the coroner had lifted the body, and the funeral home took on everything that any family of bloodline would have arranged.

They cleaned him up, dressed him, and then put him in a coffin supervised by the party secretary, which had been prepared for that purpose with oxygen conditioning through a battery system whose charge exceeded six months.

The body had been guarded for 24 hours, a day later it would be buried in the family mausoleum, which would facilitate the removal of the body with less or no difficulty, for which the party secretary had given the instruction that the tomb not be sealed, so that a group designated by the embassy and the high leadership of the party, would have the facility to remove the body to return it to the hacienda where they would practice the final steps watching the application and waiting for the final day of awakening.

Everything was already defined, the embassy would decide what they would do when he woke up, whether they would leave him in paradise or move him to Switzerland together with his relatives, meaning his wife and two children.

The next day, after the twenty-four hour funeral wake, a multitudinous funeral was held where the great potentates of Isla Dorada met and where the liberal party was able to prove its strength in case the elections had gone to be held two weeks later.

Anyway, when they arrived at the cemetery, all the users of the word let off steam through the expression, and in a supposed last goodbye, and there was no lack of those who took advantage of this democratic display by the party leaders to reinvent its ceremonial quality, So he managed to infiltrate a drunk party activist who could not be denied the use of the word for fear of anarchizing the "burial" and who did not shy away from venting his discursive spirit by intensifying tears in one and laughter in another and interrupting unexpectedly:

----- If he hadn't died he would have been president, but he died because of pendejo... Because I knew that if he arrived he would give me something to eat and drink, Viva Roger Vitine-- he would say--- he would scream, he would laugh, he would babble, so that all of this had distracted the audience a little-- Where is the widow? Don't tell me that because he died she left him? caracoles que dolor, el que crees en mujer y en político no crees en Dios. --- He said, while two bouncers from the party's security team were required to carry him and

He was taken out to restore order, and apart from that incident nothing strange had happened that afternoon in the vicinity.

Once the funeral was over, everyone dispersed and gradually withdrew to their place of origin, but the black van carrying the government emissary and the ambassador was still parked nearby. The afternoon news had begun to cause havoc, and President Ezequiel Conrado and Minister of the Presidency Frankely Buendía were being directly involved in the alleged death of Royer Vitine.

Sectors of the opposition had begun to mobilize, it seemed as if the plan of the conspirators was beginning to come out just as they had planned.

That night, under the silence of the fogs, the body of the lawyer Royer Vitine was removed from the mausoleum, first   the lid of the septic tank was removed, the coffin was pulled out, the lid was removed, the body was lifted and immediately placed on a sheet carried by the ambassador's driver, While the government emissary was in charge of placing everything as it was, looking for a way to leave no trace that would lead to suspicion, the ambassador and the party secretary kept watch in case anything unexpected happened.

The ambassador's driver carefully wrapped the body of Attorney Roger Vitine in the blanket and the government emissary continued with his cleaning operation, put the lid back on the coffin, lifted it up to the septic tank, pushed it back into its normal position, took possession of a prefabricated mixture that was ready for his

Utility, sealing the opening, and he prepared to help the ambassador's driver, and it was easy to lift him on his left shoulders, as the lawyer Vitine was thin and small.

They pushed the grating door of the mausoleum, signaled in the direction of the secretary and the ambassador to realize that they had finished, moved stealthily towards the exit door and towards the van, everything had been easier than expected, but before reaching their destination they found themselves threatened, the guard of the cemetery froze their blood:

---- Stop, or you are dead men," he said, while he pointed a shotgun at them, but he could not utter any new words. The party secretary who had positioned himself at his rear hit him hard with the handle of his .45 pistol and he collapsed, losing consciousness, which the driver and the government emissary took advantage of to get to the black van, Arranging the body of lawyer Roger Vitine in the back of the vehicle, they went again to the outskirts of the city, towards the hacienda. Once there, after arranging the body of lawyer Roger Vitine, the ambassador took possession of one of the briefcases in his possession, from which he removed a wad of dollar bills that he graciously handed to the party secretary at the time of expressing himself:

----- Take this money, find out where the man from the cemetery lives, this... watchman who was possibly injured today, check if he is injured, pay all expenses, tell them that because he put his life on the line, in the name of the party and in honor of Roger Vitine, he will help you get a visa to paradise for him and his family.

The party secretary grabbed the handful of dollars that he looked at through the fluorescent rays coming from the lights that were coming from the room's ceiling, saying:

----- I admire your calculations and intelligence, Mr. Johnson, there is a reason why you have been the best ambassador of the kingdom here in Isla Dorada, it is that you are not only a legalist, you are also a true politician, a politician with diplomacy," said the secretary with an inflated sense of pride, looking for a way to make you feel flattered.

---- He tried to do what he considered best for the cause, that, moreover, is a way of neutralizing it in case, he managed to recognize us, it is necessary to avoid any kind of scandal. The ambassador argued.

---- My car was left in the vicinity of the cemetery, I'm going to look for it, and that way I'll find out what happened to the lookout.

----- I think it's a very good idea, very well, we'll go out again, we'll leave it on the spot, and we'll continue right there for the embassy, there are still twenty-eight days left to see Royer Vitine-----'s awakening, the ambassador said, as he reflected as if thinking of something else:

---- Okay, the main thing is done, now we just have to wait.

The driver who had helped the government emissary to accommodate Royer Vitine's body, was waiting in front of the wheel of the van, the government emissary, the ambassador and the party secretary who returned to the vehicle after carefully closing, to make the return trip to the city.

 As they stipulated, and the party secretary had been left in the vicinity of the cemetery, precisely in front of his vehicle, it was four o'clock in the morning, which did not prevent the secretary from satisfying the curiosity of knowing what had happened to the watchman, This led him to enter the cemetery with everything and vehicle, and he honked on the side where the warden had been left, who, even though he had come to, felt reckless with a huge headache and an uncut hematoma between the back of his neck and the left side of his head.

He was sitting by the entrance on a granite stool, when he walked towards the door with his shotgun cocked to be shot, he shouted:

---- Identify yourself.

The secretary, who was also a well-known public man of the opposition party, letting himself be seen, dismounted from the jipeta he had left even with the engine and the light on.

-------- Oh, you are sir, you are up early, what can I do for you?

 --- The warden replied that now, because of the clothes he was wearing, he looked more like a creature from beyond the grave, a white handkerchief covered the affected part giving him the appearance of a zombie -recently emerged from a grave.

--- I was asleep and I received an anonymous call telling me that something had happened here and since we just buried Royer Vitine, I wanted to come before the press appeared to verify the veracity of the facts --- the secretary skillfully responded.

---- Sir, I cannot tell you what happened, nothing more than what you are looking at, the only thing I know is that at about one o'clock in the morning I saw two men who were moving carefully, as if taking care that no one would discover them, I wanted to stop them but they looked like two apparitions who were carrying a body wrapped in a blanket, and were covered by the shadow and protected by the devil, because when I called a halt I felt a blow on the back of my neck that put me to sleep, sir, they almost killed me.

--- Could you recognize some of them? --- questioned the secretary.

---- No sir, I told him it was dark, and after the blow, I didn't know what happened.

---- Is your injury serious?---------------------------------

---- I don't know, all I know is that I have a huge headache, sir," said the warden.

--- Do you have a family... wife, children. --- The secretary continued to inquire.

---- Yes sir, I----- have my wife, with three children, two females and a baron.

---- Well," replied the secretary, as he breathed an air of satisfaction.

He put his right hand in the inside pocket of his jacket and pulling out a business card of the liberal party he said:

--- This is my business card, after I rest go to my party office at 11 am, I'll be waiting for you, let's see how we can help you ... that injury, you will check the party doctors to see how serious it is, if your family is wondering do not go into detail, tell them you had an accident so as not to alarm them,

How old are your daughters?

---- One is 18 and the other 19, sir. --- The warden replied even though he didn't understand anything.

What's your name?

--- The secretary kept asking.

--- Pascual Mendoza, sir at your service

---- Very well, Pascual, I'll wait for you later, you're taking your daughters," said the secretary as he handed him two hundred peso bills, equivalent to five dollars, and then he added:

---- This is enough for you to cover the passage, we will finish talking later. He said, returning to the white jipeta that was still running, and with the lights illuminating the graves of the cemetery, he boarded it, reversed, and after backing up, turned north and was lost in the distance.

The warden Pascual Mendoza was even more confused, looked at the two hundred bills in his hands and said as if he wanted to be heard by the deceased:

---- If I were not a believer in God, I would believe that this luck is being given to me by the dead with the intention of helping me, too much emotion in one night, first a blow and then a prize, well, I don't understand anything, nor do I want to understand.

CHAPTER 25

— That day Pascual retired to his house earlier than usual, he left at six in the morning and the relief appeared at eight, so he thought that given the circumstances, nothing would be lost if he was absent a few hours earlier that day, because however much the thieves needed, they would steal anything but dead, That's how he decided to leave at half past four in the morning, and when he arrived at the house the first thing he did was to alert his daughters Sila and Chila that they would have to accompany him to the meeting with the secretary of the Liberal Party, and at the same moment they had been informed they went to choose the dress they would wear for that occasion.

It was easy for them to agree because as if they had been twins they wore the same number of dress, and wore the same shoe, and as the clothes were not so much by force they had to agree to alternate them, so they agreed that Chila would go in Blue and Silla in red, after making the preparations and questioning Don Pascual, they went to bed again and slept until 9 o'clock:30 to take a shower and comb their hair to be with their father at the time indicated in the local of the liberal party, which was half an hour away and 15 minutes by bus.

They attended punctually, when they arrived 10 minutes before eleven o'clock, the - - - - - - - -secretary was already waiting for them, when they were made to go inside the secretary's office, he, as a leader trained to fight with the masses, went out to meet them:

- - - - I see that you are very punctual, Don Pascual.

- - - - We tried, sir, we tried," responded Don Pascual the Warden, with deep humility, and added, referring to Sila and Chila:

- - - - These are my daughters Sila and Chila.

The secretary extended his hand:

- - - Nice to meet you ladies, please sit down- - - She said as I pointed out a deep black leather furniture.

Before they asked him what the reason for the invitation was, he stepped forward, as if he had been reading the thoughts of his guests:

- - - - I have called your father here, and I have told him to be accompanied by you, because as it is not a secret for the country, yesterday was the funeral of lawyer Royer Vitine, and because your father had an accident perhaps due to the same pressure of the day, the party has wanted to give him a medical check-up and see how we can help him," said the secretary.

---- Thank you, we have asked you in many ways, what happened to you? And he just tells us that it was an accident.

---- Don't worry, it's going to work out.

He used the transmitting phone, and had a nurse assigned to the party's medical unit come in, and sent with her Don Pascual, who in less than twenty minutes had been checked and cured, while the secretary spent time talking to the warden's daughters.

--- I have heard that you will be the next candidate of the liberal party, and surely the future president, what is the truth in that? --- asked Chila with some naivety.

---- Is that being commented on in the streets?

---- Those are the rumors that are being commented on in different sectors of the capital.

--- We still don't know, our possible candidate was going to be the late Dr. Royer vitine, now we don't know which candidate will successfully face the nightmare of

Socialism in Isla Dorada, but in any circumstance, we aspire to recover the political scenario--he said, but was interrupted by his assistant, who at that moment had entered the office to find out what was happening in the political scenario of Isla Dorada:

--- Excuse me, sir, sorry to interrupt you, but look at this," he said, as he turned on the television set in the middle of a mahogany shelf with a VCR on it, the image of the video that Royer Vitine had recorded, accusing President Ezekiel, appeared.

It was the midday news, followed by Vitine's accusations, other images of liberal party activists promoting mobilizations and calling for general strikes in different parts of the national territory of Isla Dorada appeared. They had begun to burn official vehicles and tires, however, despite the attempt

of anarchy, the government authorities had not yet decided to repress the demonstrators, the police forces were kept in the surroundings but by order of the president they did not dare to intervene, the news announced that the president of Isla Dorada would address the nation in the early hours of the night on the official radio and television networks and by all the assigned media.

The phone rang, it was the receptionist in the front office.

--- Miss, here are three reporters interested in interviewing the secretary --- He reported.

---- Wait a minute," the assistant secretary demanded of the receptionist-----, "there are three reporters waiting in the office who want to speak to you as a spokesperson for the party," she said.

The secretary exchanged a look with Sila and Chila, and ordered:

---- Tell them that the president is out of town, that I'm holding a meeting and that I won't be available for another half hour.

The assistant who still kept the receptionist on the line passed on the secretary's message and hung up.

---- I'll take care of it, sir, until you finish. ---- said the assistant, leaving the secretary's office, and as she did so she almost collided head-on with Don Pascual and the nurse, who were on their way back, they were entering as she left.

---- Mr. Secretary, mission accomplished, Mr. Pascual Mendoza is in the best conditions, we made him a complete physical examination and he came out well, in some days his bruises will disappear, these medicines are to be given to him as the mandate indicates. He said extending a bag with medicines to Sila.

----- Is Don Pascual feeling well?

---- Yes, sir.----- Don Pascual answered

---- Well, I'll leave you to it," said the nurse leaving the scene.

--- Okay... Pascual I'm happy for you, the party is going to help you, here are two thousand dollars to get your passport from you, your mom and your brother. When you have it, bring it to me, we want our friends to be well and don Pascual for his high cooperative effort deserves to be helped, but we have thought that his happiness would be greater if he could enjoy it with his family--- He said extending the wad of bills to Sila, whose equivalent in pesos would be 65,000.00 in Isla Dorada currency.

---- Thank you very much. Chila and Sila responded almost at the same time.

---- Thanks to you, when you have the passports, call me as soon as possible to bring them to me, go well, and now let me see what these reporters want.

Sila carefully inserted the money she had received into the wallet she carried, securing it, and they left.

----- Thank you, my Lord." Don Pascual said happily, turning his head as he crossed the door from the secretary's office.

The secretary did not utter a word, but nodded his head in agreement.

When they had just left, the reporters who had been lurking since the secretary had shown his body to the door, fired their camera flashes taking unexpected pictures of him, while the television reporters ran their cameras, making films of him while questioning him, there were four media outlets waiting for him, two written and two televised:

---- Mr. Secretary, we are transmitting for national television: what is the position of the party before the denunciation of the extinct Royer Vitine? ----- The television reporter intentionally asked.

----- I can't get ahead of myself until that complaint is investigated. The secretary responded sagaciously.

---- Mr. Secretary, for the 33rd news, it is said that Royer Vitine's substitute insurance and that it would contribute to avoid the socialist advance in Isla Dorada, would be you, what truth do you attribute to those rumors? ---- questioned the second of the reporters.

----- I can assure you that if I am the chosen one among so many illustrious members of the liberal party, those rumors could become true. ----- Said the Secretary, using his authority.

------ Mr. Secretary, Rhina Aramburu of Panoramic Vision, if you were chosen as your party's candidate and became president, what would be the first step you would take?

----- It would bring the country out of the economic stagnation in which it finds itself and would facilitate foreign investment, in order to reopen positions that would strengthen the nation's labor force. ---- The Secretary responded calmly.

The reporter of the 33rd insisting on his questioning asked:

----- What would be your attitude to the banking nationalization that socialism is leading?

----- Very simply, bank properties that have been nationalized would remain the same, with a small modification, they would be privatized, thus facilitating national investment. ----- The secretary responded fluently, thus expressing his gratitude for the response, which seemed to be

They were waiting to hear.

They had been so satisfied that they turned off the cameras, thanked them and proceeded to leave, at which time the secretary had received a phone call from the ambassador, who proceeded to respond with great affability.

CHAPTER 26

— At the hacienda, Dr. Colin, Ms. Makwinsy and Professor Makrowki continued to keep a close eye on the body of attorney Royer Vitine. They had placed a serum on him, they were checking his heart, they were making studies that responded to the concern that everything had gone well, anyway they had to wait the programmed time to get a final answer, that is when the nervous flow would induce him to get up and when they would proceed to the final check.

--How do you think you are responding, Professor?

---- It seems to me that everything is going well, we just have to wait... Miss Makwinsy, please change that serum and put the other one in.

Miss Makwinsy executed Professor Makrowki's order, as instructed, while Dr. Colin turned on the television.

They watched the news with interest, the lawyer Vitine, although he could not move, also listened to the information in his cataleptic state, although he was fully aware of what was being said, since the video that had been recorded for him was still being broadcast.

Something surprising and that they had not considered was happening, the lawyer Royer Vitine had urinated the shroud which announced to Professor Makrowki that without a doubt some of his formula had also just achieved success in human beings.

----- We succeeded, Dr. Colin, the man just peed himself, which indicates that he is not dead," said Professor Makrowki, full of enthusiasm.

They made a human chain between the three of them and danced in a circle of joy, while singing a chorus:

"We are reaching science, we are reaching science, we are developing it, we are developing it, we are developing it, for good, for good"

After singing that chorus they embraced, as always Miss Makwinsy entered the inner room and instantly returned with three glasses of a Scottish wine and toasted to success, but when it seemed that everything would return to normal, because they had even entered a pause of reflection, something even more unexpected happened, to the lawyer Roger Vitine in his cataleptic state and without him being able to avoid it, a fart went off and smelled so unpleasant that it took them out of their reflection.

----- What was that, Professor? --- I question Dr. Colin a little more surprised.

The teacher was silent, but frowned as if trying to find an answer in himself.

----- That was a fart Dr. Colin, and very unpleasant and the smell comes from there.----- He said by pointing to the bed where he was lying like a spilled jelly, lawyer Royer Vitine.

----- The pamper must be changed before it defecates.----- exclaimed Professor Makrowki with determination.

For his part, the lawyer, Roger, in his unmistakable reflection, thought without being able to move a muscle:

---- This was not in the script, what a shame!... but five million is five million, what does the shame matter, then I realize that I never knew what was happening, when they question me and allude to this tragedy.

Miss Makwinsy went back to the inner room, left the three empty glasses and what was left of the wine bottle, then returned with a pamper bag in her hand, limiting herself to undressing the lawyer, pulled down his pants with everything and shorts and proceeded to change the pamper that although not dirty, Because of the stench they thought he would be, for a moment he concentrated on the sex of Vitine who, for being small in stature, had a limb bigger than his feet. Dr. Colin, who was checking her and thought she was guessing the thought of Vitine, commented with a certain insinuation so that only she would listen to him:

---- It's too bad he's married, because he's not only a big shot, but a millionaire as well.

Miss Makwinsy, on feeling discovered, pretended with indifference and I just undressed the lawyer Vitine, putting on his pamper and adjusting a pair of pajamas that he had taken out of a drawer

---- The women! The lawyer thought again.

The summer was showing off, the May sun was beginning to rise. A month had passed since Professor Makrowki had been taken from Venice by the government emissary.

El mar was still waiting for a sign from God, so on Sunday morning, as Elizabeth Volqué had suggested in her last letter, she knelt down and asked the God of her being to forgive her for any disrespect she had incurred in her ignorance.

That day he had gone out early together with other prisoners to sunbathe tenderly on the chlorophyll grass esplanade, he felt that a great peace was invading the depths of his soul, from his heart a great hope was sprouting, something was telling him that everything would be fine and much better.

The leafy trees let the tender crystalline rays escape through their cracked branches.

He walked, jogged, exercised and shared with some of the prisoners who used to commission him verses and dedications for their families.

An hour later, when he returned to the dormitory, he was approached by a group of repeat offenders who did not understand why the one who had the opportunity to be out of prison had not done anything that would allow him to get out, because they thought he could accept "please Guilty" in exchange for his freedom.

However, although El mar had been dismayed by Barbarita's crying, he did not pay attention to these pressures because he understood that when someone had the water around his neck, in a moment of desperation, the first thing he did was to attract the first person who

extended his hand trying to help him, with the aim of sinking him into his own sewer

El mar knew the idiosyncrasy of those prisoners who used to feel jealous of those who arrived without guilt at the prison, because they did not like that in the pack there would be wolves and foxes, because for them the pack was for the dogs, the packs for the wolves, they distrusted those who maintained their innocence even when in prison, because they believed that they were infiltrators who tried to obtain information from them to aggravate their condition.

In any circumstance, El mar made an effort to tolerate and survive, because his sensibility was of another nature. He tried not to discriminate because he did not want to cause more pain to those who did not have the strength to endure to make their time without suffering, without pain, without sorrow, without tears.

That day, as he walked on the esplanade, someone approached him who the prisoners considered to have a sexual preference, and from a group that observed his steps and conversation, a murmur emerged that sounded more like a murmur, and one with a voice like a periquillo vine shouted at him:

- - - - "Hey, El mar, drop it and don't drop it"

El mar did not understand what Lazaro Osorio was trying to tell it.

- - - - Speak to me clearly that I don't understand you.

- - - - What I want to tell you is that it's not good to get together with him, he's a "faggot" - - - - Lazarus stated with a security accent, above the victim who, speaking in another language, did not understand what Lazarus was saying in his native tongue.

- - - - I thank you for informing me to take my precautions.

El mar.

- - - - - Well, El mar, it's time to go, they're calling us - - - said Lazaro as each one of us prepared to leave the esplanade for their respective destinations.

El mar and Lazarus left together to separate inside the building, Lazarus continued to live in J-2, El mar in J-1, and the victim in J---3.

The vice became customary and assiduously some of the prisoners used to risk to inhale some that others tubanos of marijuana that although for that then it was less persecuted than those of more drugs, it did not let provide its effects, El mar understood that those contraband that entered the dormitories could not walk arriving only without permissibility of the authorities, having by means of a rooted and strict monitoring.

The consumers for the effect used to take turns to inhale it while the custody was distracted, so that when one smoked the other watched and so on, until all the adepts of the vice managed to satiate the impertinence of their need, there "nobody was free of guilt to throw the first stone" because even El mar that did not participate in anything, he had to make himself an indirect accomplice by keeping silent, because even though he was different, and had earned their respect, he did not dare to denounce him because the law of the prison was that what someone else did in your presence, if it did not involve you, was not your business, and El mar understood this but at the same time he cried out to God to help him: accept what he could not change", because drugs came to prison because those who controlled them let them pass, especially the guards and officials who were aware of everything that moved in that direction of pride, of trials, of pain and darkness, of confusion and macho ignorance.

He remembered the anecdote of the swallow that while flying over El mar, he saw a beautiful fish that swam over the surface of the waters, and the fish also thought that no one swam over the air as gracefully as she did, they fell in love and treated each other for a while, until both realized that neither belonged to the other's world.

That was the anecdote of El mar, he did not belong to that world, where he had been forced to arrive by resorting to the action of a falsehood, which made it seem like a real fact.

El mar thought that the criminals invested with power had done him a great evil, making a case for him by sending him to prison, with a way of satisfying the crudeness of his

confused egos, because for him the wicked were cowards who trembled at the first glimmer of their shadows, but his spirit was comforted by the belief that he possessed enough skill to vent himself before the oppressor, without giving him any hint that would induce him to personalize the quarrel, because he also understood that the manipulators with

Power and guile, they used to make the guilty appear innocent and the innocent guilty, according to the interests of the turns or the gendarmes of the mayor's office.

Then courage was instilled by repeating an expression:

"He is not brave who is not afraid, but who knows how to conquer it" and then believing that imagination was the secret of genius, he confirmed that the race of life was full of obstacles, and that what really mattered was not to give up on the path, and at that moment he was ready to strengthen his faith until he achieved his goal beyond the banner of glory.

– – – – Bail you out and get out of here," said one... "This is not for you, I'm in jail for something but you haven't done anything.– – – – – Said the Mole, from whom I least expected that expression.

– – – – – Thanks Topo, thirst is a deep pain in the throat, in the sternum and under the clavicles, it's like a suffocating desperation, sometimes you have to wait for the opportunity to satiate it, thanks Topo for your suggestion, not always we human beings can do what we want at the moment we understand, however you just gave me an idea, I will investigate to see if using the resources of the system I can bail myself out – – – Said El mar.

– – – – – – Of course you can.– – – – – The Mole indicated.

El Mar immediately resorted to a custody inquiry to see if he could get ten percent of the bond, however, he was informed that since his bond was five thousand dollars, in order to post it, he would have to pay the full amount, or resort to a bail bondsman so that they could approve the full amount.

He knocked on the door of some acquaintances so that they could locate the "bailbond" for him but without any success until that moment.

Things had started to get tense, jealousy and envy were sharpening, and there was no lack of those who challenged him by inviting him to fight, now El mar would have to define a psychological action to survive, if he allowed himself to be provoked his time could be extended, most of those prisoners were common criminals who would serve long sentences, and they wanted to drag down the first of those who had arrived at the prison with less time than them, and precisely El mar had been chosen as a possible candidate for their harassment, they had already warned him that he would have to move, and he was weaning on the threats.

This is how he went ahead to apply the measures of psi coercion, he approached the custody and let him know that someone had threatened him saying that "if he didn't move he would be killed" the custody asked him who had told him that and El mar timidly indicated to the prisoner assigned to help with the distribution of the food, that he had dedicated himself to attacking him and maliciously pursuing him, being one of those who most insisted that El mar become guilty, as if he had been sent by someone with the exclusive mission of harassing him.

When the custody found out where the threat came from, he simply smiled and said in a joking tone:

– – – – – Don't worry, I'll take care of you.

Then El mar remembered the words that Barbarita expressed to him in his most recent visit:

– – – – Now I think I could marry you. – – – – – He said.

– – – – – I, I don't marry you.

– – – – – Fantastic, if you don't marry me I'll marry someone else. He said.

– – – I wouldn't marry you if you didn't forget all these problems, we've been through so much together, who else but you could marry me?

El mar squeezed his hand, and he kissed it on the lips, then he told him what was happening, the provocations he had received from the officer at the clinic, he also told him about the times he had been taken to court without being seen by the judge, he also told him that some prisoners who had heard about the offer of time served made by the prosecutor, had been pressuring him to accept it; but that he did not feel prudent to plead guilty being innocent.

Then he remembered the words she uttered in a discouraging voice, as the most intemperate sound ever heard, that if things were happening in that way, he should be careful, precisely when those who had been at odds with him began to rise against him, and under such circumstances, the same strange sensations as before overwhelmed him, this time, in the manner of pleasant distress, he was mute and petrified with an attitude, where fervor and dread were confused.

Suddenly he clearly visualized Barbarita's sphinx, approached it with a serious step, had rays of satisfaction, like those of the sun, and said without removing his eyes from it:

– – – – The rose of your hands provokes me something strange, and I would like to have you beyond your years, but you never know what will happen tomorrow, when in paradise the paradisiacal dream despairs, and ambition threatens the family stability, and it is ignored how long the magic of romance will last.

On the other hand, Barbarita, more than laconic, showed herself mute, listened in silence, had resisted with much effort the desire to cry, made efforts to contain the impulses to cry, but after trying to contain herself she broke into tears.

El mar became aware of the social conditions, where realism as Balzac once saw it, pretended to be an exact reproduction of society, he had begun to discover that Barbarita was changed and that those added words were like a pretext to justify a future resolution.

Behind her brain, eaten away by the torment of the times, were hidden collateral hands that, pulling the strings, had begun to handle her like a puppet

And she, confused, corroded by remorse of conscience, felt that her heart was trying to escape from her upright little breast.

For a moment, a light of sadness came out of her eyes, a spark of pride used to blind her. El mar came to the conclusion that this day was like the anteroom of a farewell reflection because behind her little brain of ability and brilliance, there was a worry that showed her eating away, because of the difficulties of life.

The times lived in those days were of challenge and intolerance, few were capable of giving themselves in sacrifice for the others, it was like a fight between the strongest and the weakest, the system was designed so that each one thought of him without caring about the others.

Everyone was looking for unhealthy gifts, after experiences of unsafe trajectories, however El mar was one of the few that believed that the awakening would come after the actions claiming society's teas, and that neither the rich nor the politicians, nor the mafiosi, nor the oppressors, nor the intolerant, nor the manipulators, could prevent the facts of social justice.

He understood that nothing remained static and that whatever had to happen would happen; above the will of those who had been using power to abuse and violate and manipulate the rights of the minority majority groups.

El mar insisted on remembering those happy moments when it was his turn to move under the joyful airs of the city. He saw the youthful silhouette of Barbarita, her solid and graceful body with admirable proportions and without any natural incorrectness, which obscured her details.

Gifts so prodigious that induced desire to those who contemplate teas, which qualified her as divine as an angel, and beautiful as a lady of portentous inner light.

She remembered a winter day where she had generated a truce, where the sun was exhibited with splendor, it warmed without burning, and the air, felt fresh, soft, and pleasant to the rose with the skin, she, was like the day, her eyes shone of happiness, her face was funny, her eyelids trembled with joy, she showed spontaneous, fantastic and sensitive:

--- Today is a day when I want to kiss you and hug you.

Saying this, she walked up to him and added, stopping and holding her partner by the arm: ---- I feel so good with you, I can't imagine what my life would be like without you. -He said.

El mar smiled with pride before responding:

---- That is mutual, I am convinced that with you, I feel protected.

Barbarita did not tire of looking at him, so when she heard what he had said, she stretched out, reached her lips and kissed him.

They would descend a staggered path, walking with their eyes fixed on the ground:

---- Try to step firmly because it's a little slippery.

---- Don't worry princess, this mass will not collapse.

His open hand slipped through her hair, which felt as if it were floating, as if it were hanging from her arm, her nimble little feet slipped in a hurry, little brownish spots showed on her face, she had come off her shoes and was barefoot, with them in one hand.

His voice resonated with a nice accent of harmony, he had a formal and reflexive discernment, he wanted to walk to exhaust the time in company of El mar contemplating the landscape and exercising the body.

Marvelous flowering lights spread out across the vault of the sky.

--- He murmured maliciously, to hear her thunder.

---- Maybe we love each other, because I'm not indifferent to you either.----- She replied with some pride.

His face was glowing, after a pause he returned, looking him straight in the eye- --- Are you not going to tell me anything?

El mar of enthusiasm admitted him:

------ So that, to say no, if yes.

Barbarita smiled, stretched out again and kissed him again.

He repeated with such emphasis that it seemed as if he was being flattered.

---- Yes, yes, yes, yes, yes, yes.----- He pronounced, insisting with energy. He stopped and modulated the tone of his voice-----.

If you had told me otherwise, I would have felt like I was dying.

---- he said pathetically.

Barbarita felt very well loved, and El mar was so imbued with her exploits that she did not notice when Orlando arrived and greeted him.

Orlando was his countryman, he had just arrived from court and had promised that if he managed to get out, he would look for a way to help him with the bail to leave that cemetery of living men, however he was unable to fulfill his promise,

Because he was required to pay all the money he had, he informed him of the impossibility and what had happened, and as compensation, he gave him a "walkman" radio, which El Mar was able to renegotiate in exchange for another one that was of better quality.

There everyone applied their own style to survive, and El mar had begun to develop his own, he was a type of person of an unyielding faith but had begun to feel pressure, he was unaccustomed to the lifestyle of those sectors that interacted in Vengala, so he felt that often what was most despised was what most often approached him, and at that time some of

Those who consumed the marijuana had begun to take shelter in their cubicle which was the least exposed to the bedroom chambers, and the closest to the air conditioning grills, because when they released their puffs of smoke through it the air conditioning drove it out of the bedroom and the smell was less, and it used to drift away from the nose of the guard on duty.

In this way, the nauseating smell of the grass was confused with the diverse smells of the bodies, whose variability oscillated between psychotic, fart and rook, and to achieve their objectives they appeared with two double AA batteries and two fine wires removed from the fans, or the televisions, creating a positive and a negative pole that attached to each of the batteries allowed it to produce the fire with which they lit the cigarettes that some managed to go underground, which once inhaled would produce an unpleasant smell to the noses unused.

El mar understood how harmful cigarettes were in any sense, and knowing this, every time he saw smokers approaching without his being able to stop them, he would leave the

place by going to the TV room without them noticing that he was avoiding them, or watching him from afar, since if he opposed them or had them as enemies, they could conspire and stab him while he slept.

In fact, El mar neither trusted nor trusted the "justice" of Paradise, it did not know the purpose of those who forcibly sought to criminalize it, and who under such pretext had sought all viable ways to keep it in prison.

Then also El mar thought it was necessary to take his precautions, because if he stayed close to the facinerosos and they were discovered, they could also involve him and create a charge of possession or conspiracy.

There, life, even if it seemed like it, was not the color of roses, it was necessary to learn how to survive, there was no friend and those who showed themselves as such, at the time of confrontation, sold themselves to the highest bidder, if a well paid offer appeared, a betrayal was forged.

El mar possessed a special grace that induced admiration and hate at the same time, some admired it and others hated it at the same time, it was the owner of a sensibility and a patience that made it easy for him to tolerate and successfully overcome all of life's trials, however difficult.

That ambivalence allowed him to interact and survive in that hostile environment, and he was assured that God was with him at all times, and those who dared to challenge or humiliate him, or persecute him, returned meek as a lamb to show their repentance.

Life is not always what man in his role of living it disposes it to be, but what he assumed it would be at the moment of choosing the character he would represent; he frequently stated El mar.

After the experiences of that day, El mar retired to sleep, and after the lights were turned off, it was approximately twelve o'clock at night, when he was assaulted by a vision where God revealed to him that the struggle he had fought for the custody of Mark, would not be in vain.

That night he dreamt that the boy was playing in front of an apartment he had obtained, he saw that someone approached him asking about the boy, and he gave him the answer that he had him sleeping in the apartment in front of where Mark was playing accompanied by other children, however the atmosphere he showed suggested that Celeste Chaplain resided in the vicinity, and just when he thought about it, he saw the Chaplain coming out of a nearby building with a flower-printed dress showing her pink shins with more insinuation than usual, and El mar felt exasperated and ran to prevent her from facing Barbarita Roque.

Then he found himself listening to music

From a tape that Celeste Chaplain had supplied, when he woke up he felt a great spiritual peace, he had been filled with hope, his heart indicated him that God did not abandon him and that a message was given to him for the comfort of his soul.

He felt a moving presence in his body between his neck and his head.

In the afternoon the custody called him to deliver a letter, it was from Isabel Volqué, who continued to write to him, it had arrived two weeks late, it had been sent to the address before the F-2 South block where El mar had resided before being taken to J-1 number 16.

In that letter Volqué let off steam, complained about the failures of the system, the manipulations and pressures to make people guilty even though they were innocent, so it would be easier for them, Volqué opened her soul and expressed that she did not believe in the injustice that paradise promoted as "justice", she was disappointed, depressed, and impotent, they had forced her to become guilty with a year's sentence when at first they had talked to her about six months.

CHAPTER 27

— I saw the sky clear, the sun with incandescent hues poured freely its rays on the vast extension of Isla Dorada, as if in the 15,525 square kilometers of that radiant tropical plot, there was no space where the star king stopped shining with its sudden shade of red yellow, only when it collided with the blue of El mar, the rays broke down on the foamy waters, becoming silvery shades.

Isla Dorada, a treasure coveted by all, where the poet's figurative verse could be applied:

"That place of deep blue waters, where he who amassed fortune could not smile at the moon, there where that laborer who wrestled with sweetness felt his mouth bitter.

Isla Dorada was something like the poet said, it was like a showcase in the central Caribbean, rich in fauna and flora, it produced minerals such as gold, silver and copper, among others without the lack of large oil wells, it was also favored by nature for agricultural production.

In spite of everything, there in the central Caribbean and specifically in Isla Dorada, the national political reality continued to be tense, the press continued to spread the details of the crisis generated by the opposition, which involved the President of the Republic in the assassination of lawyer Royer Vitine, having created the conditions for the destabilization of the recently inaugurated socialist government.

The presidents of other countries that had embraced the same ideology in the region, had initiated sporadic meetings to address the issue of the crisis in Isla Dorada, and how it affected them, so they would be proposing the realization of cooperation agreements between the supporters of the project socialism 20th century1, so at that time were meeting in a semi emergency regional summit, to

To evaluate the progress of bilateral projects and celebrate the independence of Equito, one of the countries that at that time were part of the socialist project century (PSS XX1).

The meeting was taking place on the slopes of Equito volcano at whose foot was the nation's capital, the celebration began when the rulers entered accompanied by the presidential guard of Equito with relief of soldiers and speeches praising and extolling the libertarian deeds with the battle of the volcano, you could see hundreds of military distributed throughout the length and breadth of the earth's space, strengthened by an air parade of fighter planes of the Equito air force.

The leaders walked escorted by children wearing folkloric costumes, representing the culture of the different topics of the nation, also participated ambassadors from different countries represented in Equito, the presidents of Equito Rety Cornier, Venemar Charly Justo, Bolimar Trebo Corrales, took hands in an action gesture to show how strength was achieved through unity and solidarity.

The project of socialism in the 21st century was a fact that they wanted to spread in the regional conscience, as a way of self-protection, they hoped that other countries in the area would adopt the socialist ideology.

Something had happened in Isla Dorada, which could contribute to the cessation of the internal pressures of that nation and its President Ezequiel Conrado.

In the office of the human rights procurator, a witness had sent a document denouncing three alleged material authors of the murder of lawyer Royer Vitine.

The action did not take long and the prosecutor looked for a way to contact the witness, with the primary objective of offering him protection.

President Ezequiel Conrado called on the United Nations to have the International Commission against Impunity in Isla Dorada (CICID) take charge of

The investigation also extended a copy of the document to an agent of the Federal Bureau of Investigation (BFI), who had come to collaborate.

For its part, the PSSXX1, had considered that the actions generated against President Ezequiel Conrado, were nothing more than a destabilizing campaign, and therefore would offer all the solidarity support that deserves before the problem of the crisis generated in Isla Dorada.

At the same time, they attributed the responsibility of what happened to insane groups of organized crime, and its consequences that had seen in the Democratic Socialism an obstacle for their personal ambitions, in Isla Dorada and in the central Caribbean, that were identifying more and more with the ideology, so much so that some rulers of those who were ascending to power in the region, By that time, they had begun to submit to their congresses, the modifications of the different constitutions, in order to embrace democratic socialism as their political tool, however in Isla Dorada, since then a series of popular protests continued to be generated with the financing of the opposition and the embassy of the kingdom.

The tragic setup by the shadow ideologues had taken effect.

On the other hand, in Bolimar some warlike exchanges had been generated, where government agents had managed to capture some and annihilate others, members of a gang, whom President Trebo Corrales had labeled as international terrorists conspiring against the stability of his government. The region had become crassly dynamic at the time.

The thirty days stipulated for the lawyer Royer Vitine to get up from the dead had passed, leaving the bed where he was kept prostrate, and above all getting rid of the pamper that had returned him to a forced childhood and a conditioned disability, where even to clean himself, he had to depend on others.

So it would also be necessary to disappear from the political scene of Isla Dorada from the first moment it could be incorporated.

The investigations were progressing, and if he remained in the country, he could take the risk that the fraud would be discovered, and since it was never known what the reaction of the enraged masses would be, it would be better to tie up all the loose ends in time.

From early in the morning, the whole team was waiting for that longed-for awakening. The body of the lawyer Royer Vitine was lying in the specialized bed where he had been since that first day of his internment.

He was never alone, next to him were Professor Makrowki, Dr. Colin, and Miss Makwinsy, always on the lookout for something deserving, they had taken his pulse for what they were commenting on:

----- Professor Makrowki, don't you think it's time you woke up?

---- He is awake when he stops resting, what we are waiting for is for the muscle blockage to be cleared so he can get up, Dr. Colin.

---- thank you for the correction professor... Miss Makwinsy, why don't you take advantage and see that when you get over the muscle block, you are ready and without the pamper... --- asked Dr. Colin.

----- I will do so, Dr. Colin.

She undressed him in the same way she did on the first day they had discovered the success of the experiment, in her action of having urinated on his clothes, changed his underwear and dressed him elegantly in a new suit that they had bought for him when they moved his personal belongings to a room in the clinic, before he was tested.

When Royer Vitine began to stretch and yawn, Professor Makrowki took a surprising leap, tapping Dr. Colin on the shoulders, all three had approached the bed at the same time, as if synchronized by an electric control.

Royer Vitine yawned again, first he shrank and stretched his legs slightly and then he got up with a programmed slowness, he was raising his torso slowly until he was supported on his buttocks still with his feet stretched out on the bed.

---- Ah, aaaaah. He grunted, and then he added:

----- Where am I?--- he asked, even with the cloudy visibility and the confused mind.

----- Welcome to your room, you are in the clinic of the hacienda.

----- How does attorney Royer Vitine feel? It's a pleasure to welcome you back in triumph," said Dr. Colin.

---- Thank you" Vitine replied trying to get up, his eyes were still blurred, he still felt weak.

----- Just a moment, lawyer Vitine, if you feel weak don't move, we will put you another serum.---- He said, while Royer Vitine who was still yawning, lost consciousness again, the professor ordered with alarmed haste:

---- He's fallen asleep... Miss Makwinsy, hurry up, please bring an H2O-R serum.----- Makrowki said looking somewhat alarmed at Dr. Colin.

Miss Makwinsy went to a cupboard in the same room and took a bottle of the required serum, while gently pushing it to Vitine for the

Shoulders, he tenderly unbuttoned his shirt, took off his jacket with everything and shirt leaving it in short sleeve flannel, they looked for in his left arm the adaptable space of the vein to introduce the needle that would lead the nutrient liquid to his

Dr. Colin took the opportunity to locate another vein in his right arm, from which she removed a blood tube, and then proceeded to install the serum.

For an hour they were passing him the serum, although after half an hour the lawyer Vitine had fully recovered his consciousness.

When Dr. Colin and Professor Makrowki deemed it appropriate, she removed the needle from his arm, while Miss Makwinsy prepared a light dinner for Professor Makrowki who had forgotten himself in his eagerness to observe, and had not eaten anything all day.

At that very moment he was checking, exploring with a pencil flashlight, the pupils of the lawyer Vitini, while he was making notes in his notebook.

When Miss Makwinsy returned from the inner room, she brought a tray with five fried eggs with a slice of toasted wheat bread, which the professor tasted with remarkable appetite.

It was seven o'clock at night when Ambassador Johnson, appeared with the government emissary, and the secretary of the liberal party.

----- Congratulations lawyer Vitine, I see that everything has turned out to be a total success, we have to drink to this --- Ambassador Johnson expressed while Miss Makwinsy returned to the inner room and returned with seven glasses and a gallon of wine, from which he poured the contents over the glass to a level that when lifted would not spill. Attorney Vitine toasted with water.

Ambassador Johnson praised Professor Makrowki, expressing the future that he had predicted for him from that moment on in paradise, the secretary learned and edified Roger Vitine about national events, and how convenient it would be for everyone if he

He left the country as soon as possible, because of the nuance that the protests had taken, and the additional complaints that were taking place, added to them the intervention of

the Organization of Caribbean States (O. E. C.), the United Nations (N. U.), and the support that the government of Ezequiel Conrado had received for the Socialist project of the 21st century (PSSXX1), which had planned a meeting in the town square, and a National Walk of Warning where it would be established that the Secretary General of the

Liberal Party, was not qualified to ask for the resignation of President Ezequiel Conrado, who had been freely and democratically elected.

From that conversation, preparations had been made for the team that developed the successful experiment to return to Paradise that very night, so that none would be exposed to discovery.

The embassy plane flew in with a crew made up of lawyer Royer Vitine and his medical team made up from that first day of the test by Professor Makrowki, Dr. Colin, and Miss Makwinsy.

An immigration commissioner and the pilot carried the instructions for disembarkation, so that everything remained in the confidential files.

As days went by, the destiny of lawyer Royer Vitine and his family had been decided, so they agreed to move to Switzerland, the same country where they had deposited the agreed five million dollars from the beginning, plus what he had managed to subtract from the public treasury during his years as legal minister of the chancellery, during the period of government of the Liberal Party, which amounted to about two million eight hundred thousand dollars.

It was money he could live with as a tycoon for the rest of his life.

Dr. Colin and Ms. Makwinsy returned to their usual duties at the central veterans' hospital where they had previously served and where they had been re-admitted, Dr. Colin as director and Ms. Makwinsy as assistant director.

CHAPTER 28

— The history of Isla Dorada goes back to a high society, product of the Rich Fruit Company, a multinational of paradise capital, which had discovered the corruptible mentality of the elite of that society, and had also visualized the fertile land, the banana and the cheap labor, combined with the ignorance of the natives, as an opportunity for enrichment.

From the end of the 19th century and the beginning of the 20th, the Rich Fruit Company (RFC) resorted to all means to bribe governors, the police force, to dispossess indigenous and peasant farmers of their land, to make local landowners associate, thus managing to build an adjacent port of the Atlantic Ocean and the central Caribbean, and a railroad from the villages to the capital, achieving the RFC, becoming the largest landowner in Isla Dorada until 1945, when the nation's radical dictatorships had been losing force, and a moderate president named Arevalo came to power who established the labor code, forcing the Rich Fruit Company (RFC) and local businessmen to make some concessions to the workers.

Later, another emerged who they called President Albenz, who had destined himself to heal the pain of the nation's deprived.

He had been elected to the presidency in 1951 and from the first months of his administration, he ordered the expropriation of the uncultivable land in the hands of the company, to which he compensated with a high amount of money, however not in accordance with the RFC, he resorted to the investors of the kingdom and specifically of Paradise, and to the "Paradise Intelligency Agency", who tactically managed to manipulate public opinion, accusing President Arbenz as an international agent of the Kremlin, which at any time would be besieged by guerrilla groups advancing against his government.

This psychological campaign had such a destabilizing effect on that government that President Arbenz was forced to go into exile, and Isla Dorada became involved in a

Bloody civil war, where the victims at the time exceeded 200,000, of which a considerable number, mostly indigenous, had been identified by the Paradise Intelligency Agency (PIA) as supporters of the destabilized government.

The historical remnants that survived that elitist management of Isla Dorada, had been represented by the fierce opposition that wanted to reorganize themselves to continue the fight against President Ezequiel Conrado, who was trying through the program of social cohesion, to improve the life of the dispossessed of the nation with dignity, And because this action was not well seen by the rich of Isla Dorada who had received it as a heresy against their sacred interests, they chose to forge a conspiracy protected by the embassy of the kingdom in Isla Dorada and select sectors of the high hierarchy of the liberal party.

This motivation had induced him to get involved in a drama where the main actor would end up being the lawyer Royer Vitine, who would lend himself as the victim of a false or supposed disappearance, in a flagrant attempt against the uncertainty of public opinion, and the innocence of the population.

As the days went by, the opposition's plans were weakened, and influential sectors of international society became visible, expressing their support for President Ezequiel Conrado and his government, which somehow helped to avoid a civil war in Isla Dorada. In any case, groups of demonstrators had congregated at different points.

The second week of May, the Secretary General of the Liberal Party asked for Ezequiel Conrado's resignation, under the pretext that he was responsible for the death of lawyer Royer Vitine. The groups of protesters had been divided into different groups, one repudiating Ezequiel Conrado's permanence in government and demanding his immediate removal from office until the cause of Vitine's descent, who was linked to the country's economic elite, was investigated.

On the other hand, in the town square, the president's supporters had gathered in front of the palace of the governor's office, to show their unconditional support for the president:

------ We are concerned about the increase in violence and insecurity, we are convinced that the solution to this conflict lies simply in the strengthening of the institutions. President Ezequiel Conrado should not resign, precisely because he is heading a government legitimately elected by a people who today say present, so that the will of the people will not be shirked, long live Ezequiel Conrado.

A popular chorus responded: ----- Let it live. —

A murmur of joy and emotion spread among the crowd, the masses wrapped themselves in it, chanted slogans moving in a circle and in half groups, some said:

----- Ezequiel Conrado-- And the others responded:

----- He has never been wrong:

----- We are with him:

------ Keep him in power.

----- The people said already.

----- Ezequiel is the one who goes.

---We are always safe.

---- Ezekiel will rule.

And so on, they created slogans until nightfall, read letters of support that came from the organization of Caribbean states (O.E.C.) of the United Nations (N.U.) and from the Socialist Project of the Twenty-first Century (PSSXX1).

From that day on, the liberal party began to be silenced; public attacks on President Ezequiel Conrado had diminished.

Meanwhile in paradise, Barbarita Roque continued to be imbued with her preoccupation, now she was going through a dilemma period where she needed to think, a lack of faith assailed her and she did not know at that moment what she wanted or what was most convenient for her, she was seen walking around in sorrow, with her eyes moistened, suddenly she discovered that she was in the vicinity of a children's clothing store where someone who knew her and saw her pass by induced her to wake up from her lethargy:

----- Hey, what's wrong with you? You move in front of me and don't even raise your eyes to greet me.

---- Oh, excuse me, you weren't looking at yourself, here I'm a little worried, they locked up El mar and I'm convulsed, not knowing what to do.

------ How did it go, explain it to me better?

Barbarita explained to him in detail letting him know the details, Margaret was a distant cousin of El mar who always lived in communication with Lency, the oldest of his sisters who because of some differences, at that time, had distanced themselves until one day when El mar found Zuly his niece and trying to greet her he discovered that she ignored him:

---- Zuly, Zuly... He was watching El mar trying to greet his niece, without her taking him into account.

----- You hear Zuly, that man is calling you.----- She was told by someone who was accompanying her.

----- I don't know him," answered Zuly indifferently, pretending not to know him.

El mar, which had realized what was really happening, thought that what he believed to be a simple pride of a spoiled little girl, had turned into an enmity; his niece had denied him as Peter had denied Jesus.

After Zuly had left, a lady who was very quarrelsome and who had not lost track of the conversation approached El mar with certain suspicions and willing to satisfy her curiosity, and questioned:

----- Do you know this young woman?....

---- Of course, she's my niece," answered El Mar, trying to justify herself.

– – – – – But she says she doesn't know him.

Seeing El mar Zuly was six months pregnant, justifying herself in the cause not to go into detail with the unknown said:

– – – – – What happens is that we expected her to get married, and since she got pregnant without getting married, she doesn't want to face me.

A few days later, something similar happened, when he was precisely walking along the same path where Barbarita was walking that day, he had tried to make an entrance to greet cousin Margaret, and confidentially he saw his sister lency pass by, who had already made an attempt to enter to greet the cousin in common, but once having noticed his presence, he decided to change course, but as he had already seen her, he decided to call her insistently, however she turned to him with an aggressive attitude and told him:

– – – – I don't want to talk to you.

El mar, which did not expect this unexpected rejection expressed:

– – – – I know that ignorance is aberrant but, courtesy does not reduce courage, I wish you the best, may God bless you and help you cleanse your soul, heart and spirit from so much ignorance, so that your evolution in healing may continue.

When El mar wanted to realize it, it was left with the impression that she did not hear what he was saying, her eyes had lost it in the distance.

The owner of the commercial establishment where this altercation had taken place, who had heard them and who also knew Lency very well, smiled at

El mar:

– – – – What a good man, watches as he blesses his sister despite the rejection," he said.

– – – – – That's right, she's a very good person but she needs to break down the grudge," he said.

– – – – – Leave it to God, he always takes care of everything.

– – – – In confidence," said El mar, saying goodbye and ready to go out into the street, the owner of the establishment came forward and opened the door for him, he left in silence, while she looked at him smiling.

Since then, three months had passed, without El mar knowing anything about them again, something had happened, El mar had been in jail for two months, he had spoken to Barbarita to go see him, he knew that for that she was incurring in a great sacrifice, because having four children and only being able to enter two, having to leave the two older ones who were 7 and 8 years old in the care of someone to be able to go visit him, and that time when El mar asked her to go, she was unable to attend but neither could she tell him that she would not go, the hour had passed when she

I used to arrive.

Then, El mar thought that that day, nobody would go to visit him; a little resigned he became ecstatic at a table in the dining room, while he read the Psalm 133, or gradual canticle of the King David entitled, in a loud voice:

THE BEATITUDE OF BROTHERLY LOVE.

"! Look how good! and how delicious it is!

Living together in harmony!

It is like good oil on the head,

Which descends on the beard, of Aaron,

And it goes down to the edge of their garments;

Like the spray of Hermon,

That descends on the mountains of Zion;

For there the Lord sends his blessing,

And eternal life"

Something really strange had happened, it had been five minutes before the custody told him that he had a visitor, El mar that thought it was Barbarita, had been so happy that he pronounced seeking to be heard by all and said:

--- That woman loves me --- he had expressed full of joy.

He went to the visiting room and without leaving his surprise his emotion increased when he saw her in the distance, there were the two who three months earlier had rejected him and embarrassed him in the presence of strangers, ecstatic at the table waiting for his departure, he was the first to express himself:

----- Oh, what a joy to see them, and what a surprise! How merciful is God, who returns in better condition and circumstances all that was thought lost," said El mar.

---- That's right, we located the facility on the Internet, we made three trips today, we hired a cab but when we entered we needed IDs and then we needed

We had to return twice from here to the city, but in spite of everything, here we are.----- Said Zuly.

---Thank you, I appreciate it.------ Expressed El mar with satisfaction.

----- What happened?----- Lency questioned.

----- It is a long story, Celeste Chaplain, Mark's custody, seeking to benefit she colluded with the city henchmen who had told her that I had fought with them, she went, and let the Yonkers family court judge know, he put an order of protection on her and the child, then the city attorney's office sent her a letter letting her know that what had happened with the henchmen of

There and I, nothing to do with the child, they lifted the order of protection, but they had me pick up the child at the precinct anyway.

---- And then? I question Lency.

---- Then? She attacked, claiming that the boy had seen me beat Barbarita, they put the order of protection back in place and wanted to reinstate my supervised visit. On November 26 last year, I took Barbarita to testify to clear up the false accusation after the department of social service had questioned her, but since her presence was going to throw the conspiratorial slander on the floor, they changed the court to November 3, When I went to the family court they told me that they had transferred the case to the criminal court, when I appeared in the criminal court they had fabricated a case for me with a guaran te, she had alleged that I had called her a whore's daughter, that false allegation was enough for them to understand that I had violated an alleged court order, they made a notification that I never received, but that they took it for granted and that is why they made me the guaran te that induced them to lock me up, and so on. --- He said.

El mar expressed everything to her with luxurious details, then told her that he had expressed his innocence to the judge from the very first moment, and that that day she claimed as

The fact that he had insulted her was not true because he was in the company of Barbarita, and she alleged that the incident had happened in front of the elevator, when it could not be possible because frequently in that place there was always a desk occupied by a court guard, so, if those allegations had been true, he would have been arrested at that very moment, none of that had happened.

On that occasion El Mar had been sent to prison for nine days, then they took him out on the condition that he attend a drug program without being a drug addict and one of violence without being violent, and then one of alcohol without being an alcoholic, to fulfill the requirements of the system he followed up on everything so when they did the urine test and found out that he was clean of all the judge's assumptions they had to withdraw him, however there was a predisposition to criminalize him, they had no intention of letting him leave the court unharmed.

At the time it was believed that those in power feared being displaced by the great masses of undocumented minorities that had populated paradise and the entire kingdom, and that there was a discriminatory disposition with the minority sectors refusing to legalize their immigration status, and obstructing those who had managed to legalize themselves, could not become citizens and for that they resorted to dirtying his tracks under any allegation or pretext that the tyrants considered viable for that purpose, and in the case of El mar that had dared to confront the provisions of the system, they were looking for an urgent reason to justify themselves, and now the opportunity had presented itself to present it as violent, and the one that was not easily left, had decided to confront it, so the conspirators had decided to violate the law to justify their purposes.

----- What happened now?" questioned Zuly.

----- I sent them a letter saying that I didn't need that program because I am not violent, and since they tried to impose it by force and I refused, they locked me up again.----- He expressed El mar.

----- But what do they want?" asked Lency.

----- Everything is clear, Lency, they want to satisfy their false ego, the first two lawyers and the third one assigned by the court have committed a series of irregularities, such as not intentionally going to court to represent me in order to lengthen my time and make me desperate to have to accept a plea of guilty.

El mar.

---- Don't worry, the blame for all this you've been through is due to Celeste Chaplain, she'll pay for everything you've done, life will take its toll, leave the boy to her, when he grows up he'll look for you.----- Lency argued.

El mar told him about the dream she had with the boy where he finally had a hunch that he and Mark would meet again one day.

----- Guided by the dreamlike warnings, sooner or later Mark and I will move together again," he said.

------ I hope so.----- Lency said and added: ---- Now we will go, we have left a cab waiting for us outside.---- He said.

---- We're going to leave you twenty dollars in your account, we don't have any more, ---- Zuly expressed.

----- It's okay, you don't have to worry, if you are going to leave it ask for a receipt. --- El mar warned him.

----- All right, write to us at p. o. box 116 in the city, and send us to tell you what we should do.

---- All right, thank you, I will.

They said goodbye with kisses on the cheek and hugs, when they left, El mar went back to J-1, from where he dialed Barbarita's number with the same mechanism as always, and left her a small message warning her of Lency and Zuly's visit.

Later El Mar went to the religious services, then the priest allowed him a two-minute call where he managed to contact Barbarita:

----- Hi Barbarita, how could you hear in the message that you left, you didn't come to see me, but God brought Lency, and Zuly --- said El mar.

----- I'm glad they've made up, the families shouldn't be angry about misunderstandings, but I talked to cousin Margarita and told her what was going on, looking for them to find out.---- Clarified Barbarita.

----- I know, they told me, you try to come on Wednesday.

----- I can't, my children didn't go to school today and they can't miss it," added Barbarita.

MARIANO MORILLO B. Ph.D.

THE TYRANTS OF PARADISE

--- Well, if that's the case, show up when you can, hopefully on the 15th you'll be in court --- said El mar.

---- Which one to the family or the criminal? --- Barbarita asked.

---- It's obvious, it's a family case, but they who have pretended to play with my head moved it to the court that defines them as criminals invested with power, go to that court, Lency and Zuly are going.

---- All right, I'll go," answered Barbarita.

---- Now I have to leave you, because they are waiting for the phone, kisses, goodbye.

----- Goodbye --- she answered barbarita as she hung up the phone.

When El Mar passed the phone to the aspirant on duty, he did not fail to thank the priest with great praise, and even let the prelate know that his patience was only equaled

to that of Christ, since he was a priest so different from others in the ministry, that more than priests, they seemed to be possessed by demons, the priest smiled and questioned:

---- because of demons?....

---- El mar answered.

The priest smiled, but nothing more was added, they shook hands, he looked like a priest in favor of the theory of liberation, El mar retired to the J-1 dormitory.

CHAPTER 29

— On the last Saturday in May, the temperature exceeded sixty degrees, the sun with its enormous brilliance was defiant.

The press reported a headline that was on the front page, alluding to a crossfire in the city where racism became the alphabet to be combined.

A black policeman in civilian clothes had discovered that a criminal had broken the glass of one of the windows of his car with the intention of robbing him, when the thief felt discovered he ran away, causing the affected officer to chase him with the gun in his hand.

At that precise moment, an undercover patrol of the anti-crime unit, composed of three white police officers, had arrived at the scene of the crime. Immediately, giving free rein to their imaginations, they interpreted that the black officer who was chasing the thief was another criminal, firing six shots at him, taking his life away from the act.

The officer sacrificed by the biased bullets had just come off duty, which had caused him to wear civilian clothes.

What had happened had caused a stir in the community, where even the Protestant church at the time was motivated to demand justice through a reverend of the Afro community, asking for a federal investigation to determine what possibility there was that those six shots were produced by an action of racial intolerance. The black agent had been shot in the left arm and in the chest, and although he had been taken to the hospital on his arrival he had been declared dead.

Tensions had begun to rise in the various lines of paradise, the crisis had increased crime again and many times it became safer for the family to stay at home than to walk the streets.

Tensions from outside reached the interior of Vengala, either through the written or televised press, or by new prisoners who had recently entered, with new criminal stories, straining the nerves of those who had been locked up in the prison for some time.

That day, at approximately six o'clock in the afternoon, a custody contingent arrived, searching the prisoners' belongings and confiscating some properties that they understood should not be in their possession; after those left, the barber appeared whose presence caused a tremendous commotion, when all wanted to use the same shift to be attended by him, first there were frictions, which later would generate altercations.

Condorito, a skinny young man of small stature who, when speaking, sounded like a man, was the first to try to disturb the order, because a list of shifts had been drawn up in order of arrival for the haircut, but as a condorito, as small as his name expressed it, had already become accustomed to anarchy and disrespect, trying to call attention, who knows whether voluntarily or by order, tried to deprive El mar of its turn, which led to that although passive, it was specified by the precise tensions of the day to demand their rights .

－－－－－ Hey, kiddo, haven't you learned to respect your elders?

The little condor, pretending not to know with whom El mar was speaking, sat down on the chair and looked at the different sides before answering with another question:

－－－－ Hey daddy, who are you talking to?

－－－ I'm talking to your spectrum －－－－－ El mar answered.

－－－－ You explained that I don't understand you. Replied Condorito.

－－－－ Don't do that, you know what I'm talking about, the turn you want to use is mine, so get down from there and don't get dressed you're not going, look at the notebook to see which name is at the top of the list.

－－－－ Mine." Replied Condorito with a voice as low as thunder.

－－－ Of course yours, because after I signed up you put it on top of mine and out of line, right? －－－ said El mar while holding his arm and made him get out of the chair, taking the turn they wanted to usurp him, little condor in front of the truth did nothing but keep silent, he retired to his cubicle and did not come out again until El mar was over, and when it was his turn.

Some hours later, when all had retired to his cubicle, Condorito, possessed by a fit of pride, began to provoke El mar to the extent that it almost lost its equanimity, and tired of tolerating it, he jumped on the wall, squaring himself like a cat ready to jump over it, but at the moment of a voice he stopped it:

－－－－－ EEEhh, El mar, you do not convert, there is a camera and you have no case, they are conspiring to find you one, leave it to me.

It had come up unexpectedly, at the moment of the discussion he was not around, and long before Condorito reacted the mole had already given him a punch that staggered him, when the mole tried to advance on him, Condorito went ahead of him, opened his arms and as the one asking for mercy said:

– – – – Ya Topo, leave it there, if the guards find out they'll drag us to the box," said Condorito with a certain amount of fear.

– – – – Let it be Mole, – – – Said El mar satisfied – – – That the dog doesn't always bite as it barks, "and it's not the same to call the Devil as to see him coming" – – – He added.

– – – – – All right, Condorito, don't go overboard with El mar again, or you'll get weighed down.

– – – – – Aaaah, are you threatening me?

– – – – – – Take it however you want, and don't forget that the one who asked for the truce was you, I don't care about the box or the turtles. – – – – – The Mole emphasized.

– – – – I asked for a truce but I don't mind killing a dog. – – – – Externally, Condorito was emboldened.

– – – – The only dog here is your dwarf.

– – – – – Yeah, leave that alone so you don't attract the attention of the custody.

At that moment, as if moved by the movements of their lips, the custodian got up and advanced to where they were. However, the custodian did not go after them, he simply moved around to do the routine check of the different phones, but when he approached them, they remained silent.

The guards were called every half hour to dial a code on the phones located at different points in the dormitory, as a way of letting the headquarters know the conditions in which the levels of controls in their jobs were developed, if they did not do so in the stipulated time, then appeared the specialized brigade called "the turtles", to confirm the conditions of service, was

One way for the headquarters to know if the custody on duty had not been attacked or kidnapped by the prisoners.

The quarrel between the condorito and the mole had gone unnoticed because when it happened, the bulk of the population was still in the dining room watching television and only El mar and they were in the area of the cubicles, where the altercation had taken place, besides everything had happened very fast, so fast that nobody outside of them could have known about it.

On the other hand, the written and televised press vehemently reported the discovery of Professor Makrowki who had taken over the direction of the Institute of Biological Sciences of the Graduate School. After the secret experiment with the lawyer Royer Vitine, more experiments were conducted than yes, the fourth power had realized that in honor of those successful results, a campaign of praise for the professor had begun.

An article with a color photo of him occupying the center of the tabloid explained that "recently it had been proven that a formula that even some time ago produced catalepsy prolonged for a maximum of ten days in dogs and cats, had developed for a month in the body of human beings.

Professor Makrowki had found a new home within the institute where he spent most of his time and where he often met with the advanced chemistry students, who came to the institute's laboratory to receive practical proof of theory and where he and Miss Makwinsy, who had been hired on his recommendation for his assistant, often met once a week to facilitate the demonstrations for the students.

Ms. Makwinsy had achieved a better salary at the Institute than at the hospital, so now she felt very comfortable working with Makrowki, during the practice she was in charge of supplying the chemicals that the students would use to mix in their verification of the theories, and from where controversial results of the theory used to come out

Applied, although the students did not always understand the particular premises and it was unsuccessful to turn theory into fantasy.

Professor Makrowki, on the other hand, stressed the need for them to resort to concentration and cunning in order to get their research under way.

The professor frequently recommended the method of spectroscopy where there was no danger of absorbing radioactive waste or being influenced by X-rays by resorting to particle accelerators, so when he spoke of death he used to explain that in fact there was no need to fear it since the matter that made up human beings were eternal branches, that from a scientific point of view, death was nothing more than the transmutation of the being through atomic particles reorganized among themselves, so he went on to explain what quantum physics was, and many of his students understood it as a fundamental premise that sooner or later would reinforce the concerns of their learning.

Sunday, May 31st was the last day of the month. El mar had chosen him to fast for freedom, in fact, on June 3rd he would serve two months of confinement and he was already uncomfortable with spending time being innocent, added to that was the harassment of those who had embraced crime as a career in their existence, and who had chosen to serve the purposes of ignorance, which every day induced them to provoke those who refused to dance their dances.

They could not tolerate that El mar seemed to be different, refusing to practice what the system promoted, which was nothing but violence, delinquency and intolerance.

That day early in the morning, around five o'clock, he had begun a fast offering it to the God of his being, followed by the ascending reading of the biblical psalms, he asked the God of his being that in the same way that he took Zuly and Lency respectively, in the same way he hoped that for the next 15th of June, he granted him freedom, for he missed his family, and he more than any other knew that this prison he was passing through was not for the correction of his spirit, but for the wickedness of those who thought themselves masters of soul and life, and who through their ignorance did not understand

That this free will they brought assigned to their lives was to glorify and liberate, not to condemn and enslave, they did not understand that the trials of the spirit glorified the soul.

From that morning until 4:30 p.m., El mar was praying, God was taking care of his family but his spirit was beginning to demand that he leave that place.

El mar understood the way things had been given, and the decision of his freedom after God was in the hands of the lawyer and the judge, but above all he was very much aware that God had the last word, especially when men exercised evil through their free will.

Something strange had happened, it turned out that even though El mar was far from where the lawyer Vitini had undergone the catalepsy test, El mar had experienced a dreamlike experience similar to the one he had had, He dreamed that he and Barbarita were in an apartment where a naked man appeared who had gone to leave him a document. El mar laughed at that little man who had the particularity of possessing a smaller than traditional penis and asked Barbarita who that man was that he was the brother of the father of her first children.

Three days later when El Mar called Barbarita, she found herself crying because the father of her first two children, taking advantage of El Mar's confinement, had begun a process to seek custody of his children, all with the purpose of harming the one he saw as a rival, had been contacted by the conspirators who had taken advantage of his undocumented status to manipulate him in order to create testimony against El Mar, Thus, in addition, they had begun to force Barbarita's will that she was somewhat disconcerted when she found out that the social service department was after her, so her ex-husband had tried to give her a court summons on more than one occasion, without her daring to open the door, so when El mar called her and asked her how she was, she answered:

----- Bad, I'm very bad," she said, as she felt her crying through the earpiece.

She explained that her ex-husband had taken her to court, that perhaps he had sent her to the Department of Social Service, that she did not know what was happening, and that she had told him that she was saddened.

---- Go to the police and explain to them what is happening, maybe they will keep him away from you until everything is clear.

- - - - All right, I'll do it. Barbarita said with a humility not often seen in her.

El mar would have liked to follow the conversation, but since he was using an operation called "three Way" which consisted of someone who had access to that service calling someone who put their handset on hold while dialing another number of a third party who would participate in the conversation, that same process was used for the conversation, so they had to leave the line free for the owners to talk freely, However, sometimes they gave him the opportunity and when the first one dialed the second one and the second one dialed the third one which in that case was Barbarita that when answering the phone the one who answered on the other side of the line was El mar, and they talked until the operator of the company that provided the phone service to the prison, discovered it and dropped the call, many times leaving the conversation between them inconclusive.

Two days later, it was Wednesday, June 3, when El mar was no longer expecting anyone to visit him, when he had begun to resign himself to living without Barbarita, who after the conflict with her ex-husband and the emissaries of the Department of Social Service had begun to move away, was being more absorbed, he felt that she was putting other things above him, and he thought that something was happening and that perhaps because she didn't care, she had decided not to tell him anything.

When El mar entered the visiting room and looked, he found no face of what he thought had come to visit him, so he looked into a corner and discovered Juny, she was the best friend of Zuly, his niece, but he did not imagine that she would lend her presence to a circumstance of that nature.

When Juny saw him enter, she waved her hand so that El mar could discover the table she was occupying. He made a gesture of surprise when he noticed that only she was occupying that table, so he approached her by walking in the direction where he had seen her sitting:

- - - - Hi Juny! I thought you'd be here any minute and look at you. He said hello to her with a kiss on the cheek, while Juny smiled at herself. Then she tried to justify her presence.

- - - - How have you been?

- - - You can see here locked up What about you? - - - He questioned El mar.

- - - - Me? Well, thank you.

El mar wondered curiously throughout the room as if trying to explain the presence of Juny, who, noticing his restlessness, said:

- - - - Only I could get in, lency is outside, she forgot to bring a proof of address and that's why she was prevented from entering.

 - - - - But how could he forget her when she knew where he was coming from and had already been here last week?" argued El mar as he managed to get in with one of the hall's guards to see if they would facilitate his entry, who dialed a telephone number with some affability, and although he showed interest in talking to the sergeant, he failed to locate him.

Zuly and Barbarita are going to court. Your ex-husband wants to take custody of the children, so he said you were hitting the children, both his and yours. That's why the city is threatening to take your children away from you as well," Juny said with a certain ceremonial act.

Although El mar was characterized by a certain serenity, at the moment of hearing that expression, he could not fake his restlessness.

He tried again to see if they would let Lency into their presence, but all efforts had been unsuccessful.

---- Now I understand why there is so much violence in this nation, it's that as Balzac said, "the bureaucracy is a giant managed by dwarves", this is an organized anarchy, look at Esteve's brigand showing itself as the rat inside, comes to accuse me of mistreating those children, look how that animal slanders me, precisely knowing that I am locked up in this place, I knew something was going on, behind that mystery of Barbarita, investigate to see if she gave cause for that guy to proceed that way.--- said El mar with some disappointment.

---- He sent Lency to say that she received her tax refund, that money is available if she wants to pay for a lawyer," Juny said.

----- It's not worth it, this is a plot against me, to pay a lawyer is to give him the chance to steal the money, everything has been planned to be generated the way it has happened, anyway tell Zuly to get in touch with a "Baild bond" to see if she can get ten percent of five thousand dollars, so that I can get out with a thousand dollars or less after someone signs, then I try to locate a litigator who I can watch, so that he won't sell to me.

Anyway, let them wait until June 15 when I go back to court to see if they will let me go without bail," said El Mar.

------ All right, I'll give him his message, I'll be right out.

----- All right Juny, thanks for coming.

They said goodbye with a hug and watched her walk away.

When Juny came out, something unexpected came up, one of the visitors introduced her hand under the table she was occupying by subtracting from her vagina a deflated balloon containing some little bags that looked like cocaine, and folding her head down she introduced it inside

Her mouth, in violation of the rules of the visit, however, could only be noticed when she kissed her companion as she passed from her mouth to his.

Her beau who had tried to reciprocate had tried to swallow it, having choked on his throat causing a surprising coughing fit, followed by uncontrollable nausea that had caused him to vomit, which immediately spread between the table and the floor, splashing those who were in the vicinity, which led to the mobilization of the ninjas, the suspension of visits and the immediate evacuation of those visitors who were still in the hall.

Furthermore, after arresting the emissary who had introduced the apparent narcotics into the prisoner's mouth, he was taken to the clinic where he was given some electric shocks until he returned the deflated balloon containing the controlled substances. They collected it by placing it in a transparent plastic bag and the substance was taken to the laboratory with him, he kept complaining while the girl was left locked in one of the cells of the prison precinct.

She had been held until the laboratory result was determined to be transferred to the court, where the charges and sentence would be determined.

El mar and the other prisoners had recently been evicted from the visiting room, so that they could not see the ninjas from the front, so they had been forced to kneel with their faces facing the wall and their hands on their heads and their legs crossed backwards for a period of more than half an hour, And when they could no longer support their arms up, they would bend their backs, bringing their heads to the ground so they could rest while the turtles continued their emergency transfer of the daring prisoner hanging by his elbows to the clinic, moaning in pain.

That foolish, perverse and daring prisoner, who had dared to defy the system, trying to distribute the drugs to the inmates of the prison, was none other than the rascal, the joker, the nice and superb Mole, who had made violence and drugs a challenge, and whom the turtles had begun to consider dangerous,

Because even though he had a minimal age of 22, he fought hand-to-hand with some guards as a warrior trained for the cause,

El Topo had grown up with Doña Sila, a single mother who also operated as a father, and who had managed to subdue him until he was fourteen, managing to get him to the 12th grade of high school, but who in turn was tempted by the need for luxury and the vanities of young people his age.

He never had a father by his side to serve as an example for him to follow, and whom he finally wanted to accept as his father, had been his mother's fifth adventure, and when she disappeared he left without saying goodbye to her but left him a note that said

"I have not told your mother that I am leaving, because I want to avoid seeing the pain in her face, but I cannot deceive you, you are my friend and I love you as my son, however I would never be a good father to you, continue your studies and take care of your mother.

I am a fugitive from justice, and persecuted by sectors that want my life, keep my secret as a gentleman's agreement, do not say anything to your mother, if you ever need anything go to the following address:

Alto del prado # 18, santa Rosa; you look in your bed's drawer, if you find something it is because you belong, attentively, to the Gladiator.

By that time the Mole was 14 years old and so desperate was he that he felt that this farewell would be forever, and so a week later, the press spread the news that the dangerous drug-trafficker gladiator had succumbed to the bullets of the police, with whom he had held a gunfight when he was discovered to be underhand, refusing to lay down his arms and give himself up.

Peacefully, they also said that his body would be used for scientific study at Santa Rosa State University.

When the information appeared in the press, Mrs. Sila refused to believe it, she had lived for more than five years next to that man and never found out about the

Gravity of his conflicts, he thought that in that nation there was such a profound hermeticism that even people who lived and shared with each other,

sometimes they used to be real strangers.

In spite of their disappointment they kept a month of mourning where both cried comforting each other, the Gladiator had rarely told him about his relatives, and when he did, he only mentioned his childhood with his parents who had died precisely when he was ten years old, being forced to grow up and survive in a children's home from where he had escaped to emigrate and they never heard from him again until he was indoctrinated by one of the drug cartels, becoming a weighted drug dealer.

A month after the end of the mourning, the Mole checked the drawers of his bed and something surprised him, there was what would be his treasure and patrimony, the Gladiator had left him a reward of ten thousand dollars, which he did not hesitate to share with his mother.

- - - - I promised not to tell you anything, but he is already dead, you can know that.

Doña Sila took the writing in her hands, with one hand she pressed it in the upper corner and with the other in the lower one, and read with the consecration of a blessed woman who was seeking salvation behind the pages of a bible, concluded her intense reading she replied:

- - - - - Why didn't you tell me this before? Perhaps I would be alive." Doña Sila expressed with a hint of exasperation.

- - - - - Mom, I promised not to say anything, he asked me, he trusted me. I'm telling you now because there's no point in keeping secrets anymore, look,

Showing her the open bundle that contained the ten thousand dollars so that she could visualize the content.

---- And where did you get that? Sila questioned with some trepidation.

--- You read the note, that's what he told me to look for in my bed drawer, I counted them and they are ten thousand large --- said the Mole with some joy.

----- It's a lot of money, what are you going to do with it?

----- I'm going to do some business, first I have to see who lives at the address

left me.----- He stated with fortitude.

---- We will go," Sila said.

----- No mom, I'll go, you can't neglect your work. -He said.

----- But you're just a kid, you're still a minor --- he specified.

----- Mom, don't worry, I can take care of myself, I'm a big boy now, and I'm the man of the house.

---- But boy....

----- Mom please stop calling me kid, look here is five thousand for you, keep it or do with it what you want, mine five are for my business.

----- And what kind of business do you want to do?

----- I don't know yet, I have to think about it, but don't worry it will be a business

Lucrative --- he said.

Three days after that conversation, the Mole traveled to the address provided by the Gladiator, meeting one who had been related to him for many years.

He spoke to him with details about him, and above all he was welcomed with familiarity, he affirmed that he was known by references because whenever they met with the Gladiator, he

The first thing that came up was the conversation about the Mole, who was flattered and could not hide his vanity.

After that empathy, the mole warned his mother not to wait for him, for a while because he was going to start a job, she wanted to oppose him but he didn't listen to her and stayed some time with the people of the Gladiator, where he learned the juggling arts of the illegal drug trafficking, the men of the Gladiator admired his intelligence, so it was easy for him to interrelate.

He had begun to traffic from the Pacific to the border of the kingdom, and by the age of 18 he was already involved in white slavery and wholesale cocaine trafficking until he became the symbol of the Gladiator's men; By that time he accumulated money that he didn't know he would make with it, but having it where they did the business, in an outing he made to visit his mother who had been very sick, in a government raid where the men of the Gladiator fell prisoners, they found drugs, and the money of the Mole in the place, taking over everything, It was when he decided to abandon Santa Rosa and stay in paradise, forced by Sila's death, that he was now left alone, and although he understood that most of the profits from drug trafficking go into the hands of the government, he didn't care, and went back into the business, starting over from the bottom.

On one occasion, while he was in one of the counties of Paradise, in a business selling clothes and communications items, he had two more people accompany him, but just one of those days two assailants appeared and tried to strip him of his possessions, one of them hit him on the back of the head, leaving him lying there, and the main partner who had gotten hold of a gun and had it where the Mole could find it, and given the ease of access,

When the Mole was able to stand up, let's say it was in a fraction of a second, he took hold of the gun and with it in his hands he went after his executioners, who before the speed of that reaction had been forced to separate, taking one on one side and running the other, in another direction.

The mole had fired more than one projectile, without managing to reach them, and one of the assailants who had met a lady on his way to buy time by pretending to be the victim said:

----- Ma'am, I called the police, they want to kill me and they are chasing me," she said.

 The lady had been so impressed that she called the police right away.

While watching the Mole and his friends board a silver-gray European model car, the lady noticed that the gun had come off the right pocket of his pants, the Mole had lost the gun with which he had fired the shots, so it was easy to identify them, when the police arrived.

When they became aware of the police presence, they saw her enter through a one-way street, which the woman took advantage of to approach them aware that for every illegal firearm reported, whoever did so would receive a reward.

----- Help, police.--- she shouted--- Here's a gun, a gun.--- She said.

Before that exasperated expression, the patrol stopped and ipso facto proceeded with the investigation, taking advantage of a pre-established law for that time, the woman for such Azaña would receive a five thousand dollar reward.

The Mole and his henchmen were arrested for illegal possession of firearms, the first were set bail of ten thousand, another five thousand, and the Mole 50,000, however he as always managed to get away with it, the store owner appeared who confessed that the gun was his, and that he used it to protect himself from assailants in the store.

In his early years, the Mole had lived an accelerated life full of adventures. At the age of twelve, he had attended a farm on one of those school experience trips, separating from the group and going around breaching an urgent dust of two of the young   teachers who were part of the group, who had gotten lost in the bushes, discovering the glory of the longed-for suffering of the one who, as a victim, asked more than what seemed to the Mole to be the torture of an abusive victim, a masochistic victim,

He became so distracted that he did not see a scorpion that had fallen from one of the bushes and was stinging him somewhere on his body.

When the professors noticed, the Mole was already shaking and foaming at the mouth, in his delirium the Mole saw a virgin who rather resembled the Virgin Mary of La Altagracia, patroness of faith in the central Caribbean, leading him to a place where they were to find the only doctor in the area.

The vehicle in which they were transporting him had run out of gasoline and a truck passed by, which two of the teachers boarded, concerned about the condition of the young man.

In his hallucination he kept seeing the virgin floating and guiding him to the place where the doctor would be, until they arrived at a place, where there was only one house inhabited by an alcoholic, the doctor, was an elderly man who had lost his license because

Drunk, and at risk of being accused, he was forced to provide emergency assistance, trying to save the Mole.

A mysterious force guided his hands to locate the place of the sting, and where fortunately he was able to apply in time an indigenous antidote to block the infection, since neither medicines were available in the surroundings, nor were there any means to go and get it in the city.

From that day on, the Mole grew up with the belief that he had indeed been reborn. The night before, before the turtles carried him hanging from his elbows, he had dreamt that he was a married man and that his wife was wearing a pair of pants so tight to her body that he induced someone to have the audacity to compliment her with malice and that he for the honor was motivated and hit   the individual, who wanting to react caused him to start shooting using two guns until they were completely discharged, at which time he woke up in anguish and with a terrible desperation.

He took a deep breath, when he discovered that it had been nothing more than a simple bad taste nightmare.

 The Mole sometimes used to talk in his sleep, because of those circumstances of life, he warned those who slept around him, to move him if they heard him talk, not to say something he would have to regret.

 He knew his main faults and was looking for the best way to hide them.

The Mole at that time was going through a certain convalescence, he thought he could swallow the balloon without inflating it more easily than other times.

Since he entered the prison of vengeance he wanted to establish his business, and he succeeded because he gave the number of his identification card to his clients who told their relatives to deposit the amount of their debt with the mole in that account.

to the hospital, and I still didn't know what the extension time would be because it was all based on the purity levels that the drug would bring.

In spite of everything, he knew in his heart that nothing would be so serious since he had made sure that those who sent the "material" to him in prison cut it to such a degree that if something like what had happened that day happened, that when it was analyzed in the laboratory, because of the cuts, they could not reach evidence that would add to his guilt, so as not to add new charges.

Now they had deposited him on a stretcher at the clinic, where they would proceed to pump his stomach preceded by the application of a serum after the wash.

 They kept him under observation for three days, gave him a $25 contravention, and released his friend because the contents of what was believed to be evidence was nothing more than bagged-up baking soda, not cocaine as the officers initially believed.

CHAPTER 30

— That night when the turtles had brought the prisoners to their knees, he boasted to a group of them, one of the guards who used to work at J-1, that she was one of the officers who was among the ninjas, who had performed that afternoon, and to make himself even more infamous he was heard to say:

– – – – So much so, that some of the residents of J-1 saw me, and trying to justify their confession, he took advantage of the fact that El mar was passing through the corridor and called him and asked him in front of everyone with the intention of having him confirm what she was saying.

– – – – How can I be of service to you, Officer Carol?

– – – – They don't believe I was present this afternoon among the Ninja Turtles.

– – – – If you say so, there's no doubt about it, I can't confirm it, I didn't see anything. -El mar answered skillfully, in case she was indirectly trying to get some information out of him.

– – – – Didn't you see anything? Who told you to turn your face to

the wall – – – he questioned.

– – – – I heard the voice, but at that moment I could not specify who had given the order.

– – – – But I was there... or wasn't I? He insisted on questioning Officer Carol.

– – – – At first I saw that the prisoners had turned their faces to the wall on their knees, I automatically imitated them, then, when everything was over and they asked us to stand up, I

Turning around I saw that you were there, but before that moment I couldn't see anyone's face – – – explained El mar, retiring to her bed, she seemed to be satisfied with the answer.

The reason for the questioning was because a misunderstanding had arisen between two 65-year-old men who were reproducing drawings that adorned the papers the prisoners used to write letters to their families, and between them what is called a competitive belligerence had been unleashed, involving, capturing and retaining clients.

The men used to draw and charge with soup or any foodstuff that would help him survive in prison, so they also sought to persuade their clientele as to which of the two drew best, and which of them should be ordered to do some illustration work.

They had assumed an inappropriate attitude for the gender and had tried to lacerate their faces with the nails, seeing themselves as the custody on duty needed to call the turtles who were waiting for the outcome to angrily burst in to break up the "riot," at the first order of the sergeant, who had entered the dormitory in the company of Officer Carol, to verify what the gravity of the situation was, and among whom the altercation was.

----- Where are the boys from the fight? --- questioned the sergeant, who, seeing that no one responded, turned with a questioning look to the custody on duty who had made the call.

---- It's the ones from cubicle 6 and 3, come on, both of you-- --Screamed the guard.

The two men got up, came out of their hiding place with a hint of shyness, like two intimidated schoolboys who had been sitting on their respective beds advanced towards the sergeant, letting the faces of frightened children show.

When the sergeant's pupils noticed the silhouettes of the spindly, aging characters, he bowed his torso, bent his head and let out a thunderous laugh of mockery.

--- The fact is that even the grandparents don't want to behave any more, aren't you ashamed to continue giving bad examples to the younger ones, as you think you can justify yourselves --- questioned the sergeant.

---- I'm sorry, sergeant, he was the one who started out charging a commission that wasn't his, and now he doesn't want to pay me back," said the one in cubicle 6.

----- It's not like that, sergeant, the client was mine, he paid me six soups in advance and I ate it, I had told this gentleman in advance that my client had paid me six soups in advance, and without taking into account my warning he made and delivered the drawing that I had to make, then when he moved out, the client told him that I had the money, the soups, this gentleman is pressuring me to pay him, whose fault is it?

---- All right, let's get this over with, you're packing up and moving out----- The sergeant told the one in cubicle 6 with determination.

While number six was packing another prisoner had dared to ask Officer Carol why she was walking with the turtles, so she sought to justify herself by revealing that she had been in training all day, because she had been transferred to that unit.

That had been the real reason she had tried to get confirmation from El mar, which was a reliable voice among the prisoners.

The turtles, as they used to call it back then, were a team specialized in prison riots. They owed their name to their relationship with the clothes they used to wear, they had some armored protectors adorned with a tester that produced electric shocks.

That night, as always, El Mar dreamed that he was walking down a street dragging a cardboard box with a detached bottom, he had entered a social service building where there was a group of social workers who discussed assistance cases with clients, and talked about the documents required for the qualification of those interested in having a public assistance case opened. When he opened the entrance door to the office where he was going, he found a white woman with a honey colored eye facing him who was questioning him:

– – – – Do you remember me?

He stared at her as if trying to decipher her essence, and discovered that her blonde hair matched her olive green eyes, but he also noticed that she was pregnant, he recognized her, he had met a girlfriend from the past, with a slight difference: in her puberty years she had the eyes of a sea blue and at that time showed him mended, which became olive green, without dissimulation he felt a disturbing curiosity to question her, then he asked her:

– – – – How many children do you have?

With a joking smile she responded with the utmost coolness:

– – – – I have nine.

The applicants who were at the ranch were gawking and blushing but celebrating the response, they commented:

– – – – There is no doubt that you are a settler of the world, with nine you form a team to play, a platoon to fight, and a chorus of various voices to praise the Lord," said one of those present.

It had been several days since the Mole incident, it was Sunday and everyone was resting in bed.

The Mole at that time was reflecting on the trials of life, and how he at his age had lived so close to danger that it seemed like a joke to him.

He remembered the gladiator fondly and without realizing that he was thinking aloud, he said:

– – – – Thanks gladio, you inspired me to be a man and you vanished from me, fearing that I would follow in your footsteps, yet here I am with the mark of destiny, who said that what is prescribed to happen is to be avoided? What you feared the most was the easiest thing that happened and here I am giving you honor.

Well expressed by El marsoned, rotten tree that is born never kills a crocodile.

He remembered his wanderings with Lazaro Osorio whom he had accidentally seen on the esplanade on Saturday and the kind of camaraderie they still used to manifest:

– – – –hey, thief, what are you doing here?– – – I had shouted at him to say hello.

– – – – The same as your delinquent– – – – Lazarus had answered him.

Both had placed their hands on their arms and danced in a circle celebrating that encounter, they had remembered their years of mischief, mainly that day when they had to leave together in search of a supposed "purity" as they used to call cocaine, to express that it was of quality, without cut and without mixture.

That day they had gone to a place where there was a window where he introduced his arm as a technique of the supplier of not letting his face be seen, and on that occasion it was the turn of the Mole who was holding in his hand four hundred dollars to pay for the order, feeling that with great care someone had received it from inside, however they had spent a few minutes waiting, with tension, without being given the goods they had paid for.

They had decided to go inside to find out why the delay, suddenly discovering that they had been swindled, found the apartment empty and with the back door open, going into the courtyard of the building they found that someone was trying to escape terribly.

Going out into the street, they followed him and saw him get into a black car, hurrying away, just as they were getting ready to go on after him, they saw someone else get off the escape ladder of the building.

A nickel-plated 25-caliber pistol in their hands strengthened their instinct, they ran after the last ruffian trying to catch him, and before walking very far they managed to capture him, rubbing the barrel over his temples and ipso facto discovering that the ruffian had urinated.

– – – Hand over the goods, condemned or not, you will not have time to count them – – – the threatening mole shouted at him.

– – – – I don't know anything, the one who left in the black car is the one who took the money, he's my friend, I was just watching, don't kill me because I don't know anything. – – – – The trapped man shouted shakily.

– – – – All right, come with us and take us to where he lives, or else you are a dead man. Lazaro Osorio warned him by holding him by the forearms.

– – – – All right, come on, but don't kill me.

They let themselves be guided by their hostage, they walked through the dusty streets of an impoverished sector of the city, they stopped in front of a building where the black car they were looking for had been seen, from the front of the area it seemed that the building where they were taking refuge was abandoned, they indicated to the hostage to knock on the door, a voice answered him from inside:

– – – – Who?

– – – It's me, open up – – – said the hostage.

Once he recognized the voice, the outlaw inside opened without realizing it, the facade of the building was old and the door had no viewfinder, so when he opened, before he could react, while the mole was holding the hostage, Lazarus took over the

A swindler, he put his hands in the bag, and there were the four hundred dollars, which had been taken from him a few minutes before.

- - - - Take what you want and don't kill us," said the Hustler.

- - - - We should do it so that they respect... We are going to give them a chance, but if the action is repeated, they will die.- - - - Lazarus warned him.

He was taken to an interior room and repeated:

- - - - Don't come out until you count to a hundred because if you try to follow us you know what you're risking.

They left with all possible caution, boarded the car and left the scene.

The Mole smiled with a certain mischief and from one thought to another, and he also remembered what had happened that same day without rules or truce, after having recovered the money as we all know at gunpoint, they went to Wanda, a girlfriend at the time, and together with her they found their friend Brenda, who decided to join the tour.

From there, they went to another dark place, far away from the population, they stopped in one place, while Wanda and Brenda waited in the car, Lazarus and the Mole entered a building, an amazing structure, they walked along the corridor to the end where they went up a staircase to the second floor, stopping at the 2K apartment where they knocked on the door.

They felt a current of air coming from under the crevice and heard someone move the hand of the

Visitor while looking outside, who was moving from inside pulled the door towards him, leaving it stuck to a chain that only showed a strip, from where the supplier looked with suspicion and somewhat alarmed asked referring to Lazarus:

- - - - Who is he? I told you not to bring me any strangers, please, Mole.

- - - - Calm down Chori, he is not unknown, he is Lazaro Osorio, my assistant, I bring him to meet you in case one day I can't come.

- - - - Well, that's okay, your thing is done - - - He told her, showing half his face through the crack in the door, still not undoing the chain, the Mole gave her the rolled-up money, Chori walked away from the door, and at once he returned with a paper bag containing a pound of cocaine, which the Mole caught with his fingertips and which he ipso fato tried by putting his thumb on his tongue.

- - - - Are you sure this isn't Copris, is this pure pun?

---- Mole, even the question is foolish, you know that my stuff is good, I don't sell garbage, I know that you want it pure to cut it, the only one who cuts the merchandise with copris and crazy drugs is you Mole.--- He said something irritated.

---- Calm down Chori, it's not a big deal, you're very nervous... Okay, see you later. --- Said the Mole.

The bag was inserted into the left pocket of the coat and they came out:

---- I saw you squeeze it between your fingers, why?

If I rub it and it disappears it is pure, and if I rub it and it doesn't disappear it is mixed with copris.---- Expressed the Mole.

---- Topo, what a criminal you are, you have become a master of banditry!" answered Lazarus in admiration and with a certain amount of respect.

---- You don't have to praise me, I'm going to pay you your money anyway, even if you don't praise me. said the Mole mischievously.

They advanced to the vehicle where Brenda and Wanda were waiting, the Mole placed the narcotics under the carpet of the car, and they began to return to the den where he would verify the content acquired.

Halfway through the road at an intersection, the mole behind the wheel tended to get distracted by crossing a red light that attracted the presence of a hidden patrol car, whose unit was made up of two agents of mistaken sexual preference, who, following behind them with the siren on, induced them to stop and made them get out of the car.

Something happened that rationalized the souls of those lesbians behind a police uniform, and being able to desire more than duty, without having to ask for reinforcement they locked the four of them in a checkpoint that had been built for such purposes in the vicinity.

They exchanged some opinions between the two before Wanda and Brenda were taken out, to which they had whispered in her ear, signifying the purpose.

---- Mole, these women are lesbians, they're making us fall in love." Wanda told the Mole in her native language, a language the agents didn't understand.

---- Follow the "current" to see if we get out of jail. --- Said the Mole.

---- What are you talking about? He questioned one who was called Chila.

---- No, I was asking my brother if he didn't think you were a beautiful and nice woman.

Chila smiled.

They then left Lazarus and the Mole locked up while they moved with Brenda and Wanda to one of the houses where the agents lived.

They looked like married couples staying in recreational cabins.

---- What about my brothers?

---- Don't worry, beautiful, we'll be up and about before five in the morning, my supervisor and I will find a solution, what matters is that you be good to us and everything will be resolved," said Chila, referring to the other officer.

The officers consumed a large portion of the seized merchandise, the other portion was left in the apartment to be consumed later, and in its place they placed baking soda, which they took to the laboratory with the objective of closing the case for lack of evidence, so that Wanda and Brenda would be satisfied.

When they arrived at the courthouse and called the Mole and Lazaro Osorio in front of the judge, the judge asked the following questions:

---- For what purpose did you possess the evidence seized by the agents?

---- For Our Consumption Mr. Judge---- Replied the Mole with feigned naivety.

---- It's a good thing you answered that, because if I had answered the opposite, you would have been sent to jail for consumer fraud, the case has been dismissed, so the process will not continue, let him go.--- The judge said.

The Mole and Lazaro Osorio went out in camaralenta, as if they were in a wedding march, but when they perceived that they were out of sight of the Judge they

They launched to run, in that way those skillful adventurers got rid of that terrible nightmare.

The Mole had lived so much in such a short time, that all those experiences had been for him like an occupational hazard.

Already when he had turned twelve as a child, he had spoken to an evangelical pastor who was heading a program where they offered five thousand dollars in exchange for every firearm that was voluntarily turned in, and at the moment the mole had appeared for the delivery he showed up with two grenades, and having changed his mind

He refused to hand her over for the sum offered, he wanted twenty thousand, and not wanting to hand her over he threatened to remove the pin from one of her if she did not pay him the sum demanded, at that moment the area was invaded by bomb experts, psychologists and persuasive talkers. In addition to the fact that helicopters flew into the area, war tanks, police armed with machine guns and revolvers, there was a great deal of movement.

Until the pastor managed to persuade him, as he was a minor they wanted to incriminate his mother, but due to the intervention of the Catholic Church that helped with the defense, they managed to avoid prosecution and to take custody of the boy who was interned in a children's home until he was fourteen years old.

After two years they let him return to the house which the mother took advantage of to move to another state, that's when they moved from Chicago to paradise.

By then everything had become a mischief of a spoiled child who had found a dangerous toy in the streets, that was his first criminal experience.

CHAPTER 31

— After what happened between Wanda and Brenda with officers Chica and Nica, certain events occurred that I will not omit so that my venerable readers will not accuse me of being an accomplice.

— Between Chica and Nica there had always been a remarkable camaraderie, now a surprising emptiness had been generated, things would never be what they were, Nica who for many years had worked as her supervisor had necessarily left her, a car accident had taken her life, leaving Chica in deep and restless pain.

— All this had led her to identify herself more and more with Wanda's understanding, they had continued to understand each other since the mole and Lazaro Osorio had been released.

— Chica had openly dedicated herself to offering protection to the Mole who had been interested in moving forward in the drug business by taking advantage of the situation. The Mole at first was upset that his girlfriend was under siege by this escape from male sentiment, but as a cunning man he finally thought it best to continue pretending that he and Wanda were brothers, fearing that a persecution would be unleashed against him if Chica came to know the truth, since for a long time they pretended to be the brothers of parents who only had each other.

— In that drama, it lasted several years until one day, unexpectedly, Chica arrived at the apartment where she shared her life with Wanda, and found that she and the Mole had been fugitives.

— The impression was so great that she could not control herself, and without further ado took her service weapon by shooting herself in the temples.

— That picture tore Wanda's heart to such a degree that she was still attending an intensive care program one year later.

— At the moment of Chica El Topo's suicide, he proceeded as if he had nothing to do with it. With the greatest patience, he called Arturito Ulloa, the new patrol member who had been assigned to Chica, who was also known to them, when Nica died, to go and identify the body, They told him that Chica had entered the house crying and that without saying anything they saw that she had taken out her regulation weapon and shot herself in the temples, as everything happened very quickly to them she did not have time to do anything to avoid it, and Arturito Ulloa did not doubt the sincerity of the confession.

— So that he would not have misunderstood what was said, the mole before Arturito Ulloa arrived at the residence, called Brenda to be present at the time of the declaration and to reinforce the testimony.

— After Arturito Ulloa saw the body of his co-worker, he called the homicide unit of the precinct where they were assigned, and in the blink of an eye, the streets of the neighborhood were flooded with police.

— A year after her recovery, Wanda chose to flee, from the violence generated at that time in paradise by the circulation of narcotics, so she decided to move to Isla Dorada where she remained for most of her life, there she continued studying until she graduated in international relations, met a Frenchman and went to Europe with him, without being heard from again.

— The Mole had achieved a successful record as a strong boy, which the young people around him admired.

— There was the summary history of all the wanderings that the Mole and his cliques had incurred, now he was in Vengala, at the age of 22, trying to redefine his path.

— El Paraíso was a nation with a conservative tone, with a pluralism emanating from a cosmopolitan population, where diverse types of institutions, corporations and ideologically diversified groups operated within a curtain of imperial neoliberalism, with certain "liberties" that some of its inhabitants misinterpreted libertinely in the expression "you must not sin, but if you decide to do so we will punish you.

— At that time, an aphorism prevailed that emanated from the fervor of the population, that "the thief judged by his condition, and the rulers for their purposes, saw in each victim a victimizer who, if he did not agree with their cause, almost always tried to criminalize him by manipulating the facts or fabricating other charges to justify the incriminating legal decisions that the system pre-established to avoid claims for damages, discrimination or harm, and at the same time to sell the image that the decisions of a "please Guilty" were voluntary, not forced.

— During the bidding process in the case of El mar, they once dared to tell him in court:

— - - - "We're going to reduce the charges to the levels of an infraction, which is practically nothing.

— - - - It is good that they reduce a false accusation to nothing, because coming from nothing to nothing there would be no reason to consider imprisonment.

— So before that answer there was a time of Reflection.

— The inhabitants of Paradise were very fearful of radicalism and the excesses of violence in modern times, and throughout its history, outside of the independence feats and civil wars that were generated within its territory, it was never known

— that other nations came to invade it, since the kingdom exported wars to foreign beaches.

— The various acts of violence that occurred or were domestic, misunderstandings between families, or crossfire between police, or actions generated by organized crime, whether gangs or common criminals.

— However, with the arrival of the new era, the twenty-first century, internal violence had increased, generating great controversy and terrorist belligerence, giving rise to two classes of terrorists:

— The conservatives, and the radicals who destroyed lives and properties in will make a relhistoric-ideological cause that induced them to assume missions of self-martyrdom.

— They used to assume their responsibilities by admitting their acts or attacks before public opinion, in order to respond to their objectives.

— On the other hand, conservative terrorists described themselves in the expression as "the kitten of María Ramos, who threw stones and hid hands" because they liked to act behind the scenes, often acting as intellectual authors, rather than mercenaries using assassins who never martyred themselves.

— When they entrusted him with a mission and failed, they were careful not to be identified, because they feared the reactions of public opinion, many times they hid in state institutions and were renowned as state terrorists.

— On Wednesday, June 10, El Mar got up early, shaved, showered and was called to the clinic for a routine check-up.

— They weighed him, took his blood pressure, read the results of the blood and urine tests that had previously been done on him, the results of which were negative and favorable, he had lost twenty pounds, and his diabetes seemed to be more controlled every day.

— After the incident that El mar and officer Caruso had starred in that time, they had not disrespected each other again, however that day, Caruso approached El mar again, this time to inform him that he had a visitor.

— Before that information the doctor tried not to keep him any longer, after he had just informed him of his favorable health conditions, El mar returned to J-1 to pick up the red card that authorized him to come to the visit, and that by the way, once he returned he would have to return it to the custody, because if it was not returned and they found it on him after the hour, they could declare it as contraband and write him a contravention equivalent to twenty-five dollars. Anyway, he went to the visiting room, and once there he met the lawyer Dino J who, although he had not answered the letters from El mar, had received them, attending the summons, one week before June 15, which was when he was assigned the new date to return to court.

— They entered a small room that was on the left side of the visiting room, along with a court interpreter who had arrived with attorney Dino J.

— While they were in there, the lawyer talked to him about what existed in the case that was nothing more than a violation of an order of protection, and that could be reduced to a minor infraction or such as a car, while he was speaking, El mar was silent and listened to him patiently, when he finished speaking El mar applauded him mockingly and told him:

— --- To your ears it is pleasant your speech, but not to mine, if I did not accept to become guilty when I was two weeks old, now that I have completed two months and seven days, less I would accept it, the only negotiation that can have or be accepted is that they vote the case and that they give me the custody of my son who has suffered so much in the middle of these difficulties.--- Said El mar.

— --- Why, did you accuse Maycol K? --- Asked Dino J.

— --- Because he wasn't representing me properly he knew all the steps I had taken regarding those programs, he was informed enough, and yet he let me go to jail, plus I don't know why they assigned me (TASC),

— Alternative Treatment for Crimes Committed on the Streets, if I have not committed any crime or used drugs or alcohol, nor am I violent --- said El mar.

— Attorney Dino J. took notes of everything he said.

— --- If the trial is done, how do you want it, alone, with the judge, or with a jury? --- I question Dino J.

— ---- With a jury, I told the judge. --- Expressed El mar.

— --- Do you want to talk? --- I continue to question Dino J.

— ---- Of course I want to talk, I want the jury to hear how this case began and why it has gotten to where we are, plus I need to be released on June 15 to prepare for the case.

— --- I'm going to submit an application to be let out," said Dino J. quietly.

— --- I hope he does, because so far, even in death I will not accept a false guilt, the reason for accusing Michael K, was precisely because when the judge told him that he was going to jail me he answered that he could not return to court for two weeks, and I was surprised that he appeared in court three days later. -El mar raised a certain thirst for justice.

— ---- They had to assign another lawyer, justified Dino J.

— - - - If he could be present for that, he could also be present before to request my freedom, those programs that were assigned to me besides being illegal, are malicious, because they are not justified by the accusation, that's why in the trial I want it to be mentioned that there was

— A conspiracy with the intention of criminalizing me, that two weeks Michael K. had proposed to return was the time they had planned to offer me as time served in exchange for a guilty plea, and for me, that is called conspiracy.

— - - - - The prosecutor will not admit a motion that there was a conspiracy," Diño J. clarified.

— - - - -But I'm going to insist that if there was a conspiracy, I want you to know all the details of this case, I want to expose the hypocrites who are behind it, and Celeste Capellán told someone in the building where we lived that the city of Yonkers wanted to criminalize me by force, I knew it and that's reason enough to denounce the conspiracy, whatever its purpose.

— - - - - Well, get ready for June 15th, if you lose your mind you'll get a year, said DinoJ, with the intention of manipulating and instilling fear in El mar.

— - - - That's important, on May 5 you told me two years, and now you say one, that means that every day we are heading more towards my innocence, that's fine, don't forget that you are my lawyer and if you persist in accepting a guilt, I will be forced to change you.

— - - - Don't worry, let's get ready for the 15th - - - said Dino J. in a mock voice, as he stood up in a combined action with the interpreter, intending to leave, they said goodbye and each went to the exit door.

— Before they left the estancia El mar asked him if he had received their letters, however although he claimed to have received them, he did not refer to any of the court papers that El mar requested from him in the letter.

— When they had moved away from El mar, Dino J. told the interpreter:

— - - - - It's not an easy nut to crack, who was the lawyer assigned to him be-fore I arrived?

— - - - - It was Mr. Smith," answered the interpreter.

— - - - - Why wouldn't he follow up on the case?

— - - - - He wanted to be released from the first day, there was some disagree-ment, because Michael K. talked to him, explained what was going on, and told him that El mar had accused him of legal negligence, and Mr. Smith didn't want to take the risk of getting involved.

— - - - - I understand - - - stated Dino J.

— They walked to the door and left the room.

CHAPTER 32

— The Mole had entered into a process of reflection where he was trying to find an answer to his life, after what happened in the visiting room, something had started to manifest itself in him and he experienced a great deal of conjecture to the extent that he was forced to knock on the wall, thinking that the connection that supplied him with the narcotics that he was distributing among the prison population of Vengala, was swindling him or sending him garbage so that the prisoners would think that he was stealing it and try to kill him.

His courage was so great that he wanted to be on the streets to go and execute those who had dared to challenge him, yet something had happened ten minutes after he had experienced that superb start.

He had entered into a reflective process that he had never experienced before in his life, and he remembered that if they had never supplied him with bad merchandise before, and at that moment, just as the incident in the visiting room occurred, the laboratory tests had reported bicarbonate of soda, as in the times of officers Chica and Nica, it must have been for a reason, since the Mole understood that nothing was accidental, and that despite his young age life had not only allowed him intense tests, but also great opportunities.

It seemed that the Mole had started to enter a period of spiritual revolution, that night he was assaulted by a reflective halo and went to sleep from the very moment the lights were turned off, and although there were other prisoners talking noisily, he could easily fall asleep by falling into a dreamlike trance that allowed him to perceive the projection of a video of his life in a movie theater in the city.

The Mole saw all the sinful things he had incurred, including the incident in the visiting room, then he also saw the appearance of an angel who announced it to him:

- - - - I know that you are aware of the tragic scenes of your life, however no merit is yours, the Lord has protected you from everything that seems bad because He wanted to preserve you for everything that humans accept as good, and from that perspective the good you practice will be greater than the bitter experiences you have incurred.

At the conclusion of the message of glorification the angel vanished, and the Mole awoke with a start, sat down on the blue painted metal bed made of iron bars and plates, and felt a sepulchral silence, everyone had fallen asleep.

He went to the bathroom and urinated in one of the urinals, looked at the custody desk and discovered that the latter, despite being called to watch, was also sleeping soundly, leaning his back on the back of the chair.

He quietly returned to bed with the greatest care not to awaken the deep rest of the others.

Already, back in bed, he reflected on the message of the revelation.

At that very moment he became lethargic again and found himself at a party that was like a big auditorium where there was a lot of people, he went on stage and the audience applauded him as if he had been the guest artist, the crowd chanted him asking him to sing, after a time of insistence, he addressed the audience saying:

---- Thank you for inviting me, if you will tolerate me I am going to sing you a song that lifts my heart, it is called prayer of love and it goes like this:

The Lord redeemed me out of love, the Lord redeemed me out of love, a little while ago I heard a voice, a voice of glory, a voice of love, a voice of the angel, angel of the Lord.

I came to warn you, I heard that he spoke to me, the Lord wants you for a mission.

Hallelujah glory to the father glory for his redemption, that I was lost and the father redeemed me. Alleluia, alleluia in the name of the Lord, alleluia glory to the Father glory for salvation.

In transit I go, I go with the Lord, making my way through redemption.

A voice told me I am your shepherd, I am the Lord, I am your savior.

In the heavens and on earth I am the Lord, of El mars and stars I am the Creator, I am God of hope, God of salvation, you can worship me with your heart.

Hear my voice and serve me, from your enemies I will deliver you, hear my voice and serve me.

No matter the arrows, no matter the battalion, I am Jehovah, I am your savior.

No matter the slander or the betrayal I am the Lord I am your redeemer, I will fight for you I will defend you, if armies come I will scatter them, if your life wants I will prevent them.

Neither by sending nor by spells can they destroy you, I am a sincere God.

I fight for you, I am your warrior.

I heard a voice that greeted me, serve me forever that I am your God. I am God of hope, God of salvation, worship me with your heart.

Hear my voice and serve me of your enemies I will deliver you, though they hate you I will lay them at your feet.

Hallelujah glory to the father, glory for his redemption, that I was fallen and the father raised me up.

Hallelujah, Hallelujah, thank you for salvation with my voice I want to offer you this prayer of love.

Hallelujah, Hallelujah, thank you for the salvation in heaven and on earth of Jesus Christ.

Hallelujah, Hallelujah, thank you for the redemption of the entire zero point universe as creator. Hallelujah, hallelujah, thank you for salvation, that in heaven and on earth Jesus Christ is Lord.

The Mole had been dreaming uninterruptedly for several hours, when he woke up, he discovered that the prisoners, were looking at his bed, because the last stanzas of the song, he was singing it aloud, and the prisoners thought he was talking while he was sleeping, then the Mole when he discovered that everyone was looking at him in astonishment, began to cry, inconsolably in front of everyone, the custody went to where he was:

----- The mole hesitated and still sobbing said to him:

---- Yes, it was just a dream, a wonderful dream, so much so that even under the effects of crying, I feel a deep happiness.

---- That's why I ask you, why did you   wake up everyone with your singing, and when we think you are happy we surprise you by crying. --- Asserted the Custodian.

---- Yes, it is an indescribable cry... it is like a cry of joy, of liberation, of peace, because now I know that my life will change, from now on all the dirt that I had accumulated in my soul will disappear, I begin to be the essence of myself. ---Affirmed the Mole with some determination.

---- I am happy for you and I congratulate you.

It is true that from that day of humiliation and joy, the Mole began to go to church and entered the spirit, getting closer to God every day.

One day they attended a service of the Protestant church with some very anointed preachers, and at the end of the preaching, they called those interested in committing themselves in conversion, to go ahead, and the first ones to stand in front of the preachers, were El mar y el Topo who that day had decided to give their lives to God, giving a turn to their trajectories, and together with them, 18 more prisoners.

Kant's arrival at J-1 was intended to somewhat disrupt the peace that El mar y el Topo had begun to experience since the day of his conversion, because Kant was one of the two who had escaped the day of the shooting when the police had arrested the Mole, but who coincidentally had had a problem with El mar a few years earlier, because of a parking lot in the city of Paradise: It turned out that

El mar had attended a journalistic event in the north of the metropolis, and as parking lots became difficult in times of large crowds in the city, it was sometimes necessary to stand in line to get it, that is, waiting for a vehicle to leave so that another one could enter.

That day, while El mar was waiting for someone to come out to park, Kant, who lived nearby, had come to the place with a certain brain disorder, so in an indecent way he tried to take over the parking lot that El mar was waiting for, so the moment a driver left the parking lot, Kant sneaked in, usurping his turn, El mar that had Barbarita and the children inside the vehicle, in the face of such injustice, tried to talk to him and leaving the key attached to the ignition key, he immediately wanted to complain to Kant, who, received him, violently and without saying a word, got out of the vehicle and attacked him in a sudden and unexpected attack.

Although El mar was a peaceful type of person, the impact of the blows led him to think that he was a radical, precisely when he was still recovering from an accident he had recently had, such blows had led him to lose his balance and he had to let himself fall, and Kant, drugged and upset, wanted to leave, leaving him stranded, but reacting in time, before he walked away moved by that injustice, when Kant already thought he was getting away with it and his mockery was settling in.

The earth shook, seized the key four in the trunk of the car, and started the breakage of all the windows of the Jeep 4x4 that Kant was driving.

That extremely angry, somewhat maddened man turned blind, found a green bottle and as an agile projectile, threw it over El mar who outlined defense skills and dodged the bottle.

Then Kant ran panting, like a tired dog with an angry look just as Barbarita was getting out of the car, as El mar had left the key in the car.

He thought of fleeing the scene, stealing the precious trophies of that father who was beaten by the action of an act of ignorance, Kant tried to kidnap May and Mark, he had started the car while El mar was running behind him, the red light defined that path and El mar that like a colt was playing its destiny, in the stop, in the light was thrown to him.

There he captured him by opening the door, forces were born where they didn't exist, from the inside of the car he dislodged it, he held it by a golden cord that he carried around his neck and that, broke in his hand, he kept it in a pocket, while Kant tried to take away the   key of four with the clear intention of hitting it, El mar prevented him, they were strongly confronted.

Pulse by pulse, step by step, side by side, from afar people were contemplating in silence, it was a horrifying scene of street violence, the high Manhattan was identified, the paradise was hoisted, then after a prolonged lapse, the gendarmes made an appearance, The police arrived and arrested both of them, Barbarita, who had run after them, found herself in front of that battle, and motivated, had called Zuly and explained the cause of the disaster, then Zuly, used a friend who was authorized to drive, ipso facto from that place the car withdrew.

El mar and Kant had been taken to the police precinct corresponding to the area of the incident, where they proceeded to search it. During the investigation, they seized a bag of cocaine from Kant's clothes, while he claimed it was for his own consumption, One of the officers who seemed to have a rose with Kant approaching him recommended that if the judge asked something related to the fight he should tell him that it was simply a joke between friends, because if El mar made a formal accusation, Kant could go very wrong if he was charged with attempted kidnapping, street violence and drug possession.

Since Kant had the first opportunity, from the collateral cell following the advice of the agent he began to flirt with El mar, looking for the friendly side in order to please him, he apologized, then both were locked in the same cell, at the time of El marrch Kant had told the agent that El mar had his chain in his possession, then El mar gave it to him so that he would go and search it among Kant's properties, in that incidental way El mar and Kant had met that time.

As the altercation had happened on a Sunday afternoon, they had been transferred to the "reception" center at the city court in paradise where they had been awake until Monday, and once the judge heard the case, he released El mar, who left ignoring what would be the fate of Kant who regretted having incurred in a "stupidity", of that nature as he expressed it, and then had to look for money to repair the broken glass; Anyway, at that time Kant had been locked up for six months, and when he got out of prison, he started working with the Mole.

Then he was convinced that people should not trust appearances because he had thought that if he abused El mar, nothing would happen because El mar seemed to have the face of a peaceful man, and so he reaffirmed it.

In many years they never saw each other again, until that occasion when Kant entered to avenge her.

Kant had been marked for jail, shortly after escaping from the raid where the Mole was captured, in his ravings he had found himself embroiled in a problem of territorial dispute, in which a stray bullet fired by him killed an innocent man.

Actually the bullet had not been intentionally directed at the dead man, it all turned out to be an accident, Jando and Kant formed a dispute because Jando had made a sale to one of Kant's customers, they argued, they shot at each other and Kant's bullet went into the body of a teenager who was walking by at the time, and that had nothing to do with the dispute.

Although Kant managed to escape, the streets would no longer be the best scenario for him, the family of the dead man offered a reward of five thousand dollars plus two thousand that the police added, it was enough to shorten El marrch, with seven thousand the monkey danced and two days after the poster circulated in the neighborhood, an anonymous informant helped the capture and there he was in Vengala, he was no longer the frightened and repentant young man that once asked El mar for an excuse.

Certainly it was not good that the victim of so much evil wanted to manipulate his truth, because the only objective of making the victim look like a victimizer is a way of creating violence.

El mar remembered the expression of the angel of the Lord:

---But that was not the case with Kant, who had a terrible history of violence as a hitman and drug lord, and finally the time had come for him to be held accountable for it.

God and society, over all the evils accumulated in their sad existence.

So when Kant meets the Mole in a process of transformation, he couldn't believe that this little guy, used to screaming and defying big men, had been transformed to the level of walking around in prison with a bible under his

arm, calling his enemies brother and paraphrasing the expressions of Jesus the Christ of "loving one another or justifying himself when something unfavorable happened to him

that "God has allowed it for something better," that was not the mole Kant had known, and it really pissed him off drastically because Kant saw the attitude of

Mole as a hypocrisy, because he thought that an evil person could not change overnight as it had happened with the Mole.

One day they met face to face and Kant couldn't find the most provocative way to radically humiliate the Mole and with all the intention of annoying him he told him:

---- "Goodbye topoyiya".

The mole reacted very cautiously, so as not to lose his equanimity, but warned him:

---- Kant, I'm a Christian, not a pig, just because I'm tolerating you doesn't mean I'm afraid of you, I love God, I don't fear man, stop bothering me and respect me in the name of Jesus.

Kant tried to hide his shame, but he could not hide his mocking and malicious smile.

Anyway, something had happened that induced him to withdraw in silence, he did not speak again.

Kant was of an elusive nature, of a difficult character, capable of capsizing at the first temptation. His relationship with the Mole dated back to those years when he was starting over from the bottom in his criminal career, in paradise, and although he was older than the Mole, he always respected him, now the Mole did not understand how Kant could go around making it difficult for him, simply because he had made the decision to change his life.

On one occasion they had agreed to go and steal five kilos of cocaine from a drug dealer who was supplying him, they pretended to buy it and when they let him in the first thing they did was to put a gun to their host's head, who

Terrified, he did not put up any resistance, they carefully checked the apartment and were awarded, they had found a kilo accompanied by 15,000 dollars, because before them the buyers who had ordered the merchandise had gone to supply themselves.

They had also found a machine gun and besides the dealer who was locked in a room, they also found a beautiful woman who, frightened, was hiding behind a door. She was a white woman with black hair and green eyes, who, faced with what happened, submitted without resisting or opposing the will of those who, seeing that she was beautiful, also planned to possess her, While Kant was watching the Mole, he was passionate about her and thought that no brain could explain the world of women's diversity, especially that of the one with tiny, translucent eyes, framed by an outline, those eyes conveyed an atrocious mystery, whose fragile character was protected in the inexplicable hybridism of its existence.

Kant, was blushing contemplating impassively the voluptuousness of her pink nipples, which at the same time seemed so tiny, like a light bulb without a socket, that emanated from her breast, producing a fight with the demons of lust, and that indifference noticed, as if she slept without dreams, attracted him with a greater restlessness, as if some indifference that she did not know she was transmitting, stimulated his hunger to have her.

When the Mole had finished wallowing, she showed a fearless and sad face that had broken the coloring that had obsessed him.

Then Kant had already lost the desire to be with her, because the distant sound of her voice reminded him of a maiden from the horror movies, from whom a thirsty vampire had taken all her energy.

Under a counter they saw a bundle that when opened and counted added fifteen thousand dollars to the contents, and before the splendor of the show, they spared no effort in seizing it.

Of that same money they gave that damsel $3,000, plus approximately fifty dollars worth of cocaine for her consumption.

They took her with them into the hallway and when they came out, they let her go there so she could decide which way to go, if she would leave or return to that place where the mole and she rubbed their skin.

CHAPTER 33

— As planned, on June 15 El mar had returned to the Yonkers courthouse and it appeared that attorney Dino J. had not done anything that had been planned, so they resorted to making him the same offer of time served that had been made in previous months, always inducing him to take the blame.

El mar kept a slight silence, saw the room clear and without an audience, only inhabited by the judge and some possible pre-fabricated jury candidates, some court guards and lawyer Dino J. More on the side of the court that gives El mar, that on having raised the sight, saw that the judge in this occasion was not less than the same one that had imprisoned it innocently, it was about Thomas B. who was serving coldly on the platform boasting of his position of major jailer, or of God's good fortune in the land, without anybody could even qualify it of racist in arrogance.

- - - - We had made a previous offer and we will maintain it if he pleads guilty.

- - - - - - Guilty of what?...if I didn't do it when I was two weeks old why should I do it now that I have two months and twelve days, however if I may I would like to ask myself a question that I had raised before.

- - - - To whom, to me or to everyone?" answered attorney Dino J.

- - - - Dino J looked at the judge as if to ask his consent, after a brief silence, he went to El mar:

- - - - can do it.

- - - - Who is criminal... the one who has the power criminalizes the innocent, or the innocent who is criminalized by those who have the power? Judge Thomas B. blushed. He looked at a blond man with red hair who was sitting at the jury table and saw that he nodded his head as if pondering the expression that El mar had just uttered:

- - - - Because how can you keep an innocent man in prison, all to pressure him into taking the blame, is that an act of ethical purity, or of baseness, would you like me to take the blame? All right, I'm going to make myself guilty, take me off, the handcuffs, I have a family and right now they're suffering, come on, make me guilty, you're going to realize who I am. - - - He said raising both hands in handcuffs to open the lock.

- - - - I question Dino J. with a certain amount of disbelief.

–––– Isn't that why they have me locked up? Come on, let me go," answered El mar.

Attorney Dino J. approached the typist who was copying the minutes of what was happening, and commented almost like a whisper.

––– He's going to make himself guilty.

Suddenly that sepulchral silence had been broken by the superb and imposing voice of Judge Thomas B. who had just come out of his adrenaline trance that had induced him to change color, he looked as reddish as an overripe tomato.

–––– I'm going to send you for a psychiatric evaluation, to see if you understand what's going on in court.

–––– I don't understand anything, you sent me for a drug test, and I don't use drugs, that's why I don't understand anything.

One of the guards who recognized him and felt a certain admiration for him looked at him straight on and said:

–––– Calm El mar.

A little later, they tightened his handcuffs again, and they were going to move him back to the waiting cell, which was located in the anteroom of the courtroom.

They sat him in a chair outside the fence, while attorney Dino J. in his plan to calm him down did turn to him and said

––– I submitted an application to be let out and fight your case from the outside, I'm trying to get the court date before July 14th, but it's been impossible.

–––– Never mind, I'll get a pardon from the governor of paradise, ––– Said El mar as I gave varying.

–––– Will you get a pardon from the governor? ––– questioned DinoJ. With some disbelief.

–––– That's right, my heart has no room for hate, but I think I hate that legal tyrant," said El mar, referring to Judge Thomas B., "I want to change him from my case. -He added.

–––– That judge cannot be changed, he is the judge of domestic violence, he waits for July 14, when the other judge will come. Said Dino J.

–––– All right, hand over the case papers, give them to me now, Dino J. is not representing me properly either, Dino J. began to retire in silence without responding to the requests that El mar had made to him, until he was lost in the corridor.

When they arrived in Vengala, a court request was going through from one officer to another, Judge Thomas B. was requesting a psychiatric evaluation, which led to his being transferred to the central clinic of Vengala after El Mar changed his clothes, where he would be seen by Dr. Colin, who in his extension service at the central hospital was evaluating all recommendations and decisions in the area of general medicine, including psychiatric pre-evaluations that arose in the treatment of prisoners in Vengala.

There was a surprising mutism; one guard had stripped him and checked him when he came back from court, to the point that even his underwear had to be taken off. After he wore his prison uniform, another guard led him down the hall to Dr. Colin's office, Leaving the impression that she had already been warned before El mar boarded the room, when he was already in front of her, she looked at him tersely and indicated by a hand signal that he should sit on the chair in front of her, and once he was seated in front of her, Dr. Colin proceeded to interrogate him:

----- Tell me, what happened in court today? --- He inquired with some kindness.

---- Well, Dr. Colin, it seems that from what I told the judge, something did not please him. El mar responded and at the same time proceeded to tell him what had happened in detail, starting with the motivations and circumstances that had led him to jail.

---- I didn't ask you to tell the whole story, but to tell me what happened in court today.

---- Okay, I told you that I asked the judge about the conditions he used to criminalize the innocent, and before that questioning he radicalized himself, perhaps because he understood that the subjects should never question the master, and perhaps because I dared such boldness he sent me for this evaluation section with you.

Dr. Colin suffered a fit of uncontrollable laughter as El mar gazed at her in silence.

---- What happened was that you talk too much, I asked you what happened today in court and you answered me with too many details.

---- I asked permission to speak, they authorized me, only they did not expect a questioning of that nature.

---- Okay, if the evaluation is decided, the psychiatrist will come to see you here, you can leave," he said as he returned to the custody the sheet he had put in his hands upon arrival.

The custodian looked at the contents of the page the doctor had given her and said

---- He didn't specify which house he was going to.

---- What house were you in? Dr. Colin asked El Mar, as she looked at him.

--- At J-1. --- El mar answered.

Dr. Colin took the reference sheet that he had in his hands, wrote down the house he was going to and gave it back to him. They left Dr. Colin's office and walked down the hall.

They went through several doors with electronic bars until they reached a desk located to the right of a door at the end of the corridor, where they waited for the arrival of the guard sergeant who checked the page.

---- Is it for the general population, or do we isolate it? --- He came forward to question the prejudiced custody.

---- The sergeant was briefly silent before responding:

---- The doctor recommended the same house.----- She said.

Before reaching their destination, El mar and other prisoners were forced to turn their faces to the wall, as the turtles rehearsed their terror tactics, appearing and disappearing in the middle of the journey, making the afternoon diversified.

Before arriving at his destination, he was held in a cell along the way for over an hour until they confirmed his reassignment to J-1, the same house he had left in the morning. He had only had his bed changed, previously he was in bed 16 and from now on he would be in bed 10.

El mar had been in court on Monday, June 15, and although he had gone with the expectation of meeting with the family, he could not confirm if they were present because that day he had seen the judge in an isolated room, he had not been able to communicate with any of them and that Wednesday he also did not receive the surprising visit he had been receiving in previous weeks.

However, on Wednesday afternoon, from the chaplaincy office, he had managed to establish contact with Barbarita, by the way, for a very short time due to the pressure of the waiting line that integrated the most prisoners, who also wanted to be able to communicate with their relatives, even if it was for one or two minutes.

That afternoon El mar had received the dose that would make him speed up a decision regarding the offer he was given, he had misunderstood that Barbarita and his children had been moved by an emissary of the government of paradise, to a refuge in the City, it seems that they had managed to break Barbarita's faith that before the pressure, manipulations and attacks had decided to put themselves in the hands of those who sought the fall of El mar, and for which they also used the participation of Esteve, her resentful ex-husband who somehow besides being angry with her also wanted to see El mar roll.

Barbarita wanted to justify herself and for that she didn't lack the courage to look for a dispute through the phone with El mar.

El mar knew Barbarita; he knew she was unpredictable; she was   one of those people that one day possessed a state of mind and the next day used to assume another posture, so he realized the condition of anguish that invaded her and that he could not dissimulate and looked for the way to evade it on time.

She then reattacked him and told him that she would not be available to see him again until her children went on vacation, so El Mar told him that she understood his point of view but that he couldn't talk to her anymore because there were people on the line waiting their turn to talk on the phone.

However, Barbarita did not allow her to hand over the phone until she told him, that she was depressed that some of those whom she believed her friend had refused to sign as guarantor for her bail, so that she could be released with a minimum amount.

From that moment he understood that very few people could be called friends forever, the modus vivendis of paradise divided, hardened the heart of those who seemed to be brothers.

A moment later, after concentrated reflection, he understood that nothing of what he experienced in his life could be more than evidence, because those whom he believed his friends had disappointed him, those, before he did so, had requested it without him being denied, but they, who being able to show an action of solidarity, for their disappointment had refused mercilessly, and even Barbarita, had begun to weaken, had begun to redefine his interests.

In the days that followed, El Mar reflected on how best to obtain justice, so he chose to file a complaint of negligent service against Dino J., whom he considered to be one of those legionnaires dedicated to blaming and imprisoning innocent people.

He would send that complaint to the ninth judicial district, he had also planned to send a report to the press seeking to foresee any kind of arbitrariness, then he knelt down and cried out to the God of his being:

Divine Father, you are the foundation of my existence. Your presence innovates my essence, your virtue renews my light. Peace of goodness you give to human happiness. Divine Jesus you are with me, with Jehovah you will intercede to grant my freedom, father of grace

And of goodness, O immaculate God, you give health. Divine lantern great friend. I would always like to be with you, and to walk in my destiny, as you have always wanted it. Father divine glorious friend. Let me always walk with you.

That night he had dreamt again, but on that occasion he dreamt that he was walking with a friend who was an artist, that they had come to a fornicated counter in sky blue, where a school principal had given him a blue-green bible, which he was to give to the artist who was accompanying him.

The director had seen that El mar had been interested in another one like it, however he warned him that he should never speak a lie, so he gave him a hard cover bible with a red wine color where there were some pages in manuscript, that El mar had written and a photograph where he, his younger brother and one of his nieces were dressed in yellow.

When El mar saw the photographs and the manuscripts, he told the director that the Bible he had given him before was his own.

Later, in another painting, he saw himself next to Barbarita in an apartment where a friend called Fred appeared. Fred had given him an aluminum thermos containing medicine and asked him to take it, then Fred went to the kitchen where Barbarita was and saw that he had given Barbarita five dollar bills.

Barbarita had hidden in a corner and from there she saw a cigarette-like smoke escaping through the door.

When he woke up he reflected again on what the message would be, he had approximately one month without Barbarita visiting him and more than two weeks without

Lency saw him, the times he managed to communicate on the phone he did it in such a hurry that he could not understand what they wanted to say.

Two days later with the favor of the priest he got a call to contact Barbarita, but that in less than two months had changed, received him with a peroration approximating the drama and accused him of all the difficulties that had suffered during his absence, that if he had not claimed custody of Mark nothing that had happened would have happened, notified him that Lency and Zuly had tried to post a bond but that until the appointed day for the new court would be impossible, told him that he was still in court fighting for custody of his first children because Esteve wanted to take him away, and notified him that Lency and Zuly tried again to visit him but again he lacked proof of address, so they could not enter.

--- Lucky me --- replied El mar.

---- You can't." Replied Barbarita.

Without asking him why she was saying that, he commented:

---- Well, I made a motion to see if I can get a hold of myself," he said.

--- That's fine, when you solve your problem I won't go back.

---- What are you saying? --- questioned El mar.

The snake had begun to pour out its venom, it had already betrayed him, so, trying to deflect the comment he added:

--- I will probably come to see you next week. Barbarita responded by changing the subject.

---- Okay, see you soon, I love you.

---- Take care of yourself. --- Said Barbarita.

El mar had given way to those who were taking turns to speak, so he waited until that afternoon's mass began.

From that afternoon onwards his heart was disappointed, he was no longer sure if he should continue to trust Barbarita, he knew that she had lent herself to the game of confusion, he thought that she had begun to think something different from what she had shown.

So he decided to tolerate it, he understood that when you run away from your loved one, love becomes a vice, vice becomes desire, and desire stops being sincere love.

His heart was beginning to despise her, she was a young woman and although he did not appear to be old, he was twice her age, now he had begun to doubt whether it would be wise to put his life in the hands of a living woman, so he chose to greet her with condescension but without trusting her, at least until he went out and checked what had happened in her absence.

El mar thought that Barbarita was hiding something from him that she did not want to tell him, he had decided to give time to investigate it on his own, he had already begun to doubt with certainty to the extent that he came to think that each visit she made was more for the purpose of obtaining information, than because she wanted to see him; information she would use for some plan or purpose, however, he agreed with Victor Hugo that "the woman was half of humanity, and the mother of the other half" but he was very much aware of the history of humanity, the events that in the history of humanity had been generated.

 It was clear to me that Adam tasted the apple because of Eve's influence, that Samson lost his strength because of Delilah, that Julius Caesar and Mark Antony had been confronted by Cleopatra.

El mar knew that the magic of women's nature made her a being that could be, as the popular adage described it: "as tasty as dangerous", and it understood it that way because it kept her in prison due to the intrigues of Celeste Capellán, a

An entity that, when contemplated, seemed to be a Heavenly Angel of those who only worshipped God, actually, it looked harmless, a display of its slenderness, genius and figure, the

It confirmed, however, that not always evil or goodness was reflected in the face or in

in his body, he always remembered his grandparents' saying: "face we see hearts we do not know", and he conjugated everything that happened as some of God's mysteries.

Then he remembered and parodied Dr. Walter L. Wilson "I only believe in what I can understand, nothing that encloses a mystery is credible to me, to which it was answered:

When a caterpillar closes in on itself, it becomes a beautiful butterfly, its hair becomes a scale, its legs become six legs, yellow becomes red, and the instinct to crawl becomes the instinct to fly.

Just as the cow eats green yerba mate to produce white milk and yellow butter, or a handful of sand that the lord buries deep in the earth, processed by the rays of the burning sun, becomes shiny opal, or a handful of clay becomes amethyst, or black carbon becomes a diamond, and the canary's eggs hatch in fourteen days, the hen's in twenty-one, the geese in twenty-eight, the wild ducks in thirty-five, indicates that everything that man refuses to understand, is proper to the wisdom of God.

The horse rises from the ground on its front legs, the cow on its hind legs.

The waves of El mar march towards the beach, twenty-six per minute in any climate. Each ear of wheat has an even number of grains, the ear of corn has an even number of rows of grains, the branches of the tree grow perpendicular to the trunk, the combination of oxygen and hydrogen as it lacks smell and taste, when combined with non-soluble carbon, black and tasteless, results in white and sweet sugar.

In reality he was delighted in the reflection, and came to the conclusion that the wisdom of God was infinite, and not always understood by the man who used to receive the misunderstood as a prodigious miracle of nature, so El mar began to understand faithfully that just as there was the self-transformation of nature,

As an expansion of God in their consciousness, so the transformation of the soul of men would be achieved in an evolutionary pattern.

In the depth of his intuition, he longed to see the beings of the world transformed, he understood that ignorance limited, and became more aware that knowledge did save, so he thought of Professor Makrowki, who had articulated that the unification of science and religion was not in fact the goal of the church.

However, he believed that everything was moving towards a language that would generate symmetry and balance in the struggle of the opposite, where light and darkness, day and night, cold and heat, God and the devil, the beautiful and the ugly, the good and the bad, would confront each other, inducing man to a vi-po-lar reflection of the powers that emanate from the same nature, would fight titanically, for the scenario of the persuasive influence that induces to balance a balance of humanitarian convenience.

In his primary years when Makrowki was pursuing a result in every experiment, he always expected an affirmative response to the existence of the human race, where God acted as arbiter of creation, acting behind the scenes, showing himself only to whom he chose, so that by faith he could achieve the miracle of redemption, thus reconfirming his existence before men, because no human being had been called to see God in his material state, without running the risk of succumbing.

That is why it was believed that it was shown to Moses in the bush or behind the parapet of a curtain in the Ark of the Covenant.

In addition, El mar, in its reflection, continued to sharpen its path to the paths of the intellect, and analyzed and broke down the contents of the profound phrases:

"With all their psychiatric evaluations and concerns," he thought, "in the same way and said that those who could not understand God, could not understand him, because many of those who in their generations would consider themselves wise, would become blind for not wanting to see, and deaf to avoid hearing, and not wanting to give their arm to twist, would make a fool of themselves before the humble, and would be ashamed by the weak, because in that way God shows his existence and his justice.

All those who oppose the good, in ignorance, oppose God, because even to be what he is, the devil must thank God that he created him.

The dreamlike conditions of El Mar had intensified, he felt that the divine spirit was manifesting itself to him in a very special way, during that week he had continued receiving revelations, he had seen that the Yamy, only daughter of Celeste Capellán with her previous relationship, was walking head down, at the age of 15 she had joined another child of her age, due to an oversight that hurried her to get pregnant, precisely when she finished the high school.

She had stopped entering the university, because then she would have to dedicate herself to work, however El mar could perceive that something else was happening, she was accompanied by someone with a double life, who while walking with her made phone calls where she ordered a hitman to kill someone.

The calls had been intercepted and the true condition of the individual was discovered.

Then she took the side of El mar, who had shown interest in helping her because of what had happened. El mar had taken off her shoes, giving them to her, who received them as an affable wife.

Then El mar went to the desk of a white woman, who gave him a reference to go to another city in Paradise, to participate in a program for parents.

Then he saw himself walking handcuffed with one hand next to an officer who was also walking handcuffed next to him, she guarded him with the caution of the one who was called to walk next to him, then he discovered that an arbitrary contravention had been dismissed that he had been assigned.

In another painting he saw a white man whom he had defeated without any effort; he was the owner of an altar invaded by several images, which he worshipped as if he were a saint.

Later he learned that his son Mark had received a blow to the right side of his neck, and had been handed over to Barbarita, because Celeste Capellán had beaten him up, had mistreated him.

All those dreamy flashes led him to think that Mark would one day return to him. When he woke up he wrote a letter accusing Dino J. of legal negligence, for coercing him to accept a guilt he did not have, the firm and waited for an answer he thought he would not receive.

The days passed under the shadow of the dungeon, the judge Thomas B. had fixed the 14th of July as the new day of the court, however already El mar had begun to feel demoralized, already Barbarita had taken the determination to abandon him in the fight, already the people in charge of the case had verified the few relatives of Barbarita approaching an agreement of intervention where they suggested her to desist of supporting for more time the whims of El mar.

First they painted a picture of how harmful this could be to them and even to their own children.

Barbarita's relatives from the other side of the border, most of them undocumented, believing that providing a service to the ideologists of paradise would help him to vindicate his migratory cause, did not spare any effort to admonish her, making her understand that if El mar wanted her and her children, he would not have gone so far as to be imprisoned for walking around claiming the son that was someone else's, they offered her economic help in exchange for her forgetting about El mar.

The persuasive fibers of bad intention touched Barbarita's weakened heart, and she agreed to abandon the house where El mar had taken her after the pilgrimage that had led her to lose her family apartment.

 All this had made El Mar so desperate that he had to make a decision that would throw all his efforts into the ground in his fight against the discriminatory abuses of the system's satraps, yet when he had to trade with members of the prison population he kept saying:

---- God's power and mercy is so great that when it comes to you, even though you are in the cauldrons of hell, you can experience peace, protection and happiness," he said.

A dreamlike sequence kept flowing, to the extent that he was convinced that no one could avoid what was destined to happen, his faith had grown, he knew that he would get out of jail anyway.

He arrived on Saturday night, only made him fall asleep, and then experienced in vision that he was accompanied by one of J-1's guards at a counter where he was passing a credit card of his property containing five thousand five hundred dollars, and from where he came out surprised because he believed that his credit had been suspended for all the falls he had had on the road, but on leaving the store he then discovered that it was not a store but the prison reception from which the prisoners who were granted freedom were processed.

When he woke up, he reflected on that dream and remembered that he had been set a similar bond in the amount of five thousand, and that he had submitted a motion demanding a reduction equivalent to ten percent, the equivalent of no more than about five hundred dollars.

He understood that through that dream he could walk in the security that his easy way out could reach, without having to use any intermediary, anyway he had to wait, because not always things in life turned out as they were visualized, but

He wanted to know what happened with Barbarita. The last time they spoke on the phone, she promised to go and see him and when she thought she would be able to meet the person who had appeared, it was Lency who had told her the sad news:

– – – – Barbarita changed her mind, and now she wants to leave you, and now she wants to give me your belongings, I refused to receive them, I told her to keep them, until you came out.

Before that expression, El mar kept silent, but he was convinced of what was happening, Barbarita had betrayed him, it was already past the month when she had not returned to him, and after she decided to sell him, all he was looking for was a pretext to justify his rampage.

However, El mar was still unaware that she was with another, although she had not declared it with her mouth, her attitude made it clear.

El mar was not surprised to learn that Barbarita had left the place where he had left her, he had a vision where she was living in a Women's Development Institution, and then he saw her confess to Kant, someone El mar distrusted, and heard him tell about the difficulties that men used to create, then when he woke up he was surprised by what he saw, because Barbarita and Kant did not know each other, besides he was in jail.

He fell asleep again and immediately discovered that he was in a large room, where from a stage Professor Makrowki was giving a lecture, and his voice coming from the pulpit was affirming:

– – – – – The reason of the will is not the same as the perversion of the senses.

In the game of life, the aim is to evolve towards new horizons, where mold and pollution do not invade the conscience, and where light irradiates the future.

In another scene he was seen leaving the room, and appeared chatting while taking a walk, and walked and suddenly a virtual schoolmate appeared, feeling

Shame on others, he not only ignored her but confused her with Barbarita, whom he was waiting for, as a longed-for miracle.

He shyly greeted those who approached, but ignored Barbarita who arrived, pretending to make the meeting seem casual, feeling intrigued and somewhat anxious to talk, but the words no longer came out, suddenly saw her leave again, but his stealthy look followed her beyond that day.

He continued to hallucinate in the distance of a wasted shade, and followed in his footsteps with stealth, unable to control his impulses and at the same time, censoring his procedure of childlike invincibility, he did not know whether to note it or ignore it.

He felt that he admired her, but she ignored him, and in the face of the dilemma he was forced to define himself between the voice of the sage and the feeling of the oracle.

Suddenly Barbarita's jovial silhouette was lost in the distance, and the hue of her passion was confused, in the glare of the moon that bathed the atmosphere, she ran after it until she reached it and between the pulses of her arms, she chained her hands.

She seemed enraged, and in a metamorphic action, showed her character, until a torrent of tears, moistened her cheeks.

Whenever he imagined that El mar and Celeste, the chaplain, came to understand each other, he could not control himself, and jealousy intensified his hormones, and his tears splashed with anger, increased.

El mar, moved by his thumb, tenderly dried the moisture from his skin, while caressing his hair and kissing his lips as fine and soft as a cotton steppe.

Sporadically, the same thing happened, so that once he became confused and questioned whether those tears were generated by pain or by remorse.

He believed that this relationship had become hostile after each attack of excessive anger in a coexistence of romantic masochism, tinged with his childish skin.

There was an inhospitable combination of adolescence and adulthood in her, which framed her sensibility, in a picture of presumption of innocence, between the pride of her appearance, and the denunciation of her presence, Barbarita Roque, was looking for the way to motivate and persuade El mar by all means, especially by making him understand that under her sleeve she was hiding two letters of introduction, which anyway would have to lead him to think that this biunivocal relationship between them, was like a stamp of history.

May, and Quincy, would be the poles of contact, where even if he lost interest in seeing her, and she carried him ignored in her life, the children born of their union, would induce them to retake the dialogue, and by then they would speak with great intensity in time.

He visualized the sweat of his hands, got up from his seat and started to turn around as if he was trying to experience the sensation of getting dizzy, hit insistently the palm of his hands as if applauding, and thought about how dangerous it would be to devote himself to immobility, since by dialectic condition, nothing remained static.

He was beginning to feel cornered between two skirts, he felt like he had grabbed a double-edged knife, with his hand unguarded, and when he was like that, it was as if the competition was directed at finding a prize that once achieved, could be hung on the wall. And abandoned to danger.

He saw himself whispering in her ear, while she gave him a tight smile, as if humor did not exist to separate his lips, he remained silent until sanity reappeared, then I hear him say:

--- Nothing will be the same, you left me alone, my heart is aching, nothing will be the same, when you solve your problem, I will not go back, I will go on without you.

--- Calm down, everything will change positively, the ways of the Lord are mysterious, and only he knows what the outcome will be, your lack of faith can induce you to make mistakes, can lead you to renounce the good, do not think only of the moment, your doubts make you weak in the face of the future, and you always have to look a little further; do not think only of you, to

Sometimes the voluntary sacrifice for your brother is worth a lot---said El mar in a speech of persuasion and reply.

----- If you do not agree with me, I will go my way so that you go yours. ---She said in a soliloquy of sorrow and manipulation, as her salty tears blocked her lips.

---- The first thing you must understand is that I did not do anything that deserved to be sent to prison, my imprisonment has been a terrible abuse of racial persecution, however I can understand that every man has various circumstances and an inevitable path that must be followed, what is happening, against my will was something I had assigned and could not avoid.

She looked at him sideways, and he thought that the chaste woman overcame her duties with the carnal temptation and understood that the chakra of divinity dwelt in the womb of the procreative woman, because God put his breath in it.

---- I don't want it to cause me any more pain," she added.

---- Do not pretend to run away from your destiny, because even if you run away or hide, you will not get very far, without meeting again the stone of your path.

----Today I'm facing you," she said with a deflected look.

A brief silence, flooded the room, El mar moved around it and added

---- Don't avoid talking to me face to face, only the fool in his blindness usually makes life difficult.

When she finished expressing herself, she felt a hint of contempt coming from the depths of her heart, as she disintegrated in the air.

At that time, custody approached:

---- You have a visit from El mar.----- He said.

For a moment he thought it was Barbarita, but then he noticed the presence of Lency, he had gone in the mood to apologize for the impossibility of helping him to get bail, he told him that because of something unforeseen he would have to travel, that Barbarita would not go to visit him because one of his first children had been injured and had to go to the hospital.

Then he remembered that he always told Barbarita that life was not easy, and that one had to be prepared to face with courage all the unforeseen events that arose.

Barbarita seemed to be the owner of an irrefutable immaturity that used to degrade some aspects of her life. By that time her trials were sharpening, she had been a dependent woman for a long time, now she would have to make her own decisions.

Not everything that the eye looks at is as exalted as you see it, not always the showcases show the best merchandise, many trinkets are usually promoted in showcases of luxury, there are paths that seem to be of light and are paths that lead to darkness, while the wise teach with their mistakes, usually the foolish attract destruction.

God instructs on the earth when generations are renewed, nature had begun to transform the atmosphere, and El mar came to understand it.v

CHAPTER 34

— On July 7, it was a Tuesday, and it was surprisingly announced that Dr. Phoenichel, a psychology specialist, had been appointed by Judge Thomas B. to conduct the psychiatric evaluation.

She was a blonde woman with blue eyes, whose age ranged from forty to thirty-eight years, she was nice looking, with a high sense of human relations.

From the first moment she limited herself to making El mar understand that more than a psychiatric evaluation, what she would do was to limit herself to asking some questions to determine if he was understanding what was happening in court and to that end she introduced herself by reaching out to him:

- - - - What's your name?

- - - - Thank you, Miss... Feta...- - - Said El mar, to which she went ahead to reply.

- - - -Fenichel.- - - She clarified, she with her answer.

- - - - Well, my name is El mar Valenilla," answered El mar, as he focused his deep gaze on the bluish iris of Dr. Fenichel's bright eyes.

- - - - Where was he born? Dr. Fenichel kept asking, taking notes on every answer.

- - - - I am originally from the Central Caribbean," answered El mar.

- - - - In what year did he arrive in Paradise?

- - - - In 1990, 19 years ago, El mar answered.

Dr. Fenichel radiated a splendid smile, while rephrasing another question.

- - - - What's the judge's name? He insisted on questioning.

El mar reflected before answering him, and without being moved, he said, still thinking:

- - - - Thomas B.

Immediately Dr. Fenichel raised another question:

- - - What are the functions of a judge?

- - - - To determine the innocence or guilt of a defendant," answered El mar.

- - - - What is the difference between a judge and a jury?

– – – – The judge makes the decisions on his own, but he must abide by the law, and the jury, besides being composed of several people, must receive the instructions that the judge must provide to vote on the individual decision, and the decision as a whole must conform to the verdict of the majority.

After a brief silence, he returned to counter-attack:

– – – – What are the functions of the prosecutor? – – – He insisted on questioning Dr. Fenichel.

– – – – Collect the evidence necessary to justify the charges against the accused, so that the judge or jury may find a verdict of guilty.

Dr. Fenichel kept writing in the notebook:

– – – – Do you know the difference between a "please guilty" and a pleabargan?

– – – – Of course, pleaguilty is a confession of guilt and all rights are lost, with pleabargan, I'm not sure, can you explain it better?

– – – El mar questioned a bit hesitant.

– – – – It's so simple that it can be understood as someone having to pay a million dollars, but can only pay five thousand. – – – Said Fenichel, as she was interrupted by El mar:

– – – – You mean it's something like a reduction, it's something less than a minor case? – – – – Said El mar.

– – – – Oh, I'm going to write that you understand," said Dr. Fenichel,

– – – – But anyway I prefer a guilty please, because being innocent it will appear as if I was forced.

– – – – What work do you do? – – – Asked Fenichel again.

– – – – Self-employment in the community – – – El mar responded

– – – – Was he an educator before? She insisted on questioning.

– – – – Yes, and I write short stories and novels, and some poetry.

While Dr. Fenichel was talking to her, she was trying to express her degree of surprise, girding her eyebrows, moving her mouth, exercising the muscles of her face.

– – – – You're going out," she said

– – – I hope so – – – El mar answered.

– – – – Are you going to stay with the same lawyer?

– – – – No.– – – El mar answered emphatically...

– – – – How many lawyers have been assigned.

---- Three, and all have been accused of legal negligence---- El mar answered, dryly.

Dr. Fenichel smiled at him again, as she extended her hand again in a farewell gesture.

---- It has been a pleasure to meet you and talk to you," he said at the end of the interview.

---- For me too, it has been a pleasant satisfaction, I hope that I have not found any complaints in me beyond those which they try to attribute to me.

---- No, everything is fine," she replied, joining El mar and leaving the small room where they had settled.

El mar retired to J-1 and Dr. Fenichel returned to her office.

That afternoon El Mar was informed of a legal letter that had arrived in his name, he had to open it in the presence of the officer who delivered it.

This was the response to the malpractice charge against Dino J. with a copy to the county bar. The letter contained the file number to which they should refer whenever that issue was addressed.

Later he managed to communicate from the parish to Barbarita's number, he found her again in a terrible bath of tears, and where she confirmed with her heart

Opened, she was forced to close the phone to Lency who, by pressing her, had shouted at her that she would be responsible if his papers and property were lost, because she had left his papers in the apartment when she moved to the shelter.

El mar told him to calm down, that he was already scheduled to go out the week of July 14th, so she a little calmer transmitted him through the headset with a halo of hope:

---- I already have money to pay the rent, but now I can't leave," said Barbarita.

---- Which direction is the shelter where they took you? --- asked El mar.

--- I can't give you the address, they're going to take me somewhere else from here.

---- Okay, I hope to go out next week, when that happens, I'll call you to talk about my kids.

---- Yes, the day you have court I can't go because I also have court for my children. --- He said.

---- don't worry, after I get out I'll help you... what did you do with my stuff? -Questions from El mar.

---- I left it in the apartment," said Barbarita.

El mar was silent about it:

---- Okay, we'll talk later, the priest will start the mass.

---- Goodbye, you took care of yourself," added Barbarita, letting out a slight sign of hope.

The priest was waiting for El mar to leave the phone to close the office and start the mass.

That afternoon he raised prayers for his relatives and for the peace of the world, the endless war between the kingdom and eastern fractions remained in force, and to understand the hypocrisy of man he recalled an Iranian proverb:

"Don't trust the whiteness of the turban, maybe the soap was taken on credit"

Then he thought of the purpose of those who had taken the path of making his existence difficult for him, sometimes waiting for him to go to the bathroom, or to go out to something to fill the little box where he used to deposit the soups with garbage, and then put it under the pillow where he slept.

He thought about what other test life would give him, and the levels of patience he needed to cultivate for tolerance, he was convinced that tolerance would be the best way to live in peace, with health abundance and love, in a world of in-comprehension, after all, all those gifts are summarized in the word God.

It was then that he chose to recite the following harangue from the heart:

Even if my enemies try to mark me, they will not be able to, if God is my shield and my sword, their evil will not prosper, much less if God continues by my side, because what seems to be an evil will have to be a good, no matter how much man tries to suppose or guess, only the author of the script knows how the work will end, God is the greatest seer.--- He said.

El mar understood that the system in paradise was designed like an invisible spider's web, where the violence of invading warriors, who in the name of their interests, enslaved and in the name of freedom oppressed, had expanded.

They were dictating sentence in the name of God; under the pretext of correction, they were imprisoning.

They promoted the glorification of God in the evils of the devil, fostering practicing religious, and ideologized evil in criminality.

At that level was the system of paradise where the dispossessed majority began to feel cornered.

Before degeneration, Paradise vehemently welcomed all those who migrated in search of the dream sold, in honor of economic freedom, and elevated the mercy of God to the aspirations of the helpless and needy from all points of the earth.

But, evil and selfishness, wrapped up and confused the hearts of solidarity and nobility, and the many good ones became bad, and the best ones were disappearing, and chaos was taking over the social political institutions, and men were losing the vision of justice and dignity, and the hegemonic struggle for control of one another expanded, and the cries of the vast majority of the dispossessed cried out to God, and great events began to be generated of which, inexplicably, the man of that generation had already lost control.

The next day the sun penetrated the bedroom behind the transparencies of the apse window, it was one o'clock in the afternoon, but they had gotten up at dawn.

They had called for the green esplanade and combined it with the orange clothes of the prisoners, who had detached themselves from their shirts to cool the collective body of their whole existence, before the imposing heat that those sun rays were causing.

The igneous rays of the star king, hit the backs of those prisoners willing to exercise, some of them gave chests, others made their bars, some did not stop beating a ball on the wall. While El mar walked, others, like the Mole, made bars by hanging from iron shelves scattered around the campus, letting themselves be carried away by the movement of going up and down, straining first of all the forearm.

Others did it on the iron bars attached to the wall and the others looked for a way to shoot a ball into the basket, imposing their chair of hardened basketball players.

Not an hour went by without most of them being exhausted, so they joined the rest of the flock who, fleeing from the sun's rays, were staying under the shade of the leafy trees on campus, and used to argue, bathing in their shadow while addressing the issues of place.

They discussed with such passion that many times the guards, dispersed in the field, used to approach, trying to notice that in the conversation, there were no personal insults, or verbal aggressions that induced physical belligerence.

In the surroundings of the Mayan hurricane, several monitors were distributed, telephones that in case of any altercation, facilitated the communication with the turtles, the group designed to break riots.

The afternoon seemed quiet and uneventful, until two opponents faced each other, an unexpected friction had lit the fuse of gunpowder, Lazaro Osorio and Kant Methylene found themselves letting old rivalries wake up, and they had shot each other up, which exacerbated their moods, and they did it so fast that no guard could notice it.

All this had been going on since two years before when Lazaro Osorio and Kant Methylene competed in the streets, rivaling each other's markets and women. Kant loved his girlfriend, she had given herself to Lazaro, and since then that rivalry was kept in her breasts.

Many of these women, especially the street girls, used to combine drugs, sex and discos, and the prettier they were, the more dangerous they were, because everyone loved them and they were worth more money to the one who paid the most.

The best bidder did what he wanted, and many times they did not protect themselves, some got sick with AIDS dragging with them in their falls, those who had decided to live the bad life, and in certain circumstances they went to the grave together.

When the guards saw the tumult, they prepared to take action, concluding the break, Lazaro Osorio withdrew to J-2 and Kant went to J-1, however, because Lazaro Osorio had managed to reach Kant with a fist, he had not been satisfied, and the next day that it was his turn to go to court, he had retired early and left without anyone seeing him leave, everyone thought he had moved to another bedroom, because they had not seen him all day, it was about six o'clock in the afternoon when someone had approached El mar and told him:

---- You're going to have a new neighbor, Kant is coming to cubicle number eleven.

El mar occupied cubicle number ten and that afternoon, El Mar played a game of dominoes with the Mole and other prisoners.

When the bedroom door was opened, one could see the silhouette of Kant, who with a mocking smile and a triumphant air, of the athlete who wins gold at the Olympics, moved into the space assigned to him.

It seemed strange to El mar that, having occupied the cubicle number seven and still being unoccupied, he had been assigned the number eleven, really, El mar and Kant did not make chemistry, El mar tolerated him because he was a human being, but Kant was a foul person, malicious and with a shrill voice and expression, when they sent him to his side he had the impression that a bad neighbor had arrived and that he had to prepare himself.

Two or three days later what was feared happened, because Kant had arrived aggressive and indecent, some of the spectators who were inside cubicle number eleven were arbitrarily evicted by him.

---- I see that things can't be the way you want them to be, there has to be more respect here.

El mar, ignoring the cries of the one who was trying to offend everyone present, remained calm.

----- You, get out, get out --- Kant shouted, addressing the audience rudely, some of those who knew him tried to calm him down.

----- Calm down Kant, one of the people told him.

---- Hey you, that game is going to end here. He said violently addressing El mar, as he touched it on one of his shoulders.

- - - - Don't touch me like that, or do you want to check if my muscles are strong? Yes, my muscles are so strong that they can melt your gelatinous skin, and stop right there, I don't want you to talk to me.

- - - - Why?" Kant questioned.

- - - - Because a person like you doesn't deserve to have my friendship," replied El mar emphatically.

- - - - Snitch. - - - Said Kant, in a spirit of provocation.

- - - - But you are a snitch, you are a chota and a calié, you are the one who insults, provokes and denigrates all those who want to be in peace, I knew that you threw the bible to the mole, but don't worry, God will take away all your evil.

At that moment Kant was silent, some prisoners who knew him had tried to appease him.

- - - - You have to respect," Kant said, addressing El mar again.

- - - - - What respect are you talking about, I'm not in your cubicle, you can't believe you're going to command in mine, you've provoked me by disrespecting me and I've left it to you

pass, avoid problems and stop looking for the four legs of the cat, which I know if you were sent from the court to produce evidence and make me another case - - - stated El mar.

Kant kept silent about the custody that had stopped the domino game and authorized its continuation:

- - - - Keep playing. He said, "I'm here and we're not bothering anyone. - - - He added.

Everything calmed down and calm returned to the bedroom, since then El mar had tried not to have any encounter with Kant, who had not stopped creating tensions by trying to irritate El mar, who continued to overlook it, ignoring him.

Regularly in Vengala, conflicts used to be generated by the slightest simplicity, sometimes by the use of the telephone or the use of the micro-slinger, or the electric oven when one wanted to heat or cook some food.

Sometimes they wanted to impose themselves on the other, and maintain control or act like gang members.

That same night a conflict was generated between El mar and one of Kant's followers, while El mar was heating up the complete dinner ration, after he had done his shift, they began to pressure him to take out the cold food he had put to heat, so soon after he did not do it they disconnected his slingshot, which caused him to be irritated:

--- He questioned   with a tone of irritation, staring into the eyes of the adversary who, unable to resist the force of his gaze, turned his face away from him, as if he had felt ashamed.

Then El mar discovered that God had endowed it with a force to impose itself on the violent without having to resort to violence.

A few minutes after the device was reconnected, a thoughtful person checked to see if the food he had put in had been heated and informed him that it was ready to be removed.

CHAPTER 35

— Destiny and circumstances were opposed, and when God has marked out a path, no one can impede the trajectory, when El mar believed that the tensions of the day had disappeared, that was when they began.

The same prisoner who one hour earlier tried to cause the altercation by the micro-slingshot, attacked again, it turned out that a few weeks before he had bought El mar a game of dominoes from another prisoner, a game that he shared inside the prison with all the followers of his cause, an act that generated envy and bad intentions, that's how Kurigo, that's how the daring one was called, in an act of provocation of the dominoes took over, alleging that they were property of the house.

El mar had lent it to someone who, although they were Kant's friends, sometimes identified with the principles of justice he promoted, had asked him for the game, having been very diligently facilitated by El mar, they played until the emotion, however when it was time to return it the black Kurigo took possession of them, under the already mentioned plea.

They had turned off the television, when El mar asked him to return them more, but the black man refused.

Even though El mar tried to dissuade him and other cliques from understanding it, he refused, seeing that it was an opportunity for him to instigate his followers against El mar and El Topo, without invitation he became part of the conversation, saying that it was so, that the game belonged to the house and that El mar had not bought anything, and he was in it until a dime was formed   and he ended up in a violent action, because Kant and his

gang members, violating the surveillance of the custody, had smoked marijuana, and having put the nerves somewhat altered, they devoted themselves to challenge El mar to the degree

If we were to induce him to lose his equanimity, even to respond to him with a certain radicalism, let us see how the conflict would become more acute:

– – – – – Men like you only hit women," Kant said.

– – – – Who are you talking to? – – – – El mar questioned as he held his right hand to his chest.

– – – – Yes, it is you and I who are talking," answered Kant.

– – – – If you're talking to me in that tone, I'm going to have to answer yes, I only hit women like you, I told you not to talk to me, but what you like to do is provoke all the problems that are generated, you have provoked it, manipulating the truth in your eagerness to confront the Afro-against me, and that is not to be honest, you well know that those dominoes I bought so that you go around agitating with the affirmation of that one, your purpose is not more than to create conflict. – – – He expressed El mar.

– – – – Not because anyone here wants to know about you, because they believe you are more than the others. – – – Kant argued.

– – – – That nothing else exists in your mind. – – – – El mar replied.

– – – – In my mind, don't you see that they want to take the domino away from you, go and get it out of its box, you say you are not a man? – – – I exclaim Kant with some sarcasm.

– – – – – Yes, I am a man and because I am a man I have looked for a way to avoid your provocations, which I know if you are being paid to do what you are doing, in order to justify your false accusations, remember that when you came from the court, the first thing you did was to provoke me and I did not listen to you. – – – Said El mar.

– – – – – Well, now you're going to have to listen to me," Kant said with some violence, going over El mar in a threatening manner.

He was determined to confront El mar, because the cameras were in their prime recording the images of all the actions in the bedroom, El mar gently slapped his face warning him:

– – – – It is better that you calm down and stay away from me," said El mar with great serenity.

Before that position, Kant did not control itself, a violent impact on El mar threw, making use of the brutal abnormal force that gives the marijuana, pushed it out of the corridor falling El mar on a metal bench of another cubicle and taking advantage of that imbalance that had taken to El mar to fall seated, El mar dodged and blocked him with its arm and feet, until it carelessly punched him, causing a bruise between his forehead and head, as well as a laceration on his back, which he had achieved by falling on the metal bench.

Once everything was over, the custody appeared to separate them, Kant, was put in the area of the phones, while El mar returned to his cubicle. Then he put the two of them together:

– – – – Tell me if you're going to be quiet about calling the turtles or what you're going to do.

El mar had a pencil in his hands that caused a certain amount of distress to Kant, who thought he had it with the intention of using it against him.

---- Look at the pencil in his hand," exclaimed Kant, calling attention to the custody.

El mar went to the cubicle and kept it in the box of his properties, and then returned to the dining room where Kant and the custodian were, then addressing Kant he asked:

----- Are you afraid?

Before Kant responded, he interrupted custody:

----- Tell me if you're going to keep fighting to call the sergeant with the turtles --- he claimed custody.

----- You can call them for me, I want them to take me to the hospital anyway. ---- Said El mar ready for anything.

----- Still, if you want, we can leave everything like that.

---- I want to be taken to the hospital reaffirmed El mar.

---- Okay, you wanted it that way.

That's how he called the sergeant who in a few minutes appeared by the door accompanied by the turtles, who since they entered began to turn everything around, no one could look at him from the front, all with their eyes on the floor, all with their backs to the bed.

They approached Kant who had returned to the telephone area and handcuffed him and then went to El mar who had sat on a dining room bench, and who had been ordered to lie face down on the floor, chained him by his feet and then took his hands back and handcuffed him, put him on his feet and walked him along the corridor to where the communication center was located, and they locked him only in a small cell with a single bench that served as the only seat inside the cell that was like a telephone booth, divided and separated by a wall, there, after taking off the handcuffs to El mar they gave him a form to write the report of what happened.

One who was in the front cell began asking questions that El mar did not answer but that Kant diligently took advantage of to continue injecting his poison.

---- You're a cop, an undercover, I'm going to tell the population so they know.

---- More shocking will be you who arrived the other day of the court, provoking, as if you had been hired to cause all these problems, since you arrived at J-1 you started to provoke me and I did not listen to you and even today I tried to avoid it, but you are an unthinking demon, it is as if I had been sent to break the pure spirits, but I want you to know that the children of God are hard to gnaw at, with us nobody can .Besides, you remember what you did, you threw the bible to the Mole in the toilet, and he was your friend, but since he decided to change and has not been manipulated by you, you want to hurt him, do not forget that no one has the power to play with God, and less with his word . Said El mar.

---- Ah, you and the mole are a couple of nuts, I heard you reading the bible in the bathroom at one in the morning. --- He said with some sarcasm.

---- Don't worry, mistakes add up to consequences, and yours are defined.

At that moment, some officers appeared in the company of Dr. Colin, who immediately identified El Mar and asked him to take him to the clinic, where he would be checked.

---- Go now, when he comes in, fill out the report.

When they opened the gate, El mar came out and walked along the corridor, escorted and handcuffed, until he was again in front of the doctor, who checked him by giving him several pain killers. After returning with El mar, they took Kant, who was as red as a tomato, and who, when interrogated, had declared that he had come face to face with El mar, because the latter had tried to lacerate his face with a pencil, seeing that he needed to knock him out.

After those allegations, El Mar was given a copy of a disciplinary report to sign that would have to be aired within 24 hours in front of the disciplinary committee for disorderly conduct.

Half an hour later they moved El Mar to the second floor of Block F, where it had been previously, there it would have a single room and would be safer, away from the population of the dormitories, however it would have to be in "Keylock" condition for 24 hours.

Under that regime of reprimand, he would be deprived of watching television, of using the telephone, however he could go to the routine check-up of the clinic, while he had under that regime, it would be the only place he could visit.

That same night, he asked the F-2 block custodian if the incident with Kant would prevent him from going home if there was a release provision in his favor.

---- There's nothing to worry about, what happened here is internal, it was proven that although you were involved in the fight, you weren't the one who provoked it, so none of that affects you in court.

Although El mar was certain that he was not in any additional danger to what had happened, because his heart was at peace, he wanted to verify that this was so, and by listening to the custodian, he felt much better.

The next day he was called back to the clinic, El mar thought he would be treated in relation to the previous night's incident, however his surprise was great when instead of meeting with Dr. Colin, he had been waited for by Professor Makrowki, whom he knew as a scientist, not a psychologist or psychiatrist, who had been assigned to provide a second opinion, and although El mar did not care about the purpose or intention, he did not stop conditioning himself for the answers.

Professor Makrowki limited himself to questioning it in terms of the same topic that Dr. Phoenicher had previously treated him, with the difference that El mar and Professor Makrowki talked in a more direct way and with more precise answers.

The professor was so satisfied with the conversation that when they said goodbye, they exchanged a strong handshake.

The following day, El mar found out that Kant had been locked up in a solitary cell for forty-five days, but he was allowed to return to his usual places: the church, the gymnasium, the library and the esplanade, and his right to use the telephone and watch TV was restored.

The second Sunday of the month was Sunday, July 13, and from very early in the morning, at approximately 6:00 a.m., the turtles again raided J-1, turning over everything in their path, turning all the prisoners with their chests on the cold floor, so that they could turn the mats over to look for contraband.

The raid lasted more than two hours, and although they were unable to seize anything significant, some prisoners were moved from their homes.

Kant continued to purge his confinement, he had imposed an alibi that El mar had tried to scratch his face with a pencil and that he had attacked him in self-defense, that he had pushed him but that El mar with some intention had thrown himself to the ground, covering his face, preventing him from hitting him, until they decided to separate.

El mar, on the other hand, gave a version more adjusted to the truth, he said that Kant was smoking marijuana, and that he had begun to insult him, the case is that the version of El mar coincided with the recordings of the camera so Kant was found guilty.

When El mar was walking in the corridor he discovered that his popularity had grown, and that all of Venice was already aware of the altercation, and the officers with their second intention asked what it was   that induced him to fight, so El mar told him:

----- I didn't fight, I just got into a fight, someone attacked me and I didn't defend myself. --- I said, and everyone was silent.

Later an officer had notified him that the contravention written to him by Kant's version was going to be investigated, and if any mistake had been made, it was not going to transcend, so El mar remembered the revelation he had had where an officer

She was handcuffed next to him, because she was carrying him to get rid of the "ticket" and she understood that the God of her being had revealed to her everything that happened before it happened.

On July 14th, El mar had been brought back to the Yonkers courthouse, upon its arrival it found a new judge and a makeshift lawyer, assigned for the occasion, Dino J. had been removed.

Barbarita's attitude and tears had led El Mar to make a hasty decision, the conspiracy had crossed the border of rationality, so he thought of a possible strategy that would allow him to fight the case from outside, he thought of pleading guilty under the conditions that they would let him appeal, that day they took him out and introduced him for more than five times to declare that he accepted to become guilty voluntarily, but whenever he got out he would add that he was innocent, but that he pleaded guilty because his family needed him and he had no other way out of prison unless he accepted the imposed guilt for the time served, and they would take him back to the cell, they had almost an hour where they would take him in front of the judge and take him out again, because he refused to accept an imposed guilt.

The weakness of the system was that even if the magistrates knew they were violating their own laws in order to impose an arbitrary criterion, having shamelessly accepted in flagrant corruption and consciously a forced guilt, they would still not be willing to give up their arms.

After the brazen show they made him sign a sheet where he voluntarily accepted the guilt in exchange for his freedom.

--- This court declares the defendant free under the benefit of time served.

Judge D. Wood was heard to say that he was joining the case for the first time that day.

El mar looking for a way to eradicate the trace of the rancor, embraced the lawyer Robert P. who had intervened that day for his vicious freedom.

One of the court custodians who looked at him with a smile said in a cautionary tone:

---- It was better that I accepted the offer, because if I didn't, I was going to last five years without seeing the light of day," he said.

El mar was silent, and it corresponded to the smile that she offered, trying to get away from that atmosphere loaded with tension as quickly as possible.

On his arrival at the apartment at the top of the city he found that one of the doors had been forced, so he went out to the street and using a coin-operated phone he contacted Barbarita, who notified him that he was in the shelter and could not leave.

The next day they met in a park near the place where she was staying, he gave her $375.00 that he had accumulated to pay the rent, while they were talking Barbarita's phone was ringing insistently, she had refused to answer, seeing that it was ringing without her answering, El mar suggested:

---- answer the call, no problem.

But she refused and kept silent, it was her new lover who was calling.

The next day and without being summoned, taking advantage of everything that happened, with the consent of Judge Thomas B. and his cliques, they gave custody of Mark to celeste Capellán behind his back, without summoning El mar, who had fought so hard in court for his child, had again violated his rights; At that moment when El mar received the news, in spite of his condition of a peaceful man, a discharge of impotence took hold of him, and he wished to be in possession of a source of fire that would allow him to melt the wrapped up scoundrels, those who stood behind the institutions to give free rein to the evils, of their hearts.

Although El Mar filed an appeal and proved that they had broken the law against them, the Yonkers court claimed that they had lost track of Celeste Chaplain; then

was appealed to the White Plains Court and after a drama of legends and criminals invested with power, the appeal was denied, the conspiracy was consummated and the

The evildoers were following their course, man had lost the ability to practice justice among them, nature would have to intervene.

After several years of waiting without a solution, El Mar had issued a statement in which he declared that he could not expect justice from a group of corrupt people who used power to abuse it, and that from then on he refused to believe in his justice, so the Supreme Court denied him an appeal. Neither Ron Stokes' efforts, nor the drama of Martin & Colin, which had been the last ones to air the possibility of El Mar Valenilla being given back its rights in its eagerness to find justice among the corrupt, were worth anything.

 From then on and during those first days when El mar had been released from prison, Barbarita continued to frequent it and on weekends she went to the apartment to join him until it was her turn to return to the shelter, and even after she had managed to get a transfer to a shelter on Walton Street, she continued to frequent it,

But he kept doing it secretly, without the family knowing anything about it, until El mar confirmed the betrayal, before they left for good he could notice that a huge scratch had invaded her vagina, with tears in her eyes she denounced herself letting him understand that something had happened.

She began to look for a reason to make a conflict, and he moved away from her.

The civil case was vitiated and manipulated by the corruption of the defenders of paradise, police brutality intended to be sold as a car accident, promoted by Rosenblatt, Frasciello a law firm that existed at the time and had taken the case but after a year had submitted a motion to the supreme court of paradise to withdraw to the detriment of El mar.

The henchmen of the city not only manipulated Barbarita's relatives, but being her the only witness of the case, as they did with Celeste Capellán, they got her to take charge against El Mar, under the allegation of domestic violence.

However, El mar was not left either; he knew what had happened:

A few days earlier, while he was still freely entering Barbarita's apartment in the shelter on Walton Street, he found a message on a cell phone that belonged to him, and that Barbarita was using it. The henchmen of the 46th Precinct invited her to come and take charge of him, who took his protective measures and took advantage of a medical report from a night he had visited her again on Walton Street, where she received him in alarm, and playing the victim, involved some neighbors she had as friends, who were at that time in her apartment.

Having fallen into a mob over El mar, they beat him, causing some lacerations, without the police making any report of the incident even though they had attended the scene of the crime, because it was all part of the plan they had forged in their eagerness to lacerate the civil claim, and in justification of the police brutality they had exercised against him a year earlier.

Then, using as evidence before the city's family court judge, the medical report of that night, he also accused her of abuse and complicity in generating violence against him, and before this formulation, she was forced to negotiate with El Mar, withdrawing the charges she had made, so that he would withdraw those he had raised against her.

Finally Barbarita and her lover got together, she met him while El mar was in Vengala, and he was always afraid that she would meet him, and even though he lived next to Barbarita Roque and the children of El mar, she never showed herself to him.

Kant had begun to experience remorse of conscience and, he remembered that once when he and the mole were still good friends, and were moving in gangs, a gunfight had formed on one of the city streets where he had been wounded, and the

The mole had shown great concern for him, which he rarely showed for anyone, chasing after his assailant, who, seeing himself lost, went into a path where he believed he would be safe.

As the mole was chasing him, the assailant was forced to hide in a pool where he used a hose to breathe while he settled under the water, with the misfortune that the mole discovered the bubbles in the pool and in order to make the assailant leave his hiding place, he fired several shots that echoed in the air, And since the shots attracted the police forces, he ran to the vicinity of the Hudson River and threw the revolver into the water, confusing the police forces without them discovering who fired the shots, but the aggressor out of fear came out of hiding, and gave himself up to the gendarmes, confessing his crime for fear of being shot.

Then the mole pretending to arrive showed that he knew the injured man and offered to take him to the hospital, while the assailant had been arrested and taken to the precinct.

He thought about how time had passed and how irrationalism had filled him with evil; Kant, too, did not explain himself about the Mole's change and condemned himself.

He remembered his radicalism where he had thrown away the Bible by flogging it in the toilet, and thought of the expression in El mar "No one defeats the children of God".

A few months later he was found guilty of first-degree murder, and although he managed and gestured, he received a 15-year sentence, and two weeks later he was taken to the state and preferred suicide to torture.

From his own strap he was found hanging from an iron bar, he slackened the word

of God and as Judas, so he died.

The Mole left two years later, by those circumstances of the life he joined with Stick and since then they left by the world hunting rebels to give it to God. Lazaro Osorio when leaving the jail dedicated himself to music, had become rapper and was making lyrics denouncing the evils of the system.

Seven years later, El Mar learned that Judge Thomas B. had been admitted to a Paradise Psychiatric Center, that a son had been kidnapped, that a ransom had been demanded that he could not pay, that first a finger from his left hand was sent, then an ear, then an arm, and then the body was left at the entrance to his house.

From then on, he was not able to continue working as a judge; those traumas caused him disorders that led him to the internment.

A terrible mystery was taking place, most of the lawyers who had defrauded El mar had perished in car accidents, except for the "Frolinger" who had been devoured by her own dog, a German shepherd with a big jaw.

Commissioner Jefri Hamilton and Captain Risk Salgado, under pressure from the population, were forced to resign.

The Frasciello's firm, which had withdrawn from the civil claim, ten years later had been accused of fraud, not only lost their license but also went to jail. El mar had managed to continue the claim of police brutality, a washerwoman named Trina Flores, introduced with a signature of Rosenberg, who had

The case continued to confuse the terms incidents with accidents, with El mar often having to redefine it when they spoke of the case.

The objective was to pass off the police brutality as a traffic accident, because after the incident the henchmen of another precinct had also hit the car at El Mar, just as it was crossing a "stop" sign, and the mystique of paradise, "a state of balance for the kingdom, cradle of wealth, justice and harmony", should never be allowed to slip through the cracks, that human rights were being violated there, and even less so by thinkers with intellects sharper than the sword.

After quite a lot of pressure, where Trina Flores introduced her hands, now indisposed against El mar, to accept gracefully and without courage some twenty thousand dollars offered, and El mar refused, warning her with a gust of his Philosophy, in a discursive peroration:

---The selfish one blinds himself rejecting the harmony of the light, it is certain that nobody will take away neither the bad thing nor the good thing, but do not confuse the malice with the wisdom, do not forget that it is not the same to serve that to serve, neither is it the same to manipulate

The only one who knows how much I have suffered is me, and now you want to sell me out for nothing.

Trina Flores got angry and marked the distance, she wanted to act as an intermediary, but it was not possible.

Finally he approached an agreement with the firm that in turn spoke with the gendarmerie and the city, they did not return to court, they had sold the case of brutality, for twenty five thousand dollars more, of those 45,000, obtained as spoils of war, the lawyer kept 10,000 and gave to El mar 35,000, although what happened would have been much more, between conspirators and evil, El mar was rewarded.

Instead, Celeste Capellán entered into a violent relationship and had to flee to Europe, seeking to rid herself of the torment; Four years later, El Mar traveled to Tenerife and heard about the descent of Doña Elude, Celeste Chaplain's mother, and Rafi the priest, and it was all through the mouth of a relative who refused to supply more information about the fate of Mark, Celeste and the Blessed, claiming that she was only looking after the house, and with more fear than shame, trapping between her fingers a business card that El Mar gave her, in case they decided to supply information about Mark, to locate him, the substitute retired.

Professor Makrowki and Dr. Colin Johnson, were united by science, in love.

Attorney Roger Vitine, who had undergone surgery and changed his name, would now be called Robert Alexander, who fifteen

Years later he appeared again in the political scene of Isla Dorada, after all, he became a senator of the Republic until he got old, the spirit left and the land claimed him.

Seven years later, when he was about to turn thirteen, Mark found out that his father had traveled to look for him, but he did not find him.

Only a few days before getting married, El mar found Jeremiah and Chari again and although he did not become the best man, he accompanied him in the marriage.

Professor Makrowki, who appreciated the talent of El mar, not only introduced him to Miss Makwinsy, but also related him in such a way that the friendship grew, and his life changed, his little novels were successful and between verses and songs they lived the love, and another girl was born, besides Quincy, Mariel was born.

EPILOGUE

— The constitution of the kingdom at that time was due to the limited condition of the planet, where in order to advance it was necessary to experiment, and in any case no one would be "free from guilt to cast the first stone".

Sometimes it seemed that the system was designed to curb the self-determination of that generation, and above all of the thinkers, so that they had to depend on the decisions of the ideologists of the kingdom, it was like a way of imposing and dictating the rules of the game, forcing him to hide behind a biting silence, which would curtail the quality of morality, so that if some tried to raise their voices on the rostrum, seeking to speak out against the status quo, that he would lack the moral strength to act by wielding the combative tools, he would be weakened

All criticism based on an adverse contextual worldview.

El mar understood him like that, he knew that this kind of trauma he had gone through, to another less strong one would have driven him crazy, he felt an imperative need to speak out, and he continued to make lyrics that Lazaro Osorio did not stop singing, and the more he wrote, the more healing he gave to his soul, he knew that the answer to everything was in not being a slave to emotions, and he wrote:

"Blue birds break the peace, they oppress too much, a gun to the belt makes them believe they have power, blue birds are a myth, to give themselves strength in their task, they inject a dose of power, some of them are malicious, they smoke marijuana or smell parakeets, that's why when they want to stop someone, they shoot the gun or kick its tail. Some of them, who are undercover, manage to catch large shipments, but remain silent, in exchange for a percentage.

If you walk down the streets of the city and look for a parking space, if everything is full and you want to wait, even inside the car you will be fined, and if you are uncomfortable you can be beaten, an infraction will make you pay, and also a criminal case can be fabricated! How brave they are!

Because of the city's uniform they sometimes think they can kill, they are creators of violence, and they hide their evil in a license.

They look for ways to criminalize you, and if it applies to a job, they try to question you, whether you are "convicted" or blessed, and so they fill your life with conflict. You have to be careful when walking, with their criminal justice system, so they don't get your fingerprint dirty. If a mistake is made against you, they need justification, to prove their perfection, to err is human and they are Martians.

Their system is designed so that they are never in a bad way, so that those on top can keep their positions, and for those on the bottom everything is a relaxing experience.

If you have a family conflict, and some misunderstanding cannot be cleared up, a case of violence can be created and you can be separated from your family.

And if you go to court and you want to fight, and a lawyer you can't afford, they offer you one that will make you commit a crime.

If your ex-wife can testify, an apartment can be granted to her, with a confidential address.

And in front of your children they will shame you, making them believe that you are a criminal, that you are a danger to them to move forward.

Your favorite son can be your punishment, they manipulate him and make him unhappy with you.

If you lose your family and are left alone, they can make your life a little more complicated.

That's why you must understand your wife, because if she doesn't study it, you can lose her, she is the honor, also the laurel, but if she doesn't learn it, you can perish, she is love and she is pain, "she is as tasty as dangerous", if you sully her she becomes a rock, if she is scorned she is like a bullet.

She warns you with her eyes, so that you understand about the play, if you bring tenderness or remain angry, if it is tasty or amalgamated.

In the city, habits are like too much, and there are little children who are poor, and live like that, somewhat alienated, the TV advertising makes you think like a great ton.

To live of assistance, for them is to practice the science of dependence, it is difficult for them to be self-sufficient, and they want the government to make them aware from the town hall, to practice the love of one day.

Either sweep the parks or become a policeman, to persecute minorities, there is also the option to get a profession, or become a lawyer or a doctor.

Single mothers are not outsiders, they can be natives or foreigners, they give birth to children for the system, the same ones that grow up and go to war, with or without a husband, it doesn't matter.

There is no one else in society, everyone has his or her own usefulness.

Some are active in the state, and others are disabled, but in reality every human being in society is located, and for that they have assigned numbers.

Some believe themselves to be free, some are locked up, and the majority are very brainless.

Over there in the kingdom it is as much as flowers, or as a bouquet, not understanding the language can be a sin, but still, no one cares how many frontiers one has to face, nor the price in life one has to pay.

 Those lyrics had given fame to Lazaro Osorio, he had reformed himself for success, El mar valenilla dragged him towards change.